burning
kingdoms

Lauren
DeStefano

burning
kingdoms

The Internment Chronicles
Book Two

SIMON & SCHUSTER BFYR

New York | London | Toronto | Sydney | New Delhi

SIMON & SCHUSTER BFYR

An imprint of Simon & Schuster Children's Publishing Division
1230 Avenue of the Americas, New York, New York 10020

SIMON & SCHUSTER BFYR is a trademark of Simon & Schuster, Inc.
For information about special discounts for bulk purchases,
please contact Simon & Schuster Special Sales at 1-866-506-1949
or business@simonandschuster.com.
The Simon & Schuster Speakers Bureau can bring authors to your live event.
For more information or to book an event, contact the Simon & Schuster
Speakers Bureau at 1-866-248-3049 or visit our website
at www.simonspeakers.com.
Also available in a SIMON & SCHUSTER BFYR hardcover edition
Book design by Lizzy Bromley
The text for this book is set in Stempel Garamond.
Manufactured in the United States of America
First SIMON & SCHUSTER BFYR paperback edition March 2016
2 4 6 8 10 9 7 5 3 1

The Library of Congress has cataloged the hardcover edition as follows:
DeStefano, Lauren.
Burning kingdoms / Lauren DeStefano.
pages cm.—(The Internment chronicles ; book two)
Summary: After Morgan Stockhour and her friends escape Internment, she
discovers that life on the ground is not safer, and that, perhaps, going over the
edge has led her to madness.
ISBN 978-1-4424-8064-3 (hc)
[1. Science fiction. 2. Utopias—Fiction.] I. Title.
PZ7.D47Bur 2014
[Fic]—dc23
2013041618
ISBN 978-1-4424-8065-0 (pbk)
ISBN 978-1-4424-8066-7 (eBook)

For
Mina
Baptista.
Here's to
the next
twenty-seven
birthdays.

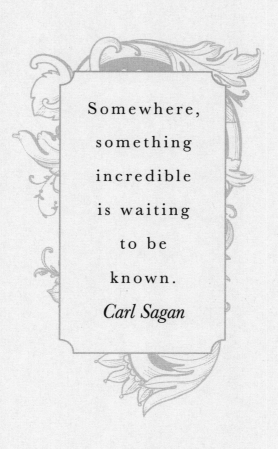

Somewhere,
something
incredible
is waiting
to be
known.
Carl Sagan

When the world was formed, the people soon followed. It has been a balancing act of life and death from that day on. It is not the place of any man to question it.

— *The Text of All Things*, Chapter 1

Snow. That's the word the people of the ground have for this wonder.

"Goddamn snow," our driver mumbles for the second time, as mechanical arms sweep the dusting from the window.

It's like a stab to the heart hearing a god referred to so unkindly. I wonder which god he means. I'd think the god of the ground would be less forgiving than the one in the sky. Vengeful. It would make sense, the god of the ground having interned us to the sky for being too selfish.

But I don't ask. I haven't spoken a word since I told Pen that it would be all right.

All the whiteness is blinding, and despite the blustery

cold, the inside of this vehicle is so hot that beads of sweat are forming at the back of my neck. There's a metallic taste to this air.

I have a thought that my parents will be worried, before I remember that they're gone. Not at home. They're colors in the tributary now, a place that can't be seen by the living.

I squeeze Basil's hand. And on the other side of me, Princess Celeste has her hands to the glass as she stares through the window. A city has begun to materialize through the snow. It's all boxy shadows at first, and then ribbons of color shoot through the sky, squares of light wink from the buildings.

My brother is in one of the surrounding vehicles. When we left the metal bird that brought us down from Internment, the men in heavy black coats split us up as they saw fit. They pushed us into the seats. They said they'd take us somewhere warm and safe. They don't seem to realize that we were banished from this place, hundreds of years ago.

The driver raises his eyes to us in the mirror. "It was swell luck that you came down before the blizzard."

I don't know what that means. "Blizzard" is a new word, and it bounces on my tongue, begging to be said.

Basil is looking up into the sky as though to chart a way back home, but the whiteness that falls from the clouds is his only answer. Now would be an apt time for him to regret following me here—regret our betrothal. Maybe the decision makers were wrong to bond us to each other for the rest of our lives; we've always cared for each other, but he's logical while I'm a dreamer. He's patient while I'm careless. And now he'll never see his parents or his little brother again because of me.

I want to say his name so that he'll look at me, but I'm afraid of what speaking might do to this odd balance between the driver and the three of us.

Our driver's coat appears to be some kind of uniform. He's a patrolman perhaps—or whatever they have on the ground. Maybe they don't keep order down here at all.

Princess Celeste elbows me. And now that she has my attention, she nods to her window. Outside, a large machine is set some distance from the buildings. It's like a giant metal bug, its legs suspended in the air. Each leg is painted a different color, and at the tips are what appear to be clouds.

I can't tell if the princess is attempting to smile. Her eyes still have their sparkle, but she is, for once, subdued.

Our vehicle rolls to a stop. I look out the window on Basil's side and I see the other vehicles stopping alongside us. I want to run out and join my brother and Alice, and Pen, who was fighting tears the last time I saw her.

But I don't move. Basil puts his other hand on my arm as though to protect me.

The driver steps out into the snow, and the cold air cuts right through my skin before he closes the door again.

The princess speaks first. "This is it? There isn't a soul in sight out there. This is what we've been banished from?"

Doors open in the other vehicles. I see Alice first. A man is trying to escort her toward the building where we've parked, but she dodges him and reaches into the car to help Lex.

The sight of my brother, pale as the snow, causes me to abandon reason. I open the door.

"Wait," Basil says.

"I have to let him know I'm okay," I say.

Basil understands. He climbs out first and keeps hold of my hand. "Lex," I call.

My brother's head immediately rises from its weary drooping. "Morgan?" His voice is panicked and relieved. "Sister?"

"I'm here," I say. "I'm right here." The words are heavy on my tongue. This cold is freezing me to the bone. I try to reach for my brother, but one of the uniformed men is steering Basil and me toward that building. Even before the door has opened, I can smell the strange and unfamiliar foods cooking inside.

I bite my lip and take one last look over my shoulder before I'm guided inside. I can see Lex and Alice, and behind them, just a flicker of Pen's blond curls for an instant, a flash, a thought I can't catch.

I hold on to Basil's hand as though my life depends on it. It might.

They bring us to a row of metal chairs, and we're each given tea.

It looks strange in its cup. Weak. They probably have different herbs on the ground. A different ecosystem, too.

I don't drink the tea. I don't trust it. But I still appreciate its warmth against my palms. Though we've come in from the snow, we're all shivering. What a sight we must be for these uniformed men: people who fell from the sky in a metal bird, sitting in a row, not a word uttered among the lot of us.

The professor is the only one of us who's missing. I heard one of the uniformed men say that he refuses to leave the aircraft.

"Aircraft" is a new word also.

A different uniformed man is sitting behind a desk, staring at us. He glances between us and an open ledger on his desk. "None of you are going to talk, are you?" he says.

Silence.

"They always stick me with the weird ones," he mumbles, more to his ledger than to us. "Last week, the caped vigilante, and this week, the party on an aircraft made of windows and doors."

I suppose he's referring to the metal bird. I got a fleeting glimpse of it as we were hustled away, for the first time seeing it in the daylight. This man's description isn't far from the truth.

"Is this them?" a man cries as the doors burst open. I flinch, and Basil grabs hold of my arm.

This man wears a long black coat that is dusted with snow, and yet his hair is pristinely combed and dry. He looks at us with the excitement of a child. "You are the ones who fell from the sky, yes?"

"They don't talk," the uniformed man says. "Don't think they understand a word we're saying."

"We can understand you just fine, thank you," the princess says. "It's just that no one has offered us an introduction." She daintily sets her cup on the ground, stands, and extends her hand to the man in the coat. She means for him to kiss her knuckles, but he shakes her hand instead, so roughly that her body jolts. But if the princess is surprised, she doesn't show it, retaining the poise that has made her an icon for all the young girls of Internment.

"My apologies, then," the man in the coat says. "I'm Jack Piper, the one and only adviser to King Ingram IV."

Delight flashes in the princess's eyes.

"I'm Celeste," she says. "The one and only daughter to King Lican Furlow." She pauses. "The first."

Jack Piper laughs, and I can't tell whether he finds her delusional or charming.

"You will have to tell me all about your father and his kingdom," Jack Piper says. "But for now, I've arranged proper accommodations for all of you."

The princess looks to me, her shoulders hunched with excitement.

She's completely mad. She knows it, too. It's her madness that made her the only one among us brave enough to speak. She means to remain a princess, no matter whose kingdom she may have fallen into.

We are whisked back into the vehicles. "Cars," I hear someone call them. They're all black with spare wheels fastened near the front doors. They emit dark clouds through pipes, and the seats rattle as we move. I try to find comparisons to the train cars back home, but there is no comparison. We have nothing like this. This is a different world.

"They won't hurt us," the princess says into my ear. "It wouldn't be civilized."

"I don't know how you can be so certain," I say.

"It's standard diplomacy," she says. "Papa says I have a real talent for it. He thinks I might even become a decision maker once I'm old enough. I'll have to find something to do with my time once my brother is king."

Decision making is one of the few professions that can't be chosen. Decision makers are scouted and trained privately. They hold our society in their palms, deciding which queue applicants will have boys, which will have girls, and who should be betrothed to whom. And that's only a small part of what they do. It's as powerful a position as one could have. Next to being royalty, that is.

I shudder to think of Princess Celeste as a decision maker. We became acquainted after she and her brother shot Pen and me with tranquilizers and imprisoned us in the basement of the clock tower.

Not that any of that matters now.

The car stops before a building barely visible in the whiteness of the storm. I can see that it's the color of sand and has curved edges, and it's larger than any of the buildings on Internment. Again, we're hustled from the cars and through the front doors.

Everything inside is red and gold.

Behind me, Alice is murmuring things into Lex's ear. He can't see any of this; I wonder if he senses the differences between the ground and home at all, aside from the ridiculous cold.

"Welcome, welcome to my humble home," Jack Piper says. He sheds his coat, and one of the drivers is standing at the ready to collect it.

Pen and I exchange incredulous expressions. Home? This place is easily larger than our entire apartment building.

"Children," Jack calls.

With the rumble of footsteps overhead, they emerge at the top of the steps, pushing and shoving one another and then, upon realizing their audience, straightening their clothes, smoothing their hair, and marching down the steps single file.

They assemble before us in order of height, all of them with Jack Piper's light brown hair. The smallest is in ringlet ponytails, and the tallest is long and lean, with round lenses around his eyes. They appear to be magnifying glasses, though I can't imagine why they're on his face.

"This is my son," Jack Piper says, gesturing to the boy with the lenses. "Jack Junior, though we all call him Nimble. Like the nursery rhyme. I don't suppose you know how it goes. And this is Gertrude." The second tallest lowers her eyes shyly. "And that's Riles." The third tallest, a boy, smirks at us. "And Marjorie. And that's Annette."

The littlest girl curtsies with all the petite grace of a dancer in a jewelry box. "A pleasure to meet you," she says.

"Is it true you came from the floating island?" one of the children says.

"Riles, manners!" snaps another.

The boy with the lenses regards us wryly. "Welcome," he says, "to the capital city of Havalais."

I don't understand that name he's just said. *Have-a-lace.* He gestures theatrically to the letters etched into the wall behind him:

HAVALAIS: HOME OF THE FLOATING ISLAND

2

"Five!" Pen whispers, after she's closed the door behind us. "I counted five children. The nerve, Morgan."

"Shh. Someone will hear."

"Oh, who's to hear us? This building has more rooms than Internment has people."

"He works for the king," Celeste says. "He could be spying. Though it isn't as though we have anything to hide."

Pen narrows her eyes. "Nobody was talking to you, Your Bloody Highness."

"I am only trying to help," Celeste says. She sits on the bed and fans the skirt of her dress around her. "As the only one among us with any knowledge about public relations."

"What public relations?" Pen cries. "You and your brother only ever left that clock tower to fire darts and arrows at things for sport." She looks to me. "I'm not sharing a room with her. I won't be able to close my eyes at night unless there is a lock between us."

The three of us have been left alone to share a bedroom as large as the apartment I shared with my parents. Jack Piper told us that we would find clothes in the closets and "a place to wash up down the hall." One of the children boasted about their indoor hot water both upstairs and down; it's quite revolutionary, he said.

None of us questioned the way we were divided up and sent to the bedrooms. We're approaching all of this with due caution.

"Pen, come here. Try to be calm," I say, patting the space beside me as I sit on the adjacent bed.

She chews on her knuckle and paces.

"All right," Celeste says. "I know the three of us haven't gotten off to the friendliest start—"

"You kidnapped us and held my betrothed at knifepoint," Pen says.

"Yes, and you tried to murder my brother. We're quite even. And despite what you may think, I do know a thing or two about people. That sign out there says that this is the home of the floating island. That means they recognize where we're from. They're interested, maybe even fascinated. They know nothing about the way our city is governed, and now for the first time they have a chance to learn. Perhaps their king and my father can do business."

"Oh, wake up, will you?" Pen turns to face us. Behind her, the white flurries are tangled in a dance within the window frame. "Their king and your father can't do business.

This was a one-way trip. We can't go home. Not ever."

"Nonsense," Celeste says. "Why would the lot of you leave Internment with no way of getting back?"

Pen looks away. Her face has turned red. Her eyes are misting.

"We had no choice," I say quietly. "We were fugitives." I stare at the floor; it appears to be made of some kind of fabric cut out into a giant oval, and it's so plush that I can see traces of our footprints in it. Even the floors are different. I fear what will await us when the sun melts away that blanket of snow. "What Pen said is true. We can't ever go back."

"You can't, maybe," Celeste says to me, "but I'll have to return. Of course I will."

Pen laughs cruelly.

Celeste raises her chin.

"We should change," I say. It's the only thing I can think of that should come next. We'll find new clothes. We'll start learning to adapt. No matter how impossible it seems.

There's a wooden screen that divides off a portion of the room. Pen and I hide behind it and change into the dresses we've selected from the closet. On the hangers are the most exquisite dresses I've ever seen—all tiers and flowers and lace. Pen helps with the buttons at my wrists, and she straightens the lace at my collarbones. And while we're facing each other, her mouth purses. She shields her eyes with her quaking hand. "Oh, Morgan," she whispers.

I wrap my arms around her shoulders. "I know." We're both as good as orphaned now. My parents are in the tributary, but she'll never see hers again whether they're living or not.

"We can't cry," she says firmly.

"No. Strength, remember?"

She nods, draws back, and pulls my hair in front of my shoulders.

I pinch her cheek, and she smiles.

From beyond the screen, Celeste clears her throat. "What sort of woman wore these dresses, do you think?" she says.

Pen growls.

"And what do you think they call this fabric?" Celeste goes on.

"Maybe they belong to Mrs. Piper," I say.

"He didn't mention a wife at all, did he?" Celeste says.

I step out from behind the screen, and Pen follows. "Maybe they don't have wives here," Pen says. "Maybe the women just come around to lay eggs and then they leave."

I can't help laughing. "Be careful what you say," Celeste says, but she's laughing too.

"I'm quite serious," Pen says, assessing her reflection in the oval mirror that hangs wreathed in dry flowers. "What kind of woman could birth five children? Can you imagine? It isn't human."

"It would be rude to ask," I say. "We'll have to look for a ring."

"He had a ring," Celeste says. "A metal one. It was the same shade of gold as the curtains downstairs. Gold is an odd choice for a wedding ring, isn't it?"

"We can't ask," I repeat firmly. "If we were to offend our host, we could well be tossed out into the snow, and then what?"

Pen walks around me, dragging her finger through my hair so it rises and falls. It's so straight that it falls immediately back into formation. "What if he killed his wife? What if we're next?" Pen says.

"Are you always so grim?" Celeste says.

A knock at the door silences our chatter. I loop my arm around Pen's.

"Excuse me." It's one of the children. A girl. "Dinner is being served downstairs."

The thought of food nauseates me. For just a moment, I nearly forgot the magnitude of this ordeal, but that strange affectation in the child's voice has reminded me.

"Thank you," Celeste says sweetly.

"Should we try to eat any of it?" Pen whispers into my ear. "What if it's poisoned?"

I'm not eager to relive the experience of the poisoned sweetgold. "We should at least pretend to," I say.

"Let's let Her Highness eat it and see if she survives."

Celeste, who is fixing her braided crown, pauses to glare at us in the mirror.

Jack Piper is a man who strives for order; that much is clear. His children do all things in order of height, which includes taking their places at the largest dinner table I've ever seen. He gives them a nod, and they shake open their folded napkins and lay them in their laps.

"I have to compliment you on your gold curtains," Celeste says. "We don't see much gold fabric back home."

Back home. What a notion.

Riles's snorting laugh says he think we're the strangest things alive. "You don't have gold fabric?" he says.

"What else don't you have?" one of the younger girls asks.

"Don't be brats," Nimble tells them.

"Yes, gold is popular down here," Jack says. "It's a precious metal."

I've never thought of any one metal as being more special than the next. They all come in handy for something or other.

"Do you have ham?" the smallest one, Annette, asks. She isn't teasing; she really wants to know. "Because that's what's for dinner."

"I don't think so," Celeste says. She doesn't seem to mind speaking on behalf of us all. "What is it?"

"It's from a pig," Annette says. She presses her nose upward with her finger and makes a snorting sound.

"We don't have those," Pen says, speaking before the princess can get in another word. "And we don't eat animals very often. Only on special occasions."

Annette looks at her like she's never heard such a thing.

"That's enough inquisition," Jack says. "Our guests have come a long way and they've earned an evening of relaxation. There will be plenty of time for all of us to get acquainted."

Lex and Alice are missing from the table, as are Judas

and Amy. I look through the doorway, and all I see are infinite doors, and a staircase that leads to even more of them.

A fireplace is crackling. I can feel the warmth of it from the next room. It's an effective enough way to stay warm, but most of the buildings on Internment have been outfitted with electric heat in the past decade, thanks to the sun's energy being harnessed by the glasslands. I'd thought the ground would be much more advanced than we are, given that we borrow so many of their ideas through our scopes, but we seem to be on par, if not a bit ahead.

One thing the ground does have is space. A house practically the size of a whole section of Internment, and as many children to a family as they please. Dozens of windows and curtains, and closets fat with clothes, no matter if anyone can be bothered to come along to wear them.

The food is brought out by a young woman in a black dress that is dripping with metal buttons. She lays each plate on the mat with precision, and uncovers all the hot dishes, which are heaping with enough food to feed twice as many people as are seated.

The smallest Piper volunteers to say grace, which means we all bow our heads as she recites some sort of poem that begins with "Thank you, God" and goes on to list all the things at the table. She adds in "please" and "bless" copious times. It ends when she says, "And bless Mother, too. And tell her to please send a telegram."

"We don't ask for things like that," Riles says.

"Says you."

"I thought it was a fine prayer," Nimble says. He winks at his littlest sister and she grins.

Everyone wields utensils and begins helping themselves. Pen, Basil, Thomas, and I take a modest portion of everything, but we aren't brave — or perhaps stupid — enough to try eating it.

"Your accent is lovely," Gertrude says, forcing the words out all at once as though she's been building the courage to speak. She's the second oldest, with soft rosy cheeks, and hair that covers one eye as it falls over her shoulder in waves.

"Accent?" I say.

"Yes. You don't know that word? It's the way that you speak. Everything has an upward inflection. You all sound so inquisitive. I think it's pretty."

"Thank you," Celeste says brightly. "Where we're from, everyone speaks the same way. It hadn't occurred to me there was any other way."

"There are lots of ways to speak," Nimble says. "Though King Ingram prefers to war with the one nation that speaks the same language we do." He looks at Celeste. "You come from a political family. Does that seem smart to you?"

"That's enough," Jack Piper says, dabbing his lips with a cloth napkin. "Your depiction of our king is unwelcome in this home, Nimble. We've discussed this."

Nimble's gaze rolls from one side of his lenses to the other. The younger children are giggling soundlessly at their plates.

"Are you at war?" Celeste asks.

"The dinner table isn't the place to discuss politics," Jack Piper says. "Perhaps tomorrow, once you've all had a chance to rest." He leans back so that he can see under the table. "And speaking of inappropriate, what have I told you about rolling your stockings, Gertrude?"

She blushes. "Yes, of course," she says. "Sorry, Father."

During the meal, Jack explains to us that this building is something called a hotel during the warm seasons. It's winter now, he says, and so it's closed for business. There's something called a theme park nearby, and people will travel from all across the nation in a season he calls summer to visit it and catch a glimpse of the floating island. They have scopes here on the ground, too, though Internment's position and altitude prevent them from seeing much besides the bottom of the city.

"It's flattering to know you've taken such an interest in our humble city," Celeste says. "I—we would all love to see this park."

"Well, then I—we—will have to show it to you," Nimble says, and the way he's looking at her actually makes her blush.

After dinner, Basil and I find a moment alone in the hallway that holds my bedroom. We're standing in something called the east wing. His room is in something called the west wing. So many words for one building.

His eyes meet mine, and at the same time we both blurt out, "Are you okay?"

He puts his hand on the wall by my head, and I feel so safe, so very safe in his shadow and in the smell of him, like home and bottled redolence and sunlight.

"Yes," I say. "I'm okay. Are you?"

"Is that the truth?" he says.

"Can't we just pretend that it is?" I say. "What else are we supposed to do?"

"Morgan—"

I put my finger to his lips. "Don't. Please. I can't be pitied right now."

"All right," he says.

I nod to the closed door beside us. "They're making Pen and me share a room with the princess. Pen thinks she'll kill us in our sleep."

"I should sleep with you," he says.

"You know we can't change where they placed us," I say. "It might insult them. They were kind enough to take us in at all."

"You're right," he says. "And sooner or later they'll come to collect on that kindness."

"What do you suppose they want from us?" I say.

"If it's a way up to Internment, they'll soon be disappointed, won't they?" He makes an effort at a smile. "I'll see you in the morning, if the princess doesn't kill you and Pen, and Judas doesn't kill me."

"We must survive if only to see what poor animal the Pipers cook for breakfast." I rise on tiptoes to kiss him. "Good night."

As I reach for the doorknob, he grabs my wrist. "I also think we should take an opportunity to get familiar with this kingdom," he says. "In case we have to run."

"Run." I try not to laugh, but it's so absurd. "Basil, where would we go?"

He seems worried, though. "Don't you think it's strange that they've built a theme park just so they can gaze at the 'magical floating city' and yet when the lot of us falls down from it, the king wants to keep us a secret?"

"It is strange," I say. "But everything about this world is strange so far."

"All I mean is, what's to stop him from killing us all if he pleases? No one would be the wiser."

"I hadn't thought of that," I say, and I feel a chill. "Oh, Basil, do you think that could happen?"

"I didn't mean to scare you," he says. "But we should keep that in mind."

I nod. "We'll familiarize ourselves with the city. Pen could even draw up a map, I should think." I force myself to smile. "It will work out, Basil."

He gives me the same sort of distracted smile. "Good night," he says.

After I've washed up and changed into one of the many nightgowns hanging in the closet, I look for Alice and Lex. They'll surely be together. When I get to the door at the end of the hallway and I knock, no one answers. There's light coming from under the door, though. "Hello?" I say, and turn the knob. "Alice?"

"Quiet," Judas says. "Close the door behind you."

He's knelt on the floor beside Amy, whose skin is red. Her hair is damp, and I recognize that dead stare in her eyes.

"I came in to check on her before everyone went to

dinner, and I found her in the middle of a fit," he says. "A bad one."

"She's been lying on the floor like that since dinner?" I touch her forehead, and she flinches and gasps, but there's no real awareness about her.

"I'm afraid to move her," he says. "Daphne would always say never to move her while her eyes are still open, to wait until she looks like she's sleeping."

Daphne aspired to be a medic before her murder, and I'm sure she knew how to care for her sister's fits, but it doesn't seem right to leave a sick child on the floor like this.

"I'll get Lex," I say.

"No." He grabs my arm and pulls me back down. "She needs to be kept calm. She doesn't like when anyone sees her like this; it makes her feel weak."

"She's ill, Judas. Look at her. She needs a doctor, and Lex is the closest we've got."

He looks at Amy. Her lips twitch like she's talking to one of her ghosts.

"She needs a doctor," I repeat.

"You don't understand," he says. "You just don't. If you want to help, bring a cold cloth from the water room and let's try to break her fever."

I do as he says and drench the green towel from the water room.

"Her parents hoped she'd grow out of this," he says, dabbing at her cheeks and behind her neck. "It's only gotten worse as she's gotten older. And the pills and meetings with the specialist have caused more harm than good." He looks at me. "Want to hear something crazy?"

"What?" I say.

"She's got me believing in apparitions with all of this. She swears they talk to her."

"I don't think that's crazy," I say. "Our history book doesn't account for the unexplained, but that doesn't mean it's not there."

Her eyes have closed now. She's surrendered to whatever dreams haunt that troubled mind of hers. I hope for all of this snow to be gone soon. I hope for a morning bright with sun. If she can see that the sunlight is the same whether we're on Internment or the ground, it will surely help. It has to.

Pen catches up with me as I'm leaving the water room. "There you are," she says. "You left me alone with Princess Fancy. It's a wonder I didn't kill her." She leans closer to me. "What is it?" she says. "You look troubled."

I tug her into the water room and close the door behind us. I tell her about Basil's theory that Jack Piper and the king could be hiding us away in case he means to kill us.

Pen hardly seems surprised. "Yes, I've been thinking that as well," she says, scrubbing her face at the sink with a cloth. "For all we know, these people have a history of killing outsiders. Or one another. Or anyone. It's a strange thing to be in a world and not know a thing about its past."

"So what should we do?" I ask.

"As you said, familiarize ourselves with this kingdom as best we can," Pen says.

"Do you think you could draw a map?" I say.

"If they have a library, it likely already has a map of the kingdom. I could copy it and add my own notes," she says.

"Jack Piper's eldest daughter seems close to our age," I say. "Maybe we can befriend her and gain some insight into the family."

Pen shrugs. "We could. I doubt that she'll be privy to her father's politics—he seems annoyed with his children at best—but she could probably teach us a thing or two."

She sits beside me on the edge of the tub. "I think we'd be wise to learn from her, but not to trust her," she says. "We shouldn't trust anyone in this world."

3

There is sunlight come morning, but it's not the same.

Pen stands at the curtains, parting them with her hand. Beyond the window there is nothing but white.

Celeste, still sleeping, turns away, muttering in protest at the light.

Pen nods from me to the window. "Come and see," she whispers. "It's like we're inside an unfinished sketch."

Even the water on the horizon is gray and white. It sparkles as it fades into the distance. There is no train framing this city. There is no limit. It could well go on forever, to a horizon it would take ten lifetimes to run to.

There's a draft coming through the window frame, and my skin swells with little bumps.

"I can hardly stand to look at it," Pen says excitedly.

"It's beautiful," I say. Pen looks at me, and I grin. She

knows what I'm thinking. "You know we can't," I say. "We'll freeze to death."

She runs to the closet, a skip in her step, and she throws a heavy coat at me and takes one for herself. "What good is all that brave nonsense we've been feeding each other if we don't act at least a little crazy?"

"What are you blathering about?" Celeste mumbles from under her blanket.

"Nothing," Pen says. "I got lost trying to find the water room. Woman troubles."

"Thank you for that charming announcement," Celeste says.

We stand still until we're sure she's asleep, and then Pen opens the door, wincing as it creaks.

It's still early and the hotel is silent. The soft floor helps to conceal our footfalls, but we move slowly anyway. "Would you look at these colorings?" Pen says. "The frames are taller than we are."

I tug at the lapels of my coat, struggling to adjust to the weight on my shoulders. "Do you think they're portraits of real people?" I say.

"Look at the colors," Pen says. Her fingertips hover over the portrait of a woman whose shoulders are cloaked in fur, but Pen doesn't dare to touch. "They're so rich. If I had colors like this, I'd want a canvas this size to work with too."

The next step creaks under my foot, startling us both, and we hurry the rest of the way to the door.

Overnight the snow has accumulated to knee height, but

the cold is surprisingly bearable. Pen spreads her arms and falls forward into the white powder. When she emerges, her face is red and there are clumps of snow turning to water on her skin.

"Not as soft as you might've hoped," she says, and pulls on my arm. I go toppling down beside her with a shriek.

"There's so much of it," I say. "When it melts, the whole world must be soggy underneath."

"Our little clouds have been holding out on us," Pen says. "Who knew?"

We make a game of chasing each other, bogged down by the weight around our ankles. We splash each other like it's the water of an enchanted, glittering lake.

Pen kneels and tries to draw a floating city with her finger, but snow proves to be an unsatisfactory canvas.

I look at the sky, and all I see is more whiteness. I've never known the sky to be any color but blue.

And then, as though I willed it, I see a bit of blue in the sky. Moving.

"Pen!" I gasp.

"What? What is it?" It takes her a moment to see what I'm pointing to, and then she's silent. We both stare at the thing, and turn our heads to follow as it flutters up and out of sight.

"Was that—"

"A bird." My heart is in my throat.

"It was the most perfect thing I've ever seen," Pen says. "Do you think it will ever land?"

"Not if it has any sense."

The moment is broken by a noise in the distance. Along the side of the building, a girl is attempting to scale a tree. We walk toward her until I can better see her wavy hair and the sharp seams in her brown gloves.

"Gertrude?" I say.

She drops from the foothold, a hand to her chest. "Goodness, you scared me half to death," she says. She gives us a sheepish smile. "You can just call me Birdie. Everyone does."

"Were you going to break into our bedroom?" Pen says.

Gertrude looks up. "Is that where you're sleeping? Sorry, girls, that room has the strongest tree outside. You wouldn't mind my traipsing through every now and again, would you? I'm kind of a night owl."

"Well, we wouldn't," Pen says, "but who knows what Her Royal Stinky Highness will do from one day to the next? I wouldn't let her catch you."

Gertrude looks contemplatively at the window again. Her breath comes out in little clouds. She's wearing a coat that seems too thin for this cold, though she has enough beads around her neck to constitute a scarf.

"Your princess is a wet blanket, huh?"

"That's one way to put it," I say.

"Once she senses a weak spot, she goes for the jugular," Pen says. "Here's a silly idea: Why don't you use the door?"

"Father locks it," she says.

"It isn't locked now," I say. "We've just opened it."

"If you give us a heads up, we'll make sure it's unlocked

when you want to sneak out," Pen says. "That way you won't have to sneak through the house or climb through our window and scare everyone senseless."

"You'd do that?" Gertrude says.

"Back home, I used to sneak out all the time," Pen says. "There was this little cavern in the woods. Remember, Morgan?"

Remember? How could I not? It was only last week and a lifetime ago. All I can do is nod. I suddenly feel that I'll cry if I utter a word.

Gertrude smiles. It is a sincere, girlish smile, one that's unaffected by her heavy eyeliner and blood-red lips. "Well, thanks," she says. "I should get washed up before Father wakes us for breakfast. I must look like a ragamuffin."

She's a shy girl in a rebel's garb. The ground is her home, but it's still a big place, and I think she must be like Pen and me—trying to figure out this strange world as it reveals itself, bit by bit.

I think Pen was right, and that Gertrude Piper—Birdie—will have little insight into her father's political dealings, but I would still like to get to know her.

After she's gone inside, Pen looks at me. "What's a night owl?" she says.

I shrug.

By the time we're summoned for breakfast, Birdie is as fresh-faced and bright-eyed as her brothers and sisters. Not a drop of cosmetics on her face. After a night of no sleep, I'm not sure how she manages it, but no one suspects a thing, though I see Nimble elbow her as she takes her place beside him.

The plates are laid before us. Something yellow and fluffy, accompanied by little gray-brown cakes. "Eggs!" Annette says happily.

Pen can't hide her skepticism. "The eggs of what?" she asks. We've never heard of eating something in egg form.

"Chickens," Annette says.

"Chickens are birds," Nimble says, watching to see our reaction.

I tuck my hands under the table. I was already having difficulty forcing an appetite, but now there's no hope for this meal passing between my lips.

"We don't eat a lot of plants," he adds.

"Can it, Nim," Birdie says under her breath. She clears her throat. "Where's Father?"

"Otherwise engaged," Nimble says. "He's with a few of the king's finest, trying to talk that crazy old man out of that ramshackle plane."

"You should talk to that little girl—what's her name?" Celeste says. "His granddaughter."

"Amy," Judas says. "And she hasn't woken up yet. The trip exhausted her."

"How exhausted could she be?" Celeste says. "We're all recovered by now. Except for your brother, Morgan."

At the mention of Lex, my hands turn to fists. She speaks so casually of people she doesn't know at all. She doesn't understand what it's like for Amy and Lex. She doesn't understand blindness or crippling fits or what it means to be anything but royalty.

"Is Amy all right?" Basil whispers to me.

I shake my head at my plate of strange food. I don't know. "I'll go and check on her," I say.

"You have to ask to be excused first," Annette says.

"May I be excused?"

"Yes. You may."

When I open the door to Amy's room, I find her standing at the window, her hair tangled from sleep.

"Here we are," she says.

"Here we are. I went outside this morning. Didn't realize how cold it truly was until I came back inside and the feeling started returning to my fingers."

"It sounds wonderful," she says. Her voice is subdued, though, and when she turns to face me, her eyes are cloudy.

"Would you like something to eat?" I say. "The food is strange, but the princess seems to like it. Pen has sort of been using her as a poison tester."

Amy shakes her head. "My stomach is still recovering from the trip. I am getting restless, though."

"Well, then, how would you like to go outside?" I say. "They could use your help talking the professor out of the bird."

Her eyes brighten at that.

"And speaking of birds, I saw a real one today," I say. "It flew straight across the sky and disappeared."

"You didn't," she gasps.

"There are bound to be more. Maybe we'll see one. Hurry and get dressed."

"Will you come too?" she says.

"Sure, if you want."

"And—could you tell Judas not to tag along?"

"I can talk to him, but—"

"If you want me to try and convince my grandfather to come out, those are my terms," she says. "Let me get dressed."

She shoos me from the room and closes the door.

"Glad you're feeling better," I mutter to the knob.

Judas doesn't take kindly to being left out, but it's enough of a relief to see Amy up and about that he concedes to her demands, though not without grabbing my arm at the door and warning that he will kill me if anything happens while she's in my charge.

It isn't the first time he's threatened me in this way, but it is the first time I believe him. Now that his betrothed is dead, Amy is the only thing he has resembling family. Her frail health and stubborn bravery give him good reason to be concerned.

"I'll guard her as if she were my own," I say.

"If you had given birth to me when you were five," Amy says snidely. Her way of reminding us that she isn't a child.

"Don't worry," Nimble says. "I'm an old pro at driving in this weather."

He drives slowly, glancing back at us in the mirror every now and again. "I couldn't help noticing the tracks outside this morning," he says.

"We've never seen snow before," I say.

"Then this must be a real shock," he says. "What do you get? Rain?"

"Rain?" I ask.

He laughs, turns the wheel against his open palms. "Oh boy."

No matter how far we drive, we never seem to get any closer to the city in the distance. We do pass the field of strange machines I noticed when we landed, though. "What are all of those?" I say, nodding to the machines outside my window.

"Rides," Nimble says. "That's the theme park. Roller coasters and biplane rides to give you the sensation you're flying higher than airplanes. For a penny you can get a look at the underside of the magical floating island through a telescope."

"The magical floating island?" Amy says, scrunching her nose. "That's what people call us?"

"What do you call it, then?"

Amy says "Internment" at the same time I say "Home."

"Internment," Nimble repeats several times, testing the word on his tongue. "As in 'confined.' Creepy."

"It isn't creepy at all," I say.

"Maybe it is," Amy says. "Not at first. You'd have to be there a while to see it."

She's quiet after that.

We pass what appears to be a sort of garden made of rocks, and Amy's breath catches. Her chin snaps up attentively and her eyes are sharp.

"What's wrong?" I ask. "Do you feel another fit coming on?"

She climbs onto her knees and watches through the back window as the garden gets smaller.

"That place gives me the heebie-jeebies too, kid," Nimble says.

"What is it?" I say.

He raises his eyebrows at me in the mirror. "Where do you put your dead on Internment?"

Amy's voice is small and fading when she says, "We burn them. Until they're nothing and nowhere."

I try to explain the tributary to Nimble, how we burn the bodies of our dead so that all the bad in them can fall away, while all the good becomes a mass of colors in the sky that can't be seen by the living. I've believed it all my life, but now that I'm on the ground, it doesn't make as much sense as it once did.

Down here, they bury their dead. Mark the spot with a stone, with dates and names. Leave flowers to remember.

It must be nice to have so much space to squander.

"Have you ever buried anyone?" Amy asks.

"Can't say as I have," Nimble says.

That must be nice, too.

"Here we are," Nimble announces, stopping the car. The bird is several paces away, surrounded by men in coats who appear to be convening.

"Morning, boys," Nimble says, and opens the door for Amy and me. "We all figured you wouldn't have much luck talking him out, so I've brought someone to help. This here's the old man's granddaughter."

After a brief discussion, Jack, who seems to be heading this unsuccessful operation, agrees to let Amy inside. "Go with her," he tells Nimble.

"No," Amy says. "It won't do any good unless I go alone. He's quite stubborn."

The men all exchange glances. Jack hesitates. Amy nods to the red metal funnel that's in his hands. "May I?" she says.

He's so perplexed by her straightforwardness that he hands it to her. She holds the funnel near her mouth. "Grandpa, it's me. Amy." Her voice is magnified. "I've come to talk to you."

She hands the funnel to Jack. "Thank you," she says.

Nothing happens for a few seconds, and then there's the unlatching of locks. Amy breezes past us and opens the door, disappearing into the darkness and then closing it behind her.

The men are all astonished. With a few words she's managed to do what they've been trying to do all morning.

Nimble folds his arms. "She's a real firecracker, isn't she?"

I don't know what that means, but it sounds apt. "She's hard to stop . . ." My voice trails as I step back and look at the bird. Just as the ground looked like a patchwork quilt of land, the bird is a patchwork of metal in varying hues. It's at least three stories high, it tilts to one side, and it stands on legs that are made of blades for burrowing through the soil. The wings are folded now, like a beetle that has fallen dead.

It doesn't look like it would fly so much as hurtle through the sky and then destroy the ground it hit. But I am still astounded by the sight of it. Astounded that such a thing could be designed, assembled, welded, and created in secret, quite under the king's nose. It was a refuge for us. It's the embodiment of our rebellion, our liberation. It's the thing my parents and Amy's sister and countless others died for. It was nearly a lifetime in the making.

I understand why the professor won't leave it.

In my observing, I've wandered away from the others, but Nimble has followed me. "I'm impressed that it flew," he says.

"Me too," I say. "I might not have boarded it if I'd had much of a choice."

I shut my mouth immediately. I've said too much. What will Jack Piper and his family do if they realize we're all fugitives? All of us but the princess, anyway, and Thomas, who was dragged along as her hostage.

Then again, what would it matter to anyone down here how the people carry about on that tiny floating rock so very high above them?

"Sounds as though there was some trouble in paradise," Nimble says.

"Paradise?"

"Your perfect little island," he says, nodding upward. I follow his gaze, hoping for a glimpse of Internment. But there's only a sky heavy with clouds. These clouds are not like the ones I know—light airy things that soared around and over me every day. These clouds are burdened and gray, and I sense that they are grieving.

"There are no perfect places," I say. The clouds move away from the sun just enough for the light to blind me, and I shield my eyes.

"You know that and I know that," he says. "Try telling our king, and you'll be run out of the kingdom. He thinks that if we plan an aerial attack over the right places, once the ashes clear, we'll be in our own utopia."

I don't know the capabilities of a bomb, but surely it wouldn't take much to destroy a small city like Internment.

"Firecrackers, bombs," I say. "You people sure do like things that burn."

"I imagine there aren't many fires on Internment?" he says.

"Even a small one is cause to panic," I say. I suppose something like the fire at the flower shop would be nothing to the people down here, but it was enough to throw all of Internment into upheaval.

I can feel his gaze on me as I look for a trace of Internment in the sky. I know what he's thinking. That we were foolish to come here. We left our safe little island and descended straight into a kingdom at war. But while they fight with explosives down here, different battles are being waged in the sky. Silent revolutions. Equally silent murders.

"You don't know anything," I whisper. I'm not sure if the words are for him, or for me.

The door of the metal bird creaks open and Amy descends the ladder alone. She's talking to Jack and his men, and by their disappointed expressions it becomes clear that her attempt to lure the professor out wasn't a successful one.

"All right, all right. It looks like there will be another storm coming. Let's reconvene once I've spoken to His Majesty. Nim, please see our guests home."

"Can do, Father."

Once we're back in the car, Amy says, "My grandfather will come out in time. He's just got an awful lot of love for that metal bird. He's afraid they'll destroy it if he leaves."

"What makes you so sure he'll come out, then?" Nimble asks.

"He'll run out of food soon. He asked me to bring him some more just now, and I told him that if he wants to eat, he'll have to come out." She dusts the snow from the shoulders of her plaid coat.

"But if he's so stubborn, what makes you sure he won't starve to death rather than come out?" Nimble says.

"He won't. He's far too curious about this place. He'll be taking a magnifying glass to the insects and collecting soil samples soon enough. You'll see."

The car starts to move. Overhead, the sky has begun to darken. The sun is behind the clouds like light trying to hatch from an egg. I feel as though I'm being smothered.

Amy seems better now, though. Her eyes are their usual blue and her mouth hangs open as she watches the city in the distance.

"What did you call that place where you bury your dead?" she asks.

"A graveyard," Nimble says.

"Can anyone visit?"

"You want to visit the graveyard?" he says.

"If I can."

"I guess it can't hurt," Nimble says. "It's not much to see, though. People go to visit their loved ones, and kids go at night to spook each other, and that's all the action these places get."

"Do you always bury your dead?" I say, trying to hide how appalling I think the whole thing is.

"Not always," Nimble says, his tone cheery to the point of sarcasm. "Sometimes we cremate. I'm guessing that's what your kind does up there, with so little land."

"It makes the most sense," I say.

"It isn't that we don't like to burn stuff down here," Nimble says. "Most homes have a fire altar. There's one at the hotel, in fact. Even guests use it."

"You burn bodies out on your lawn?" I say, my stomach beginning to turn.

"Not bodies. Offerings," Nimble says. "If there's something you really want to ask of our god, you burn something that's of equal importance to you."

At last a ritual I don't find wasteful. It seems poetic, even. "We have something like that on Internment," I say. "Once a year we burn our highest request and set it up on the wind to be heard."

"Once a year." Nim whistles. "You could burn things all day down here if you wanted. People have no shortage of things to ask for."

"So you burn things often, then," I say.

"I don't, personally. Don't take much stock in it."

As soon as the car has stopped at the graveyard, Amy is gone, leaving the open car door behind her to fill the car with cold.

"We won't be long," I say apologetically. I don't expect

him to understand a girl like Amy. He can't appreciate what the edge has done to her.

I expect some sort of judgment or another remark about how odd she is, but "I'll keep the car warm for you," is all he says.

The graveyard is framed by hedges, and the entrance is through a pair of elaborate iron doors ingrained with flying children holding some sort of stringed instrument.

Amy is knelt in the snow when I find her. She clears away the brambles until the words on the headstone before her are revealed. "Lila Pike. It says she died the year she was born," Amy says.

"That's miserable," I say.

"I wonder what happened."

I don't.

I look up from the stone. It is only one among hundreds of untold stories. Names, dates, flowers in vases left to wilt under all this white.

There's so much land on the ground that they can make a garden of all their dead. It's no matter whether anyone ever comes to visit.

Amy looks over her shoulder at me. Her brow is raised. "What do you think happens when they bury you here, and years pass, and everyone who knew you is dead? Who comes to visit? Or do they mow this down and start over?"

"I don't know," I say. "It seems like such a waste—all of it."

"Maybe not," Amy says. "If there were a place I could go and visit my sister, talk to her—I think I'd like that."

"I don't think I could visit my parents in a place like this," I say. "There are no spirits here. Only stones."

"There are spirits," Amy says with certainty. "But these spirits aren't our spirits."

I don't know what she means. She's a peculiar little girl who says peculiar things, but her outlandish remarks are different from the kind that other children tell. She speaks assuredly. And when she awakens from her fits, there's real sadness, and that sadness lingers with her for days.

And though I don't entirely believe in the things she claims, I don't think it's all her imagination. A normal girl would want to imagine happy things.

A breeze disturbs the bare branches and I hug my arms when it reaches me.

I'd much like to leave now, but Amy may well miss out on much of the exploring, due to her fits and Judas's overprotectiveness, and if this is all she wants, she should get to see it.

The wind picks up, as though it means to force us away. The rusted gate swings on its hinge, an invitation to leave.

But the squealing gate isn't the only noise. There's a low whistle, and then a crack so loud Amy jumps to her feet. "What was that?" she says. Another crack. Louder, so much louder, than the thunder that horrified us the other night when we heard it for the first time.

Straight ahead of us, the headstones make a path to the horizon. They offer no answers. And they have no reaction to that black billowing smoke where a building stood only seconds ago.

I think of what Nimble said. Bomb.

"Come on!" I grab her arm and run for the gate. I don't look back. She's gasping for breath beside me, but she manages to keep up. I have a fleeting thought that this could trigger one of her fits, but I don't know what caused that explosion or if there will be another.

The day the flower shop caught fire, I thought it had the power to end my little world. How was I to know that there were bigger fires happening below us? I don't know what it would take to end a world this size, if anything could. All I've seen are more terrifying ways to destroy, to no end at all.

Nimble is speeding away even before I've had a chance to close the door. The car lurches and swerves on the ice.

"Looks like you ladies arrived just in time for the fun to begin," he says.

4

The black clouds are visible from the hotel by the time we've returned to it. I see them rolling in the distance, moving the way that giant body of water moves, snuffing out the bereft gray clouds. The sun has made a wise decision to hide from us completely.

The car jolts to a stop by the front door. "Go on inside," Nimble says.

"Aren't you coming?" I ask.

"After I park," he says. "Aerial warfare's bad for the paint."

The front door swings open and there the Piper children stand, perfectly in order, all of them with the same frightened eyes. "Nim!" Birdie calls as he speeds around the building.

"Where's he going?" Riles asks.

"To park in the carriage house. Him and his love for that stupid bus," Birdie says.

"I'll help," Riles says, but Birdie catches him by the collar as he tries to run outside.

"Don't be a pest." She ruffles his hair. "Leave the door open for him."

"What happened?" Basil says.

Everyone is full of questions. Everyone is talking. The words bounce off my skin, never reaching me, not really. I move to the nearest window and I step behind those gold curtains to watch the smoke blend into the sky.

"It's like the flower shop fire times a thousand, isn't it?" Celeste's voice startles me. She's standing beside me, both of us tented off from the others.

"You wouldn't know, would you?" I say. "Or did you see it from your clock tower window?"

"I was out hunting with my brother that day, I'll have you know," she says. "True, we were some distance away, but I could smell the smoke."

Snapping at the princess won't do any good. Even if her father and his henchmen did start that fire in an attempt to cease the rebellion, she had nothing to do with it. She hasn't made her sinister side a secret, but when she held Pen and me hostage, I got a sense for how little she knew of her father's plans. She wasn't interested in or aware of any of them. She only wanted me to help her get to the ground. Nothing more.

"So this is what you left your floating kingdom for," I say, nodding ahead. "Are you glad you came?"

She takes a deep breath, straightens her shoulders. "I understand that you're frightened, so I'm going to let this bitterness slide," she says. "But I'll have you know that you're beginning to sound like that brazen friend of yours, and I know you're better than that. Anyway, I wasn't looking to argue."

"What were you looking for, then?" I say.

"I wanted to check on you, of course," she says.

I look at her from the corners of my eyes.

"Oh, all right. I also wanted to ask what you saw out there."

"I heard an explosion and then I saw the smoke," I say. "Nimble called it an aerial attack."

Celeste arranges her thumbs and index fingers like a frame and holds them to the glass, considering. "Do you suppose this has been going on below us the whole time?" she says.

"I don't know," I say. "I don't know how anyone can live in a world where this happens frequently."

Celeste looks at me. Her smile is toothy and bright. "Then we've come just in time to save them, wouldn't you say?"

I bring a tray of food to Alice and Lex. I can't think of any other way to make myself useful. I tell them about the explosion, and the smoke. And I tell them about the graveyard.

How much can the people of the ground value life when they have so much land with which to bury their dead? What's a few more stones? But I don't say that. "The princess thinks we can help them," is what I say.

Alice looks concerned. "Did she say why she came with us?"

"No," I say. "But she seemed pretty desperate. Enough that she interrogated Pen and me, and held Thomas at knifepoint so we wouldn't kick her off the bird."

Lex's transcriber sits on the floor near the bed, and the lack of smell that its coppery motor usually emits tells me he hasn't used it since we arrived. We all left in a hurry the night I was poisoned. I was unconscious and dying in Basil's arms. But Alice thought to grab the one thing that will surely keep Lex sane; she must have known there would be no turning back.

Lex sits on the floor beside the thing, his legs folded, worrying a square metal clock in his hands. The ticking provides an anchor, reminds him that even in his persistent darkness, the seconds never cease. He doesn't need to know the hour; he only needs to know that they're still passing.

"This war may just be getting started," Alice says.

"Basil says that the Pipers will want to collect on their kindness in taking us in," I say. "I've been giving it a lot of thought, but I can't imagine how we could help. It isn't as though we have any more ties to home than they do. We can't go back."

"They don't know that," Lex says. His head is down, and his voice is scratchy. "We'd better hope they don't figure out how powerless we are."

Alice frowns into her tea. Then she kneels before Lex and replaces the clock in his hands with the cup. "Drink this," she says. "And then we should eat something. We're going to need our strength."

"Strength for what?" Lex says.

"For living," she says, with that persistent vivacity I've always loved her for. "I don't know what's to come, but we'd better prepare ourselves to face it." She brings the cup to his lips, forcing it on him. She kisses his forehead when he scowls at her. "Drink it."

Hours pass and Jack Piper doesn't return. The smaller children occupy themselves with some sort of game that involves a board of squares.

Nimble enters through the front door.

"I didn't realize you'd gone outside," Birdie says, looking up from her mathematics sheet.

He's tucking a cloth into his pocket. "There was a smudge on the seat of the car that was nagging me."

"You risked your safety going outside for that? After a bombing? Sometimes I think you value that car more than you do us."

"Don't be silly, Birds," he says, and flicks her hair. "Of course I care more about the car."

She rolls her eyes, blows at a bit of eraser dust on the page.

That car is his only haven, I realize. The Piper children live in this very large home, and yet every corner belongs to their father, and every move they make is scrutinized. That small place belongs only to Nimble, though, and it can take him anywhere he may ever wish to go.

Some phantom part of me keeps expecting a patrol-man to come around and turn on the screen so there can be a broadcast with some news. But there are no patrol-men. There are no screens. There's only something called a transistor radio, the knobs of which are arranged to make a permanently startled face. And it isn't giving us any news right now. It's only playing some sort of jaunty music that reminds me that this is not my home.

Celeste and Nimble sit by the fireplace, stacks of books between them. The pages are open in their laps, but they're looking at each other. I catch bits of what they're saying. Kings. Death. Something called a biplane. She is fascinated and excited.

Basil, Pen, Thomas, and I sit together on the lush floor. A carpet, they call it; it's nothing at all like the tiny rugs my mother and Lex used to weave from old clothing scraps. "You know what this reminds me of?" Pen says.

"Don't tell me you can liken a passage from our history book to this," Thomas says.

"Of course I can." She raises her chin. "This is like the story of the dark time. Hundreds of years ago, Phinneas Hart discovered a way to store the sun's energy and use it as fuel. He knew it would revolutionize the way Internment worked, but his greedy brother, the banker, advised him to charge money for the new technology. The god of the sky was so displeased by this display of greed that the sky filled with clouds, and the clouds covered the sun completely. Crops wilted. Children and the elderly grew ill first, but slowly the illness began to overtake everyone.

47

"Phinneas recognized what was happening, and he abandoned his brother's ideas, and he toiled for months laying the groundwork for the glasslands, and he wouldn't take a page of money for it."

"Yes, I've always found that story a bit hard to believe," Thomas says.

"Because you're a heathen," Pen says. "In any case, the god of the sky returned the sunlight with a warning about charging for what should be free. If people were going to be greedy, he could take the source of that greed away. That's why it's against the law for any king to pass a bill that would charge for wind or solar energy."

"Why does this remind you of the dark time?" Basil asks.

Pen stares at her betrothal band, twisting it round and round her finger. "Because," she says. "This is what happens when there's greed. Everything gets destroyed until there's nothing left to take."

Thomas puts his arm around her shoulders, and in a rare display of fondness she leans against him.

"It isn't as bad as all that," I tell her, though I don't entirely believe it. "The ground is much bigger than Internment. These bombs couldn't possibly end it all."

"Don't you see it?" she says. "All this space has made them cocky. Look at how big their houses are. Look at how many children they have. A cloud of smoke and a few explosions are only the start, Morgan. These people are doomed, and it doesn't matter where we're from. We're along for the ride now, all of us."

"I'm so fortunate to be betrothed to an optimist," Thomas says.

She sighs, irritated. "Don't take me seriously, then. You'll see."

"I do take you seriously, Pen. I just worry you'll go spiraling if you talk like this."

She opens her mouth to argue, but I say, "Let's see if the others will let us join their game."

For me, Pen relinquishes her side of the argument.

The board games are all simple, quick, and mindless. Birdie often forgets it's her turn because she's staring worriedly at the door. When it finally opens, she about jumps from her skin. She rushes to take her father's coat.

Nimble looks up from his book. "What did you find out?"

"The banks are gone," Jack says.

"The hospital?"

"No, though it may only be a matter of time."

Marjorie, Riles, and Annette are wide-eyed, and Jack smiles at them. "Nothing to be alarmed about, children," he says. "It's all just a game that our King Ingram is playing with King Erasmus."

"What will the winner get?" Annette asks.

"Something very precious," Jack says. "A very important place." He nods to Celeste, who is rising to her feet from across the room. "Princess, if I may speak with you privately," he says.

"Certainly," she says. She follows him from the room, Nimble at her heels. Birdie rushes after them, only to have the door closed in her face.

She scowls and presses her ear to the door, nearly stumbling when it opens and Nimble pokes his head out at her. "Father says to go on and have dinner without us."

"But—"

The door closes again.

"Riles," Birdie whispers. He has already read her mind. He scales the back of the couch and climbs onto her shoulders. He's just high enough now to reach a crack in the plaster wall. He presses his ear to his drinking glass to amplify the sound, and listens. Clearly the two of them have this down to a science.

"Anything?" she asks.

"Not if you keep yapping."

He listens a few seconds more, and Birdie arches her back uncomfortably. And just when I think she can carry his weight no longer, he climbs down.

"No one died," Riles says. "That's all I could get. That's good, isn't it?"

Birdie looks worried. "I don't know," she says, and then she blinks away her melancholy. "I owe you some ice cream after dinner, but don't tell your sisters."

"Pleasure doing business," he says.

5

"I don't like this one bit," Pen says, scouring her face with a wet cloth. "Her Duplicitous Highness has been at conference with Jack Piper for hours now."

I lie back in the drained tub, letting my legs dangle over the edge. "What do you suppose they're talking about?" I say.

"If she's smart, she isn't telling him all about the way Internment is run. But she's as dumb as a rock, and she loves to hear her own voice." Pen begins furiously braiding her hair. "When I think of my mother and all those people up there, I just—I can't stand it."

"What?"

"How powerless they'd all be against something like what I saw today. One bomb, and it would all be gone. And down here they fire them off like it's nothing."

She drops her braid and struggles to fix it, but she can't seem to steady her hands.

"Pen." I reach for her. She sits on the edge of the tub, sulking. I fix her hair. "There's no sense thinking about it. All the bombs they've got on the ground can't reach Internment. Nothing can. Not even that bird we saw this morning."

"Not even us," Pen whispers, broken.

I wrap my arms around her waist and pull her into the tub with me. I was hoping to make her laugh, but she flops unceremoniously against me.

"Tell me another story from the history book," I say. "What about the tree that grew endless fruit after the infestation killed the crops?"

"It wasn't an infestation," Pen says. "You always get that part confused. It was a drought. The lakes weren't replenishing. The people were losing faith in the god of the sky. Fish were rotting in the sun."

"And then?" I say.

"You know the story," she sighs. She flails until she's able to free herself from the tub. "I'm going to bed."

She reaches her hand out to me, and I let her pull me to my feet. I'm not tired at all, but there isn't anything more to do. The sooner we sleep, the sooner it will be morning. And maybe there will be some answers then.

Celeste still hasn't returned by the time I turn out the light. Pen's bed and mine are separated by a small table that holds a black book and an alarm clock. The ticking feels louder in the darkness, drowned only by Pen's tosses and turns.

I don't move. Guilt has made me fear the days to come. If experiencing this war is the price I must pay for my curiosity, then I accept. But Pen never asked for this. Nor did Basil and Thomas. And they're all here, one way or another, because of me.

The door creaks open, letting in the faint glow of the fireplace down in the lobby.

"About bloody time, Princess," Pen mutters. "Don't even think about blinding us with the light."

"It's me," Birdie whispers. "I'm sorry, but Father is still downstairs and I—I need that tree."

She sounds as frightened as I feel.

I sit up. "Is it safe to be out there?"

"I don't care about safe," she says.

"We have something in common, then," Pen says. "Take us with you."

"Or you'll tell on me?" Birdie says unhappily.

"Of course not," Pen says. "I just think it would be the decent thing for you to invite us. We are letting you use our window and all."

Birdie hesitates. "You won't find anything suitable to wear in this room," she says. "All these clothes belonged to my mother. Let me go see if I can't scare up a couple of dresses."

We stuff our beds with pillows. Birdie is impressed with the deftness by which Pen and I can descend the tree, even with the icy branches. "We're all a lot of natural climbers," Pen says, hopping to the ground. "After a while there's nowhere to go but up and then back down again."

"Where to now?" I say.

"We have to walk for a bit," Birdie says apologetically. "But then we can take the ferry once we reach the harbor.

Used to be it would close by nine, but since the war the king has resolved never to let the city sleep. Makes us superior to King Erasmus, he thinks."

"Even if a bomb has just gone off?" I say.

"Especially then. The Cranlin will be open until sunup. That's our cinema. Do you have moving pictures on Internment?"

I imagine an image, blurry and monochrome, like the school portrait of Daphne after her murder. I imagine the image moving, her stoic eye blinking, and it gives me a chill. "Sounds terrifying," I say.

"Not at all!" Birdie laughs at Pen's and my startled expressions. "They're the bee's knees." She loops her arms over the backs of our necks as we trudge forward. "Seems I have a lot to show you, girls."

She introduces us to the harbor, and the roaring body of water she calls an ocean. "Is that like a big lake?" Pen asks.

"Much, much bigger, and full of salt," Birdie says. "And the sea has more creatures than lakes. Whales and sharks and mermaids—they have human hair, you know."

"Of all things," I breathe.

Birdie bounces on her heels, looking at the lights coasting across the water toward us. "That's the ferry," she says.

Pen elbows me. "Look!"

But I'm still trying to imagine what sort of fish could have human hair, and when I look at the water, every bit of light now seems like it could be filled with strands.

There's a tea-steeped moon above us, cratered and beaming. Strange how it looks as near now as it did when we lived in the sky, even as the clouds meandered alongside the city.

The ferry pushes out into the water, leaving my stomach and lungs on dry land. How easily I forget this afternoon and all the fears that came with it. Pen and Birdie crowd me at the railing. We are looking for mermaids and fins.

Pen looks between the harbor and the city lights in the distance. I know her. She's charting the course, memorizing the details most others would miss. She'll be drafting maps of it for days. Even as a child she would pen maps of every place she'd been, on the back of her hand and on walls if she couldn't find paper in time. It became a part of her, as obvious as the green of her eyes. And one day it became her name, and no one ever questioned it, it was that certain.

"There's one!" Birdie points to where the water has become crowded with bubbles. There's a head of hair as silver as the light on the water, and once it's under again, there's the flicker of a fin as long as my forearm. Pen squeaks with delight.

"They never come near land and you probably won't see their faces, but they like to flirt."

"Have you ever seen one up close?" I say.

"Once. I was fishing with Nim, and his hook got caught up in her hair. She let out this wail, I swear, that could be heard from the heavens. Scared him so much, he dropped the pole, which may have been what she was after. They like to collect human things. Which reminds me, mind your jewelry. I saw one jump up and snatch the beads right off a woman's neck." She presses her hat against her head at the memory.

Pen and I close our fists around our betrothal bands.

The ocean waves slap against the ferry, more turbulent than any of the lakes back home. It's no wonder; the ocean is filled with so many creatures swimming about.

"There could be cities underwater," Pen says. "A whole society with buildings made up of human things."

"There's more shrimp than you could ever eat," Birdie says.

Pen makes a face. "Do those have human hair, too?"

Birdie laughs. Out here, her eyes aren't downcast. She isn't all "please" and "thank you" and "yes, Father" this and that. She tells us about all the sea creatures she can think of—hard little fish that look like stars and crawl like hands along the ocean floor, and whales that could swallow a village if they had a mind to.

"A fish big enough to swallow a person." Pen is giddy. "What a hilarious way to die, in the digestive tract of a fish."

"Whales aren't fish," Birdie says, which is all the more absurd a notion.

"You live in a strange world, Birdie," Pen says.

The ferry comes to a stop, and once we're on land again, I topple dizzily into the two of them, which sends us all into giggles. We collect a few stares from passersby, but they mean nothing. We are young and enchanted and clattering with beads. We are untouchable.

I find myself very aware of the ground under my feet. It's unlike the cobbles back home. Rather, it's solid and black, and its paths branch out like a flat tree, all of them leading to bright lights and music and possibility.

"Cinema's this way," Birdie says, tugging us by the wrists.

"It hardly seems like you're at war," I say.

"That's how King Ingram prefers it," she says.

"You've met him?" Pen says.

"Lots of times. Father has him over for dinner when there are matters to discuss. It's a real honor. The king's paranoid about poisons and he doesn't trust a lot of people to prepare his meals."

"Our king doesn't come out of hiding much either," Pen says. "He and his family live in a clock tower that's full of dungeons."

"How medieval. Here we are, girls!"

The cinema is a wedge-shaped building, the top of which is framed by a strip of light, and the words "ETIENNE JONES DOUBLE FEATURE."

"What an unusual sign," I say.

"It's a marquee," Birdie says. She hands silver coins to a man behind the glass and we go inside. She leads us into a dimly lit room that's full of chairs and already crowded. "You're going to love it," she says.

Pen is eyeing the girls in the front row who are passing a bottle among them, taking swigs. I can smell from here that it's some kind of tonic, which wouldn't be allowed in public back home.

Nobody here seems to mind.

I clear my throat loudly. "What was that name on the building?"

"Etienne Jones," Birdie says. "She's the biggest star in the kingdom. Wait till you see her."

I stare at the giant screen that takes up the wall before us like a giant image waiting to be developed.

Then the screen goes black and music starts to play. Pen loops her arm around mine and squeezes. The world doesn't seem so scary now that she's in good spirits. It's not all warfare and doom.

The moving picture is gray and jumpy. Lips move and then the words appear for us to read. Etienne Jones has bobbed hair and ringed eyes, and when she walks down the street, she kicks her heels, and all the men watch, dropping hatboxes and getting elbowed by their wives.

But the image is merely a projection. The screen is only fabric. And though our screens on Internment are much smaller and are never used for entertainment, they are more advanced than this. I wonder how it could be that our tiny floating city could be ahead on any of the technology.

For hours, we watch the antics of the upbeat actors on the screen, our laughter a roar that blends in with everyone else's.

By the time we make our way back to the streets, I have no idea what the hour may be.

"I heard that story you were telling earlier," Birdie says. "About the dark times and the solar energy."

"It's from our history book," Pen says.

"She knows all the stories," I say.

"Have you seen the ginormous black book on your nightstand? That's *The Text of All Things*," Birdie says. "Father insists on leaving one for all the guests. Thinks he can save everyone's soul. I think it's all a lot of baloney, myself. Most of it, anyway."

"Was it written by prophets like our history book?" Pen asks.

"Prophets, yes."

"And the god of the ground told them what to write?"

"Well." Birdie checks her reflection in a shop window and begins twirling a lock of hair. "We don't say 'the god of the ground.' It's just 'The God.'"

"Just the one? For the ground and the sky and everything?" Pen asks.

"I think so," Birdie says.

Pen looks at me like this is the stupidest thing she has ever heard, and maybe it is. I scan the city, hoping for something I can use to change the subject. Thomas is right. This is the sort of talk that can send her spiraling.

Whether or not it's a welcome one, a distraction finds us in the form of brassy music streaming through a door that's been left ajar. Pen stops us from walking and looks inside. There's the smell of smoke and tonic. Giggles and clatters. Sparkling drinks floating on trays.

Pen is hypnotized. "What is this?" she says, swatting me when I try to pull her away. I follow her gaze to a woman who is gyrating on a table. Her beads swish around her throat in shimmering ovals, and she kicks her leg in an arch right over the head of some lovesick boy. Her lips are red, and I see now what Birdie has been trying to model herself after.

"It's a brass club," Birdie says. Her voice is almost too soft to hear.

Pen, stars in her eyes, takes a step forward, but Birdie pulls her back. "We can't go in there," she gasps.

Pen looks with heartbreak at the hand that's holding her back. "Why not?"

"We just . . . can't," Birdie says.

"It must be late," I say.

"We're already going to have to sneak back in," Pen says. "Why not have a little more fun?"

Birdie stutters and looks worriedly over her shoulder.

"Don't hold out on us now," Pen says. "I saw you come home after the stars had gone to bed." With that, she plunges into the crowd.

"I'm so sorry, Birdie, she can be like this," I say, and hurry after her. I can't imagine the trouble Pen could get into in a place like this, with tonic shimmering in glasses everywhere.

Pen has already progressed through curtain after curtain of smoke. She's made a direct beeline for the dancing woman, who is tall and so skinny, she's concave. A man at the table holds what must be her shoes.

The dancing woman smiles at Pen, and it's as though they have a sort of kinship somehow, for in the dancing woman's eyes is a melancholy under all that cosmetic.

Or maybe the melancholy belongs to me. I can't be certain.

The music doesn't cease, but it changes. The dancing woman climbs down, and as she does, the man who holds her shoes leans in for a kiss. "Sorry, Mac," she says, smiling with all her teeth. "The bank's closed."

Birdie stands beside me, both of us watching the dancing woman talk to Pen. We can't make out her words, but she wraps her long arms around Pen's shoulders and says something before kissing her cheek. And then she's gone, waving her shoes above her head, to begin another dance.

Pen spins around to face us, giddy.

Birdie and I are on her at once.

"What did she say?"

"You have to tell us!"

"She said, 'Now is our time to be queens.'" She stands a bit taller for having repeated it. "And then she told me not to take any wooden nickels."

I don't know what that means—any of it—but Pen is glowing. With a single hand she lifts three nearly empty glasses from the dancing woman's table and hands one to each of us.

"Pen!" I say.

"What? It isn't as though anyone is still drinking out of them. Come on, a toast." She raises her glass. "To the coronation of three queens. Oh, don't look like that. You aren't going to make me drink alone, are you?"

Birdie raises her glass warily. I believe she's never had a drink before, though nobody here would suspect it by the looks of her; she's made up so confidently. I raise my glass to show her it won't be as bad as all that.

"What's it like?" Birdie asks.

"How should I know?" Pen laughs. It's a beautiful, free laugh. "This is your world, not mine."

"There now," I say. "Bottoms up."

The tonic of the ground has a greater burn than anything I've ever tasted on Internment, even from the myriad of bottles Pen and I found after we'd picked the lock in her mother's cabinet. Birdie coughs, and Pen pats her back sympathetically. "Come on," Pen says. "We'll look for something yellow or pink. Nothing pink is ever menacing."

By the fourth or fifth glass, Birdie has stopped spluttering the stuff back up before she can swallow it. "I can't hear myself think in here," she says.

"Isn't that the point?" Pen says, mimicking the dance moves she's been observing all night. They make her look deranged, like she's trying to stomp invisible bugs.

I laugh. "What is that supposed to be?"

"I don't think anyone knows." She snorts, which sends us all into hysterics. "The dancing and the music and the hair and the dresses—it's all so brilliantly tacky."

"We really should go," Birdie says.

"For a girl who sneaks out at night, you really are no fun," Pen says.

"Birdie's right," I say.

"Morgan, you more than anyone should be glad we're here. Isn't this exactly what you've been dreaming about all your life?"

She's right and she's wrong all at once. I have dreamed of the ground for as long as I can remember, but the most talented imagination in human existence couldn't have foreseen this. It's all so bright and fast and terrifying.

"Dance with me!" Pen says, grabbing my arms. I backpedal, pulling her for the door.

"You, my friend, are ossified," Birdie says, and giggles at Pen. I don't know what that means, but I suspect it applies to her as well.

When we burst outside into the cold air, Pen opens her arms and throws her head back and says, "I can't believe we could get away with that in public."

"There aren't any speakeasies on Internment?" Birdie asks. She slips on a patch of ice, and I catch her by the arm.

"Only bottles and locks and drawn curtains," Pen says, trying to balance on the edge of the sidewalk, to little avail. "This cold is drawing the burn right out of my veins," she sulks. "I think I'm already sober."

"You aren't," I assure her.

"I don't know how you're both holding it so well," Birdie says. "The ground is tilting."

"Isn't it great?" Pen says. With a shriek she topples into a pile of snow. "Morgan is a sensible drunk," she tells Birdie as she picks herself up.

"Some sense," I say. "I don't even know where we are."

"I do; everything's jake," Birdie says. "You've done this kind of thing before?"

"Now and again," I say. "Not often."

"Not often," Birdie echoes, rolling my accent down her tongue.

"Only when we're together," Pen says. "We have a pact. Never drink to combat our sorrows and only drink when we're together."

"Why?" Birdie says.

"Because it's dangerous otherwise," I say, fighting off a chill that is not entirely brought on by the wind. Lex. I had my first sip of tonic the day we learned Lex would never see again. My parents kept vigil in his hospital room, and they sent me home to an empty apartment. But Pen was waiting for me on the steps; she took me by the hand and she led me to our secret cavern, the bottles clinking in her satchel. That day was an ocean in itself, filled with creatures that wanted to pull me to uncertain depths.

It's as though Pen knows what I'm thinking, for she wraps her arm around my shoulders and kisses my cheek.

Pen looks to Birdie. "I should like to know more about your lonely god."

"That part is boring," Birdie says. "The divinities are the only parts I ever liked in my studies."

"What are divinities?" I ask. I had hoped to keep Pen from mourning our own faraway god, but if we're to live in this world, we should learn about its faith.

"They're like guardians," Birdie says. "They keep the elements safe. They're the first creatures to have existed in the world, and everyone descends from them."

"So the divinities are human, then," Pen says.

Birdie shakes her head, loses her balance and giggles as she stumbles. "There's Aresi, who doesn't have a body. She lives on the wind and can be thousands of places at once. And there's Terra, who makes things grow, and when living things die, it's her job to guide their spirits up to the afterlife."

"So it's her fault Internment is floating in the sky, then." I laugh.

"She must not have liked us," Pen says.

"Maybe she thought we were dead and the whole city got stuck halfway to the afterlife," I say. And after I've said the words, I realize with certainty that I'm still drunk.

"Growing up by the water, I was made to learn a lot about Ehco," Birdie says. "When the world was created, he was the first creature of the sea, and he was as small as a worm. And he asked God why he was meant to live in that whole huge body of water, and The God told him that when he put mankind in the world, mankind would sometimes ask The God for things he wouldn't be able to do. And mankind would grow angry with him—and they would grow sad, and that anger and sorrow needed someplace to go, and so it would be Ehco's job to consume it and keep it in his body so that it didn't destroy the world. He was a small thing then, but soon the ocean would be the only thing big enough to contain him. And eventually he divided himself into pieces—a bit in each ocean."

Pen cranes her neck to get a view of the water in the distance. "Your ocean does seem to go on forever," she says, "but I don't think it's big enough to contain all the anger and the sorrow in the world."

"They're only stories," Birdie says. "People live their lives devoted to them. My father made us memorize passages from *The Text*, but even as a girl I never believed them. Except maybe for Ehco."

"Why just Ehco?" I say.

"Because when I see anger and sadness," Birdie says, "I can't believe it's for nothing. I like the idea that there's a great monster in the sea who keeps all the bad thoughts so we can let them go."

She has slowed a pace behind us, and Pen and I stop to take her hands as we make our way back to the hotel.

I had worried about sneaking past the princess upon our return, but her bed is empty and neatly made up. Early gray light follows us in through the window.

"She can't still be meeting with your father," Pen says.

Birdie opens the door and looks out into the hallway. "Nope. Fireplace is out," she whispers. "Father is always the one to put it out before he goes to bed." She lurches in an unfortunate and familiar way, and, hand over mouth, she staggers off for the water room. They call it a bathroom down here, but that doesn't make much sense, as the bath is only a small part of the room's purpose.

Pen falls facedown on her bed with a groan. "I'd say I'll feel this in the morning, but it's already morning, and I already do."

I help her under the covers. "What do you suppose that princess is off doing?" she mumbles into her pillow.

I fall gratefully into my bed. "Whatever it is, we can't let on that we knew she was gone."

"She's only a princess," Pen says. "We're queens now, remember."

I close my eyes and see Internment cloaked in silver. Everyone has black lips and ringed eyes. The train pulls across the screen, and I'm not awake to see the last car go by.

6

"Up and at 'em!" Annette says, knocking on our door as she makes her rounds through the hotel. She's done this every morning since we arrived. I hear the phrase echo what seems to be a thousand times as she knocks on all the doors.

Pen whimpers and pulls the blanket over her head.

Celeste stirs in the bed across from mine. She must have come in sometime after Pen and I snuck in, and though she makes no complaint, I can see by her heavy feet and her bleary eyes that she's worse off for it.

"Morgan," she says. "Did your father ever mention anything about the glasslands to you?"

"Why would he?" I say. I crane my neck to have a look at myself in the mirror, and what I see is enough to make me want to stay in bed.

"I just assumed that as a patrolman he might have been called there."

"He didn't discuss his work with me," I say. The throbbing in my head steals my attention from the aching in my chest; she speaks so casually of my father, when her father is the reason he's dead.

Celeste moves behind the changing screen, and moments later her nightgown has been flung upon its edge.

"Don't suppose you'd know much about your father's work there, Margaret," she says.

"Never call me that," Pen says from beneath her covers. "And what would you know about my father's work?"

"I make it a point to know about the people of Internment," Celeste answers pertly.

"Well, then," Pen says. "You know I think you should take a running jump from that window there."

"He works there, doesn't he?" Celeste says, her condescending cheer undeterred by Pen's tone. "Today I have an audience with the king, and I only thought, if either of you possessed knowledge His Majesty might find useful, I could invite you along. I'm a little too nervous, I admit, to go alone."

Pen sits up. Her hair is an electrocuted blond animal atop her head. "The king? How did you manage that?"

Celeste emerges from behind the screen and reaches for the brush on her night table. "Despite your opinion of me, Pen"—she says her name pointedly—"I am the daughter of a king. And this is a war. I'm the only one to negotiate on my father's behalf."

Pen is all at once very sober. She throws back her blankets and stands. "You can't really be saying you mean to involve Internment in this mess down here. You can't think that's what your father would want."

Celeste laughs at the mirror. "I think I know my father much better than you. And I intend to convey his support to King Ingram. My brother, the prince, would back me up." Her eyes linger on Pen. "But he isn't here."

Pen is clutching her collar, twisting the fabric in her fist. "This is not Internment's war," she says. "Thank goodness the people of the ground can't reach Internment, or they'd destroy it."

Celeste smiles. It is a daydreaming, hopeful smile. "Oh, but soon they will," she says. "They have mechanical birds—planes, they call them—that can go nearly as high as Internment. And they're learning more and building upon them every day. It's only a matter of time."

Pen looks as though she'll be sick. She's right. Internment would be very easy to destroy; it's no match for the ground's warfare.

What has my blood going cold is the thought that Celeste is right, too.

"So, Pen is clearly not interested," Celeste says, turning to face me. "What about you, Morgan? I could use a fellow citizen from the magical floating island." She can't help giggling at the name they've given us. "And as the daughter of a patrolman, surely you know more than you give yourself credit for."

"Yes," I say. "I'd like to go. Thank you."

Pen opens her mouth to speak, but then she closes it and stumbles from the room at a run. I wince at the sound of the water room's door closing.

Celeste sets her hairbrush down. "See you at breakfast," she says cheerily.

I find Pen sitting on the edge of the tub, red-faced and watery-eyed. I can smell that she's just been sick. It isn't just the tonic—she can hold that quite well—but the thought of losing her home for a second time.

"They can't," she whispers. "Tell me they can't reach Internment."

"I'll find out all that I can," I say, running a cloth under the cold water and then handing it to her. "Let's not panic until I've seen the king."

She stares at me, horror in her eyes.

"Pen? I'm going to find you something to wear, and we're going to have breakfast, and we aren't going to panic."

She nods dazedly.

"Say it."

"We aren't going to panic," she repeats.

After a deep breath, she's ready to face the morning.

We find Basil and Thomas at the bottom of the stairs. "Morning," I say, perhaps too brightly. I kiss Basil's cheek.

I nudge Pen, which prompts her to give Thomas a flat, if troubled, stare. "Good morning," she says. It puts her under his immediate scrutiny. I can see as much in his eyes.

Basil is looking at me the same way.

"Oh, all right," I say. "Birdie showed us where the tonic was last night and we were up late in her room talking and sharing a bottle."

I'm startled by how easily the lie comes. I've never lied

to Basil. But while the people of the ground find magic in the floating island, they are perhaps too blind to see the magic that hides in this city, in silver screens and brass clubs and the beautiful thieves that live in the ocean, who carry stolen trinkets from the human world to depths beyond even the sunlight's reach.

I feel an inexplicable need to protect that magic. Or to keep it for myself, buried in the blood that rushes around my beating heart.

Pen has no trouble with the lie. Secrets have always comforted her. "Don't look at me that way," she tells Thomas, and shows him the back of her ring hand. "I didn't lose my virginity in a card game. I'm still your betrothed, no matter how far we both fall from the clouds."

I've no idea why I find this so funny. Perhaps she said it to amuse me.

Thomas clears his throat and then looks between Pen and me. "Word is this morning that you're going to meet King Ingram."

"Morgan is," Pen says. "I want nothing to do with all that whatnot. It makes me sick."

That's all she cares to say on the matter. She pushes between the boys and makes her way toward the dining room. That's what they call it. So many rooms that there's no need to eat in the kitchen, where the food is prepared.

Thomas frowns after her.

In the car, Celeste hooks her arm around mine and lets loose a squeak of excitement.

Two schoolgirls. What an audience we are for the king of more land than any one person should control.

Jack Piper drives while Nimble points out landmarks for us. He's in high spirits, but all I see are more possibilities for bombings. There's been minimal talk of the banks, and no talk at all of what casualties could have occurred.

"There's our hospital," Nimble says. "Saint Croix."

If the hotel is the size of a city, the hospital is the size of ten. "Morgan," Celeste says. "Your brother is a medic, isn't he?"

I don't like the liberties she's taking by discussing my family this morning.

"He was," I say. "Before he lost his sight."

"The one who never comes out of his room?" Nimble says. "That's your brother? Married to the redhead?"

"Yes," I say, and then quickly, "How long has your hospital been here?"

"Went up the year Riles was born," Nimble says. "They seem to be expanding on it every year."

Celeste leans in to me. "I wish for us to be friends," she says, softly so that only I'll hear. "I'm a great judge of people and I have a sense about you."

I haven't forgotten the hours I spent shackled in the clock tower while she and her brother brought me grapes like I was a pet, or a game. But it seems so far away now. It happened in a place I can't even see when I look for it, it's so cloudy all the time. "I think it was brave of your parents to be a part of that metal bird's creation," she says. "I am sorry that they aren't here. Truly."

"Thank you," I say, for lack of fitting words. My head aches and my mouth feels stuffed with sheep shavings. I am thinking of Pen, inebriated and dancing in the smoke and noise, trying to forget what we've had to leave behind. And of the blue bird that sailed over our heads, unaware of its own brilliance, indifferent to whatever silly worries the humans may have.

"I'm sorry about your brother, too," I tell Celeste, because it seems like the right thing to say. Even if a part of me thinks he deserved what Pen did to him.

Celeste smiles mischievously. "He'll be so jealous when I tell him about this place. We've always been rather competitive."

"Have you considered the possibility that we won't make it back?" My question just slips out.

"Not at all." The princess doesn't miss a beat. "Have a little faith."

"In what?" I say.

"Well." She draws her eyebrows together. "In the way of things, I suppose. And in me."

I return her smile. We are all doomed.

We drive through the streets that Pen, Birdie, and I haunted the night before. We pass women in long coats that are a trove of buttons, hats that look like shells or folded paper, all of them with flowers and big white beads that Birdie calls pearls. They, too, are a treasure of the sea.

Celeste gasps, palming the glass as we pass a storefront full of fur coats. "What animals do you suppose have such pelts?"

Nimble looks back at her. "You like fur?"

"Not just fur. Any part of an animal is useful to me if I can kill it myself," she says. "My brother would carve charms for me from the bones."

She says this as though it's a perfectly normal thing.

"Waste not, want not, eh?" Nimble says.

She smiles and tugs at a bit of her hair.

The city is arranged like some sort of giant, scaly, sleeping creature. The buildings rise and then sink in height, and then they dwindle until there is nothing but a field of snow that goes on for ages. How frightening, all that nothingness. I feel that if I should leave the car, it would swallow me whole, and I'd become nothing.

Jack and Nimble are talking about the banks. Celeste says nothing, but I can tell that she's listening, absorbing every bit about it that she can. Money seems to be the apex of the way things are run down here, while on Internment it's hardly a thing to worry about; as long as we have jobs, we're outfitted with an apartment, and a few pages a week to buy food and whatever frivolous things we like. The idea of anyone being without that much reflects horribly on this king, and I haven't even met him yet.

There is another city on the horizon now, its reflection in the surrounding water like a jealous twin.

"Is this the capital of Havalais?" I ask.

Nimble chuckles. "This is the king's castle," he says.

If Pen thought the hotel too grandiose, this would have her absolutely livid. What could possibly fill all those rooms? A king could live his entire life in that place and still not have time to look from all its windows.

I pretend that it is a city. I pretend the water is the sky and that we are going home.

"This is lovely," Celeste says. I think she means to pretend that as royalty she wasn't raised in an archaic clock tower. But in our world, castles are a fantasy, perhaps even a myth. We are witnessing something beyond what we've been taught to imagine. She and I have that much in common.

We drive through a series of gates, and as we cross the bridge that separates the king's castle from its kingdom, men emerge from doors as big as an apartment itself and direct Jack where to park. Celeste waves to one of them, and he catches her gaze but doesn't acknowledge her. The king's men are stoic.

It takes five men to show us to the doors, two men to open those doors, and four to take our coats. We're led down a pathway of patterned carpets, past portraits and flowers and wallpaper whose flowers and swirls glimmer where the sunlight touches them.

"His Majesty will see you in a moment," one of the men says, with the most rigid of bows. "Please seat yourselves."

I'm not certain why Celeste feels so strongly that we should be friends, but she keeps playing the part rather dutifully, sitting close beside me on the paisley sofa, straightening my skirt hem. I think of what Birdie said about these clothes belonging to her mother. Surely Jack Piper recognizes them, but he gives no indication. Maybe the women really do stick around only long enough to lay eggs.

"What are you smirking about?" Celeste asks.

I clear my throat. "Nothing."

"Don't be nervous," Nimble says. "King Ingram is informal. You won't have to curtsy or anything."

I wonder at their definition of "informal" down here. King Furlow wouldn't have expected a curtsy either. And while this castle is sprawling, it seems silly that I once fantasized about ever visiting one. It's unreasonably large, and soulless inside. Maybe I'd hoped for something magical or historic, but all I see is greed. I'd much prefer the clock tower, which was laid stone by stone hundreds of years ago, not only for the king and queen, but for our entire city.

My parents died trying to reach the ground, and my brother and Amy damaged themselves forever trying to catch only a glimpse of it. But I wonder now if things on Internment were as bad as all that.

I feel guilt for being so angry with my parents and brother, and it silences my thoughts.

The doors open with a theatrical groan. Celeste rises, pulling me along with her. Her eyes are bright. "Your Majesty," she says, with a nod that is the perfect mix of cool and cordial.

The king, for all the grandeur of his home, is unremarkable to look at. He is short and slight with hair that is slicked back to curl up at the nape of his neck. He wears a dark suit with elaborate copper-colored lapels that disappear over his shoulders. While Nimble wears a pair of round lenses over his eyes, King Ingram has only one, attached to his pocket by a gold chain. He brings it to his left eye as he studies us.

"I guess I'm in the presence of two princesses?" He sits at an armchair in a beam of light that seems all too planned.

"You flatter me, Your Majesty," I say, and the words are sour on my tongue. "But there is only one princess of Internment, and she's standing beside me."

"Celeste Furlow," she says. Her smile has gotten tight. She is accustomed to formalities, but even she can't be sure what to make of this king's behavior.

I'm beginning to like him.

"They've been our houseguests," Nimble says, winking at Celeste when he thinks no one will notice. "And the princess was especially interested in helping with the war effort."

"Mr. Piper tells me you're from the floating island," King Ingram says, and waves for us to sit. "I've been out to see the thing that brought you to our humble kingdom. What kind of airplane is that?"

After a silence, I realize I'm the only one in the room who can answer.

"The professor has never called it an airplane, Your Majesty. Actually, that's a word we don't have on Internment."

"What she means, Your Majesty, is that we haven't built any sort of aircrafts, yet," Celeste says, eager to preserve our city's integrity. I can hear in her voice that she's embarrassed, and it angers me. Internment is a brilliant place, and she should be proud to have called it home. She should miss it at least marginally. How could she not? It's a knife to the heart every time I look up and find that the clouds conceal it from my view. I feel ousted.

"Internment had no intention of building an aircraft," I say. "There are winds that surround our city, and anyone who tries to leave is either injured or killed."

"Nonsense," the king says, though he looks at me with interest. "How are you here, if that's the case?"

I'm not sure I want to tell him about the rebellion, or the seedy behavior of King Furlow. I question Celeste's motives, but I'm not ready to dismiss her claim that the two cities can work together somehow. So I only say, "It was an experiment several decades in the making. The professor devised a way to burrow through the bottom of the city. He doesn't believe it would be possible to return. Not in his machine, at least."

Behind its lens, the king's eye brightens with intrigue. And I realize that I've just said too much even before he says, "You all left Internment expecting to never see it again?"

"What she means to say—" Celeste begins, but the king interrupts.

"She doesn't need you to speak for her. She isn't a mute. Go on, Miss . . ."

"Stockhour," I say. "Morgan Stockhour, Your Majesty. And I only meant to say that—well, you could consider us explorers, I suppose." It's a weak attempt to bandage what I've done.

Celeste moves in quickly. "We have scopes—much like the ones you use to see the stars and our island—and the kings of Internment have been studying your technology for generations. We felt confident that you would devise a way to reach us soon. We thought it should be time to greet you, so you'd know a bit about us."

Flawless. She must have been planning what she was going to say. She raises her chin, quite proud of herself.

"So you came down to welcome us," King Ingram says skeptically.

"There was something else," Nimble says. "Her Highness is too modest to bring it up unprompted."

"Oh?" the king says.

Celeste's face becomes guarded. She sits, prim and rigid. She folds her hands in her lap. "As you can imagine, Internment being so small, there's only so much room for advancement." She lowers her eyes, composing herself, and then she looks at the king. "My mother, the queen, is rather ill. She'll die soon if she isn't treated."

And with those few words, it all makes sense. The tranquilizer darts, and holding me hostage while demanding information. Not telling her father or the patrolmen the truth when we escaped and injured her brother in the process. The stowing away, holding a knife to Thomas's throat so we wouldn't cast her out.

She wasn't a bratty princess discontent with her tiny paradise and striving for grander things, and she wasn't trying to torment us like the game she hunted for amusement. She was desperate.

King Ingram takes this as a bit of politics. "We know you haven't got a sister," he says. "Is there a prince?"

"Yes, my older brother." Celeste hesitates. "He's incapacitated at the moment."

King Ingram tucks his lens into his breast pocket, pats it into place. "So I have Internment's heiress presumptive in my parlor?" he says.

"Yes," she says, with some difficulty. "If you'd like to call it that."

"It isn't a matter of what I like to call it," the king says. "Your mother is dying, and your brother isn't fit to inherit the throne—"

"Not at the moment, Your Majesty, but—"

"So at the moment, you are it." He smiles, all the lines in his face spreading out, making him a drawing of himself. He breaks into a laugh that is startling, coming from a man so small in stature. "I think you should embrace it," he says. "You're your kingdom's only hope. Yes, I believe we can work together. I'd be a fool to say no."

I don't know what this means. I only know I've given up the idea that I'll like him.

There is talk of airplanes and biplanes and altitudes and atmospheres. According to King Ingram, Internment sits above the troposphere at thirty-five thousand feet, in a zone called the stratosphere. The most powerful planes the kingdom has to offer right now are hardly capable of leaving the troposphere and are unable to endure the stratosphere anyway. But there is talk of a new sort of plane that may be able to reach Internment. A jet, he calls it.

"We had a lot of fancy hopes about visiting the floating island," King Ingram says. "But then the war began and we've had bigger fish to fry. There is an archipelago that sits between the kingdom of Havalais and the kingdom of Dastor. King Erasmus and I are having, shall we say, a disagreement about who should have it."

"An archipelago is a cluster of islands," Nimble tells us.

"Yes, thank you, I gathered," Celeste says, though I'm sure she hadn't. We would have no cause to know something like that. I've only just learned what an ocean is. Celeste looks to the king. "Am I to understand that this war is all about a cluster of islands?"

"It isn't the islands," the king says. "They're too small to be inhabitable. But they contain something precious. There is a substance that occurs naturally beneath its soils, called phosane. When it is in rock form, it isn't of much use. But once melted down and refined, a few gallons could fuel a city for a year."

If the war seemed absurd when I thought it was being fought over islands, I think it's doubly absurd now that I know it's being fought over fuel. Sunlight is always free and fuels Internment, and there's plenty of that to go around. But I don't say that, for I will surely talk myself into a corner again.

"I'm certain my father would love to help, speaking on his behalf," Celeste says. "If you were able to return us to Internment and your doctors were willing to help my mother, I'm sure he would allow you to use Internment as a sort of base. It's quite a vantage point, you must agree."

This is exactly what Pen was against. My heart palpitates at the thought. How could Celeste be the daughter of a king and truly not see the risk of what she is doing?

Or perhaps she sees it, but the alternative is to let her mother die.

And now I'm thinking of my own mother, turned away from me in what I thought was sleep. Wouldn't I have saved her if I could? And my father, killed in the melee. And Lex, who was once so full of energy and life but who is broken now. I would want to save all of them, and the last thing on my mind would be the cost.

7

Celeste is quiet during the drive back to the hotel. She catches herself fidgeting several times and tries to still herself.

Havalais passes by our windows, less intriguing now that we've seen it all before. The sun is bright and the snow is beginning to puddle. I can see traces of sidewalk and grass. I wonder if the grass could ever recover from such a long burial, but I don't ask. Everyone in the car is respecting this tight silence.

Once we've returned to the hotel, Jack leaves us at the door and drives off to park in the carriage house.

Judas and Amy are in the distance, heavily clothed and fashioning some poor animal out of snow. They meet my eyes, expectant, inquisitive.

"Morgan," Celeste says. Her voice is uncharacteristically gentle. "I see no need for everyone on the ground to know about my mother. As someone who has endured her own hardships, surely you can understand why I'd like to keep something like this private."

"Of course," I say. And I do. It's the first time since the night she dragged me, paralyzed, to her tower that I feel I understand anything about her.

"Especially not that incessant friend of yours." She can't quite look up from the snow.

"Celeste?"

"Yes?"

I touch her shoulder. Startled, she looks at my hand against the plaid wool. But she doesn't move away. Maybe some part of her understands that this is it, our fate, and small comforts are the only reward she will have for her valiant efforts. "I really am so sorry about your mother."

She almost smiles, and offers the very slightest of nods.

"I should see what Nim is up to," she says. "Excuse me."

As soon as she's gone, Pen and Birdie burst through the front door. It's nice to see that they've both recovered so well from last night's adventure. Pen throws a string of pearls around my neck and then tugs them, harnessing me to within a breath of her face. "You have to tell us *everything*," she says.

I glance behind her to the open door, where the younger children are chasing each other around the lobby.

"It doesn't have to be here," Birdie says. "We can go anywhere. I'm all caught up on my lessons for the day."

I nod to Judas and Amy, who are still making some

effort at that snow animal while pretending they aren't straining their ears. "We should invite them along," I say. "And Basil and Thomas."

Pen makes a sour face. "Must we bring Thomas?"

"This will concern them, too," I say. "I'll talk to Lex and Alice tonight."

"Why don't they ever leave their room?" Birdie says. "I only catch the redhead when she's on her way to the water room. She's a real doll. So gorgeous. And my sisters love her."

Birdie can't know how sad it makes me to be reminded of Alice's beauty, and the things she and my brother could have had, if only.

"It's complicated," is all I can say.

Pen comes to my rescue by shouting to Judas and Amy, "Come on, then! We all know you want to." She goes inside to find the boys, and as Judas and Amy approach, I turn to Birdie.

"Can you borrow the car?" I ask. "Or should we take the ferry?"

"Nim would be fit to be tied if I even asked about the car." She rolls her eyes. "Now that the sun's out, I thought we could rent an elegor."

"What's an elegor?" Amy asks, excited.

"A very big and very slow animal," Birdie says. "We could rent one for the day, and for a few rubes the boys at the rental place will hook a cart up to it."

"What do they look like?" Amy asks.

"They're nifty; you'll love them," Birdie says. "They're

bigger than a car, and they have dark silky eyelashes that are as long as your hand." She holds up her gloved hand. "And they can't go very fast, but they love it when you talk sweet and feed them sugarcane."

Basil, Pen, and Thomas meet us outside and we start walking. Birdie is telling Amy about the pen of elegors in the city, how they like to be patted on the cheek, and how very human they can be when it comes to emotions.

I walk between Basil and Judas, and my silence must be torturing them, because finally Judas says, "How doomed are we?"

"I don't know that we are," I say.

Pen is skipping over the cracks in the sidewalk. "I've been thinking," she says.

"What's that, darling?" Thomas asks.

"Once all the clouds clear up, we'll see Internment again. I was thinking it can be our star." She nearly crushes a limp weed that has grown through a crack. She will let it live, in case it should bloom when the weather turns warmer. "I was thinking that would be better than not having it at all."

True to Birdie's description, the elegor is much larger than a car. I keep imagining that if Internment had such heavy animals, it would never manage to stay in the sky; that it would hover above the water, shuddering and tilting, depending on where these things walked. Its short, squatting legs are as thick as tree trunks. There's a folding ladder attached to the cart on its back.

I should be frightened, but any worries I have about the

security of the cart are abated by the creature's cooing murmurs as we board. One of the boys at the rental house pats the elegor's face, and the elegor curls its large, ropelike nose in pleasure.

Judas is trying to give Amy a boost up the ladder, and she's swatting at him, telling him she feels fine and to lay off. I don't blame him for worrying; it takes so little to provoke one of her fits.

Pen climbs after them. "You've got to come up and see this," she says, waving a red silk cushion she's taken from one of the seats. "We'll be set up like royalty."

"When we ride them, my little sister Annie likes to pretend we're princesses," Birdie says.

"No, not princesses," Pen says, pulling me up as I reach the top rung.

"Queens," I agree.

"Absolutely," Birdie says, emphasizing each syllable, looking back at us as she takes the reins. She seems so brilliantly happy when she's outside the hotel.

Basil and Thomas are eyeing us suspiciously. They can see that they're being left out of something. When Basil sits next to me, I pat his knee reassuringly. He has placed himself directly between Judas and me, making his opinion known. Basil hasn't forgotten that Judas was accused of murdering his own betrothed, Daphne, and a part of Basil still believes it to be true.

The elegor starts to move with a lurch, and I tense.

"Don't worry," Birdie says. "The cart is fastened on about a dozen different ways. It won't fall off."

Basil is watching me closely. And when he can see that I've calmed some, he says, "What did you learn this morning?"

Much more than I was prepared for, that's certain.

I tell them about the planes and the altitude and the phosane. I tell them everything but that the queen is dying; that part isn't my secret to tell, and I'd like to think my promise to Celeste means something.

"Fuel?" Pen makes a face. "That's what this war is about?"

"It isn't just any fuel," Birdie says. "Phosane is naturally produced by the soil in that one archipelago. It would take thousands of years for it to run out, if it ever did. It's a real world wonder."

Pen looks thoughtful. "What does it take for this phosane to work?"

"Heat, I think," Birdie says. "The king's men have been the world over, and there's nothing like it anywhere else. You can find about a billion pictures of the stuff, but no one's mined for it yet."

"If so little goes so far, why can't they just share it?" Amy asks.

Birdie tugs on the reins. "That's the million-dollar question, isn't it? King Ingram and King Erasmus are both afraid that if they share it, the other kingdom will use it to enhance their warfare. They both want it all to themselves to ensure that doesn't happen."

Even Amy, a young girl, can see why this is appalling. "They're having a war to prevent losing a bigger war that may not even happen?"

"That's about the size of it."

Pen has gone quiet, body jostling with the elegor's steps as she watches the city. I nudge her with my foot, and she offers a weak, distracted smile.

"What is this King Ingram like?" Judas asks.

Birdie shrugs. "He's a politician."

"So, awful, then."

Birdie laughs, but doesn't deny it.

The conversation turns to Havalais's capital city and what the theme park is like in the summer. Having heard not a word of this, Pen blurts, "Birdie, do you have libraries down here?"

"Of course we have libraries," Birdie says. "Did you need to find something?"

"No," Pen says. "Just looking for similarities between here and home." She cants her head back against the railing and stares at the sky until the clouds move from the sun and she's forced to look away.

She's trying to be together about it, but I fear what will become of her without her home. I worry that all those years she's invested in our history book will unravel, and she'll be left holding the tangled threads she once thought made up a god.

And, strangely, I worry for the princess, whose mother will die without a doctor from that sprawling hospital. What will it do to her to know that she can never go back, that she left her kingdom for nothing?

But greater still is my fear of these things they call airplanes. Because, whether or not Internment has anything to gain, King Ingram and his army may find a way there soon enough. Even without our help.

It is the worst worry, the helpless sort.

Birdie has begun playing tour guide, and the grim conversation turns to a lighthearted geography lesson. Basil leans close and speaks at a volume only I will hear. "It doesn't bode well, does it?"

I shake my head. "I can't see it ending well for anyone. Internment can't handle a war."

He has more to lose than I do. His parents and little brother are still up there, oblivious to what is going on below their haven. And that's what it was for us: a haven. The king was putting people to death for trying to leave, but while his actions were deplorable, I'm beginning to think that he saw this as his only way to protect the city. Keep the people safe. Keep them in the sky. Maybe he saw through the scopes what was happening on the ground.

And where does all of this leave my parents? Surely they only wanted my brother and me to be safe. Internment was our home, but its edge blinded my brother, and its government took away his and Alice's child before it could have been born. Internment is an imperfect world that sits atop another imperfect world.

"I feel that we have nowhere to go," I say to Basil.

"We're here," he says.

"For now," I blurt.

Pen breaks free of her brooding to say, "All this moving around is making me ill."

I'm immediately concerned. While the food has been an

adjustment for all of us, uncertainty and sullenness have taken Pen's appetite away completely. The tonic at the brass club is the most she's consumed of anything but oxygen since we arrived. It was only a matter of time before it caught up to her.

Thomas frowns and places the back of his hand to her forehead. "Do you feel sick to your stomach? I've told you that you should try to eat more."

"It isn't my fault vegetables are hardly so much as a garnish down here. I should love something that didn't have to die for my appetite at every single meal." But she rests her head on his shoulder, and all he can do is fret and worry and insist that she go straight to bed.

I don't mind that our elegor ride is cut short; after all I've learned this morning, I think I'd like to lie down as well.

But as soon as we return and I've followed Pen into the bedroom, she closes the door behind us. "You must tell me everything you learned about phosane," she says, with all her usual verve.

"Pen! You're feeling all right, then?"

She waves my question off. "There's no time for that. Thomas will be up in the time it takes to boil broth and toast bread for me, and I need this to stay between the two of us. What did you learn?"

"Only what I've already said. It's a substance that can be used for fuel once it's melted."

"What does it look like?"

"I didn't see a picture," I say. Her anxiety is palpable. "Why? What do you know?"

"Possibly nothing, but we'll have to go to the library before it closes. After Thomas leaves, I'll pretend to fall asleep and we'll use the window."

"We could have asked Birdie—"

"No. One. Can know." Her words are slow and deliberate. She climbs into her bed. "I looked in one of the tourism pamphlets in the lobby, and I'm sure we'll be able to find the library on our own."

"How do you do that?" I ask.

"What?"

"Just be able to navigate your way through a strange city."

She shrugs. "No matter which city you're in, it's all buildings with numbers. It's easy."

Sure enough, Thomas is soon at her side with a tray of broth and toast. I would think it dishonest of her to make him worry, but his doting on her will do them both some real good. He's also brought drawing papers, which for Pen has always been the greatest medicine. As I'm leaving the room, I see her wield the pencil, and I know that she is going to begin a new map.

It's nearly an hour before Thomas comes downstairs carrying a tray and a worried expression. "She isn't running a fever," he tells me, "but she's sleeping. She asked me not to wake her for dinner. All of this ground business has taken its toll."

"I agree," I say, and that's the truth.

"Morgan—" He hesitates, looking very uncomfortable, and I know what he's thinking.

"She hasn't had any tonic," I say. "She's only tired."

He nods, though it doesn't seem to put him very at ease.

By the time I'm able to steal away on the pretense of taking a nap, Pen is already wearing her coat. She can't make it to the library fast enough. We have no money for the ferry or an elegor, so we're forced to walk. I can't tell one city block from the next, but Pen navigates them as though she's lived here all her life. She has said time and again that she always needs to know where she is, and she makes it her business to be familiar with her surroundings.

"Here." Pen hands me a folded handkerchief when she's had enough of my sniffling. "You should really carry some on you. My nose has hardly stopped running, thanks to this cold."

"It's like living in a cold box," I say. "I feel like the god of the ground is trying to preserve us like food."

She gives me a wan smile as she opens the library door. "So you still believe in the gods, then? Or is it just a habit now?"

"I don't know," I confess. But then, I haven't known that for some time. "It's hard to believe in this one or that one when the answer is silence all the same."

We step into the library, and Pen closes her eyes, takes a deep breath.

"Are you all right?" I say.

"Books smell the same down here," she says.

The books are arranged around us in circular tiers accessible by ramps and ladders. The cataloging system is similar to the system in the libraries back home, and it takes Pen only moments to find what she's looking for. Soon we're sitting at a table before something called a world atlas and several texts about minerals, chemical substances, and fossil fuels. I can't help being distracted by the smoothness of this paper. Perfectly white pages with bold black ink. It hasn't been recycled and there are no ghosts of the pages' past lives in other books. These books, filled with topics I scarcely understand, are the most beautiful things I've yet encountered in this world.

Pen retrieves her latest map from her coat pocket and smoothes it against the table.

"What's it of?" I ask, as she flips through the atlas.

"This is Havalais here, and that's Dastor, and here between them is the archipelago. Or at least, my nearest guess." She holds the page near the open atlas, and the likeness is astoundingly similar. She points to a small land mass hovering over the ocean near Havalais. "And there's Internment. It's a ways off from the archipelago, but you said the archipelago's islands are all too small and misshapen to be inhabitable, right?"

"That's what the king said."

"So what if this is where Internment once was, before it became a part of the sky?"

"But it's all the way over here now, thousands and thousands of paces away."

Pen shrugs. "Internment broke away from the ground and has spent several hundred years in the sky. Is it so hard to believe it might have drifted?"

"Maybe not," I admit. Her eyes are bright, and it's nice to see her interested in this world the way she was interested in Internment. It gives me hope that she'll be able to adapt. That we both will. "What made you think of all this?"

"It's the phosane," Pen says, lowering her voice. "Grab one of these books. Help me scare up a picture of it."

We both scan the glossaries and the pictures on the pages until I find what she's looking for. "Here," I say, laying the open book between us. There's an image of a cavern taken at the archipelago. The image is gray and white, but the jagged clumps of phosane are clearly visible along the walls and ceiling. I had pictured a black rock, but it's more like quartz, clear and sparkling.

Pen turns to the next page, where there is an image of a scientist who discovered a way to refine phosane for fuel. He holds a rock of phosane in his hand.

Pen's lips move as she reads the text under the photo, and soon all her brightness fades for worry. She looks at me. "The reason I think this archipelago is left over from when Internment broke away is because it has the same sort of soil. It's not like regular dirt. It produces this substance. Down here they call it phosane, but on Internment it's sunstone. All it needs is heat and light to make energy."

"We have this on Internment?" I say. "Where?"

"It can be dug up from almost anywhere," Pen says. "But you've looked at it every day of your life. It's what the glasslands are made of."

"Are you certain?"

"Absolutely. My father brings hunks of it home all the time for his work. It's hardly a commodity before it's refined." She taps my betrothal band. "It's used to make these, too. It's nearly indestructible, far better than glass."

"I had honestly thought our betrothal bands were made of ordinary glass."

"Most people think that," she says. "I suppose you'd have no reason to question it."

She's a genius, and here we sit, surrounded by people who have no idea what she's found. The splendor and the horror it can unleash.

"This is why you wanted to sneak out," I say.

"We can't tell a soul." She grabs my wrist, and her knuckles are white from the strain. "Morgan, no one can know about this. They'll cause an upheaval looking for those rocks."

I stare at Pen's handmade map. It's the work of a prodigy, and at the same time a homesick, wistful girl who has taken the time to draw mermaids and starfish in the water and clouds in the sky. The clouds form a protective barrier over Internment's surface, curtaining it from what is happening below.

Pen stares at the map for a moment, and then she folds it in half and begins tearing it apart.

"Suppose we should tell the professor?" I ask, as we make the long trek back to the hotel.

Pen shakes her head, and her curls shudder in agreement. "We can't trust him."

"I think we can," I say. "He's risked so much to get away. He wouldn't be for a plan that would get anyone back up there. He won't even come out of his bird."

"No one," Pen insists. "You're the only one I trusted enough to share my theories with. That means no Thomas, no Basil, and no professor. Don't even inter it to your diary. I'll draw us a proper map of the city that we can hang on to for reference."

"It's just . . ." I hesitate. "Pen, what if it isn't as bad as all that? What if Internment and Havalais can help each other?" Against my better judgment I am thinking of Celeste and the dying queen.

Before I can take my next step, Pen has grabbed me by the shoulders and pushed my back against a stone fence. "Listen to me," she says. I can feel the warmth of her breath. Her fingers are clawing into my shoulders. "You're forever trying to help everyone, and I love you for that, truly, but no good can come of this. If this king knew he had something so powerful hovering right over his greedy head, Internment would cease to be the magical floating island and it would fast become a mining opportunity. It would be finished. My parents, Thomas's and Basil's families, everyone we've ever known would be annihilated. Do you see that? Tell me that you do."

Her eyes are red and brimming, and I brush the first tear that falls with my thumb. "I see it," I say.

She releases me, dabs at her eyes with a handkerchief

and clears her throat. "Are you all right?" she says. "I didn't hurt you?"

I touch her shoulder, and she flinches. "You couldn't ever know how sorry I am that you were dragged into this because of me."

"It's my own fault." She sniffs. "If I hadn't attacked the prince, I wouldn't have had to run away. And anyway, I wouldn't have wanted to be left behind."

"Oh, Pen, don't cry."

"I'm not." She blows her nose. "Really."

But the tears still come, and at the sight of them I can hardly hold myself together. Soon we're both sniffling and embracing each other.

A frigid wind cuts through us, howling as though it has anything at all to say about the secret that now fills our troubled minds.

8

When we return through the bedroom window, the sun has just begun to set. Pen changes into a nightgown and returns to bed as though she never left it.

"Do you want me to bring something up for you after dinner?" I ask.

"No matter," she sighs.

"I hate to see you like this," I say.

She hugs the pillow and buries her face in it. "Everything's roses," she says, her voice muffled.

"Maybe Birdie will go out tonight," I say. "Take us with her."

"I'd like that," Pen says. "If you don't mind, I'd like to be alone with my thoughts for a while." To bring her point home, she sighs theatrically and flops onto her back, arms sprawled. "And do turn out the light."

I think I hear a laugh in her voice, but I can't be sure.

I walk toward the water room—no, bathroom. That's what they call them down here, and I may as well get used to it. If I had any hope of returning to Internment, it's turned into hope that I never will. I know that Pen is right. So why can't I stop thinking of Celeste coming all this way to save her mother's life? I can't accept one reality or the other—a ruined Internment or an unattainable one. I can only conclude that there must be some way to make everyone happy, and once I've found it, I'll tell Pen and she'll agree. She'll be glad for the chance to return home.

An arm grabs my waist from behind and a hand covers my mouth, and I'm about to try to scream, when Judas whispers, "Quiet."

I wrest away. "I hate when you do that!" I whisper. "There are other ways to get my attention."

"I didn't want anyone to hear." He's got me cornered against the bathroom door. "I saw you and that contemptuous friend of yours sneaking out earlier."

"Pen isn't contemptuous, Judas; she's bereft. Like the rest of us."

"Not all of us," he says. "And I don't trust her."

"I am sure she will be heartbroken to know. And why are you being so judgmental all of a sudden?"

"Because I think the two of you are up to something. Did you go to talk to the professor?"

"Not that it's any of your business, but no," I say. "We only went to the harbor to look at the mermaids."

"You left in the opposite direction," he says.

"So you're writing a spy novel now? I don't see why you should care whether we leave or where we go."

"I am only—" He pauses like he's swallowing something bitter. "I was only worried that she might have talked you into doing something stupid."

I should be offended, but he's averting his eyes and I can see that this was difficult for him to say. He adds, "The last time you snuck off in the night to meet with her, both of you were kidnapped by the prince and princess."

"That was hardly our fault," I say. "And I'll remind you that on another venture, I did possess enough brain cells to push you into the lake and hide you from those patrolmen. Though you're making me question my decision now."

"I'll remind you that this isn't our world," Judas says. I suppose he's trying to sound firm. "What you think is safe may not be. And you can never know who may be watching."

"We were only looking at the mermaids," I repeat. I can see that he doesn't believe me, but I look right into his eyes to convince him. I've never been much of a liar, but the promise I made to Pen overrides that.

"I once knew a girl who had your degree of curiosity. And greater still, your desire to do good, to take things on that were much, much too heavy for one girl's shoulders," Judas says. "She was killed for her efforts."

He's the first to move his eyes away, and they betray his pain for only an instant. He means Daphne. The girl he was betrothed to. The girl he was accused of murdering when she was found slashed on the train tracks. "I'm telling you to be careful," he says, already walking away. "That's all."

All through dinner, I see Daphne Leander's school image. Her sage almost-smile, her glitter cosmetics. And I remember the day the train moved backward and that small change in my routine filled me with dread. I couldn't have known then how much my life was about to change. I couldn't have known that Daphne's life was already over.

Jack Piper rambles about politics despite his eldest son's glazed expression, and I wonder at what's in store for us while we stay here. There has been no evidence that King Ingram intends to kill us, but all this waiting has me nervous.

Basil tries to entice me with a starlit walk, but I tell him the cold air has left me congested and excuse myself to bathe and go to bed with one of Birdie's books. True to his word, he has frequented the city on his own, familiarizing himself with the layout, but since the bombings I hate the thought of him going out there alone. Am I any better, though, sneaking out with Birdie?

I find Pen sitting on her bed, drawing something she keeps shielded from the view of the princess, who sits on her own bed, struggling to transform yarn into a garment.

Celeste huffs. "Aren't we a cheerful bunch," she says.

Pen erases at the page, blows away the dust and resumes. Her silence is pointed.

"Nimble says the banks should be able to recover from

the bombings." Celeste says. "It was more of a warning than a substantial attack."

Pen slams the pencil against her drawing. "I can't concentrate with your babbling," she says.

"I was just trying to make conversation," Celeste says.

Pen nods to the yarn. "Is that an activity that requires a lot of talking, then?"

I feel two pairs of eyes on me, but I don't look away from my book. Some watery love story of a mundane girl who has caught the heart of an equally mundane boy. Still, I would like to know what happens. All the marriages on Internment are arranged at birth. Sometimes before then.

"Be that way, then," Celeste says. "I'm going downstairs, where my company might be appreciated."

"How? Is there a staircase that will take you to another world even lower than this one?"

"Pen," I snap.

She looks at me, surprised. "Did you have something to add, Morgan?"

"You're being unnecessarily harsh, is all."

"Excuse me. I didn't realize I was in the presence of the princess and her familiar."

The words wound, and I'm sure there's nothing I can say that won't make it worse. It's the heartbreak talking, I tell myself. I look back to the open book, but I can't retain a word of it, I'm so hurt.

"You're being vicious tonight, even for you," Celeste tells Pen.

"Vicious?" Pen says. "I'll tell you what's vicious: a

father who is responsible for the murder of a schoolgirl. Remember Daphne Leander? And that's just to name one of your father's victims. Vicious is kidnapping two innocent people and holding them hostage like they're toys for you to play with. And vicious is being willing to destroy an entire city filled with people just so you can play queen and save the day. You are nothing but a selfish, selfish brat."

"I am not"—Celeste pauses to regain herself—"playing queen. I am only trying to make things better."

"Things were fine the way that they were," Pen says.

"If you can say that, then you don't know anything about Internment," Celeste says.

"I know that it's separate from the ground for a reason," Pen says. "I know that the only reason we're here is because your father drove us out. And I know that you had no business muscling your way along. You don't belong here. You belong in that bloody clock tower, hunting your deer and playing your stupid games and knowing positively nothing about life."

"Pen," I say.

"And you!" she cries. "Your parents were killed. Don't you care that she's to blame?"

"She isn't to blame, Pen. The king is."

"There's no difference!"

"There is a difference," Celeste says. Her voice is quiet. She's looking at the floor as she gets out of bed. "And I won't listen to this." She draws a shaky breath, and I believe Pen has actually reduced her to tears. But she won't let us see them. Yarn and needles and all, she leaves the room, her steps still maintaining all the poise of a princess, whether or not this is her kingdom.

Pen smoothes the blankets over her knees. She doesn't look at me. "I won't hear a lecture from you," she warns.

"You've a right to be hurt," I say. "But you never have the right to use my parents as props in your argument. I won't say it again."

I close my book and settle in my bed, turned away from her.

She says nothing. But there is no scratch of the pencil to paper. No sound to indicate she's moving at all. Eventually she gets up and turns out the light.

Sleep doesn't remove Daphne from my mind. I see her in my dreams as well.

The door creaks open, startling me awake.

"Are you awake?" Birdie whispers.

"Yes. Careful not to wake Her Oh-So-Royal Highness," Pen answers.

My mattress dips with Pen's weight as she crawls over me, peels the hair from my face. "Are we friends or enemies right now?"

I grunt, and she shakes me. "Come out with us. Please? Please, please, please."

I'm still sore, but I suppose this is as much of an apology as I'll ever get, and maybe I did deserve some of what she said.

"Get off me, then, so I can get dressed."

There's a chill when Birdie opens the window, and

Celeste murmurs in her sleep. Pen grunts as she reaches for the strongest branch and begins her climb down. I follow, and then Birdie, who closes the window without a sound.

"Picture show?" Birdie says.

"Brass club?" Pen asks hopefully, dancing as we make our way for the ferry.

"We shouldn't," Birdie says. "We're underage and someone might recognize me and tell my father. People love to beat their gums in this city."

"What else is there to do?" I ask.

Birdie cants her head to the stars as she walks. It's as though the cold has sharpened them and they shine more brightly for it. "Oh!" she says, and grabs our wrists as she heads back in the direction of the hotel. "Neither of you have ever been to a theme park, have you?"

"Can we go on the rides?" Pen asks.

"Well, no," Birdie says. "I have the key only for the gate, and it'll work on some of the restaurants. Nim is usually the one who handles the rides."

"Can we sit on them and pretend?" I ask. Even that is more than we've ever done.

Birdie laughs. "Sure, if you want."

"What about the telescopes?" Pen says.

My skin swells with little bumps at the idea of looking through a lens, of maybe seeing home. I don't know how it will feel, if it will make things easier or impossibly harder.

"Sure thing," Birdie says, like it's any mundane attraction. I suppose, to her and everyone else on the ground, it is.

Though the park is filled with elaborate rides and restaurants, the telescopes are the main attraction. They sit at the heart of everything, atop a tower that contains a gift shop. As we climb the stairs that wrap around the tower, Birdie prattles off a list of things that can be bought there: key chains, toy planes, shirts, and fake passports so people can pretend they are taking a trip to the magical floating island.

"It may be the silliest thing I've ever heard," I say.

"Don't spoil it for the girl," Pen tells me. "If she wants to think we're as interesting as all that, let her."

"You *are* interesting," Birdie says. "I've always wondered what kinds of people lived up there. What language they spoke. If they had green skin and antennae. Who'd have thought we'd be so copacetic?"

"I've thought the same," Pen says. "The antennae part, I mean."

At the top of the tower sits a row of telescopes affixed to the railings. "You might not be able to see much," Birdie says, fishing coins out of her coat pocket. Even the sky costs money here. "It's still pretty cloudy."

"Maybe I can see a star up close; I've always wondered if they have faces," Pen says, squinting one eye as she looks into the telescope. I stand back, unwilling to admit how frightened I am to do the same. Birdie drops a coin into a slot by a sign that reads BEHOLD THE FLOATING ISLAND.

"Do you see anything?" I ask.

"Stars," Pen sighs. She moves the telescope around, trying to find her way home.

"Maybe you can see another planet," Birdie says.

Pen draws away from the telescope, blinking. "A what?" She looks to me, as though I should know, but I can only shrug.

Birdie is staring at us like we truly do have antennae. "You're from the sky," she says. "How can you not know everything that's happening in it?"

"Clouds, sun, moon, what's to know?" Pen says.

Birdie seems to pity us for this. I know what she's thinking. "We spent all our time looking down," I say. "Not up."

"You know what?" Birdie links her arms through ours. "I have a restaurant key, and I think this is a conversation that would go well with some gin."

I'm nearly finished with my second glass, and the warmer I feel, the more believable it seems that the ground is not, in fact, a flat plane below Internment.

Pen traces her finger around the brim of her glass. "If this planet is round, does that mean people are walking around upside down on the other side of it?"

"It's relative," Birdie says. "To them, it's not upside down. Everyone is right-side up." She tops off our glasses. Pen diminishes her drink in seconds, and she throws back her head, staring upside down at the window behind her.

"How can you bear it?" Pen breathes. "There's so much out there. How can you bear it?"

I think she's brave to even face the stars. They no longer seem the same to me. How many gods must there be? How many planets, moons, suns?

Perhaps we are upside down. I have lost the sense to tell.

Pen sits upright and nearly topples out of her chair. "Your eyes are unfocused," she tells me.

"I feel like I'm floating," I say.

Birdie squints at the label on the gin bottle. "Really?"

"No, I mean, I thought the ground was it. I thought this was the very bottom. But it isn't. There is no bottom at all, is there? Just stars forever and on into the abyss."

"Maybe it loops back around again," Pen says. Her eyes are wide and I can see that I've frightened her.

"One day we'll know," Birdie says. "King Ingram says a man will walk on the moon."

"Perhaps not," Pen says. "Maybe it's one of those things we're not meant to know."

"Not anytime soon, obviously," Birdie says. "We have a war to think about. And getting to the moon will cost money and take years and years even if they started on it right this second. Who knows? Maybe if I live to be a hundred, I'll see it."

"Or a thousand," Pen says.

"Doubt it'll take that long, doll."

"But it might."

"You know what I think?" I say. "I think we should ask the professor about it."

"What would he know?" Pen says.

"He knew a way to get to the ground. He knew not to listen to King Furlow's rules all the time. It stands to reason that he'd at least be interested."

Birdie holds the gin bottle up to the light, watching the way its patterns illuminate. "Father says he won't come out of that contraption."

"Bird," Pen and I amend in unison.

"I know how we can make him talk to us," I say. "Amy said he'll be out of food soon. I bet he'd open the door if we brought him something."

Pen shakes her head. "Just tell him that there's a universe that goes on and on forever? He wouldn't believe it."

"We believe it," I say.

"We are drunk," Pen says.

"It'll still be true when we're sober," Birdie says.

"That's tomorrow's problem," Pen says. She pushes her chair away from the table and walks behind the counter and drags her fingers over the bottles as she paces. "This is getting depressing, all this talk of planets and forever."

"We could sit on the rides," I say.

"Novel plan, if Birdie's up to it."

"Sure," Birdie says, and with the word comes a loud hiccup. She slaps both hands over her mouth, mortified. But it makes us laugh. And laughing makes us forget what we were talking about. "You are terrible influences," she says. "Is everyone from your floating island like this?"

Pen squeezes my shoulders. "We're two of a kind," she says. "We're just like a double birth."

Birdie scrunches her nose. "A what?"

"It's when two babies are born at the same time, and they look just alike," I say.

This makes her break into hysterical laughter. "Oh," she says. "You mean twins! I love the way you girls speak. I swear, I could just listen to you all day."

"Glad to entertain," Pen says, managing a graceful

curtsy. "Even if nothing we say is that funny."

"I know something that's funny," Birdie says.

"What is it?" I say.

"It's a huge secret," she says. "Nobody in the kingdom knows."

"Well, now you have to tell us," Pen says.

Birdie regards us with wide eyes, and then she snorts with a laugh and says, "I'm royalty."

Pen claps her hands together. "I love it," she says. "Let's all be kings for the rest of the night."

"We can't be kings," I tell her. "We're girls."

"So what, we're girls?" Pen says. "We can be anything we want, and tonight I want to be a king of this mad world."

"No," Birdie says. "I mean I really am third in line to the throne. King Ingram is my grandfather."

The laughter has left her face. I lean closer to her. "How can that be?" I ask.

"Years and years ago, when he was still young and his wife was alive, King Ingram got a servant pregnant. He paid her off and she raised the baby herself. My father."

"You're making that up," Pen says giddily.

Birdie's hair swishes as she shakes her head. "And as it turned out, the queen was completely barren and they never had any children. So now my father is the only prince. But it's like this huge secret shame and no one in the kingdom can ever know."

"But who will inherit the throne when King Ingram dies?" I ask.

"My father," Birdie says. "It's already all planned out.

The story will be that the king left the kingdom to his trusted right-hand man in lieu of any heirs. No one will ever know my father is really his son."

"You're a princess," I blurt.

She giggles, takes another drink. "I am." She stands, pushes in her chair. "Let's go and explore the kingdom, shall we?"

She takes our arms and leads us to the theme park. Bits of metal on the rides glint in the moonlight like earthbound stars.

We spend the rest of the night climbing into the seats of rides that take us nowhere. I keep imagining that one of them will come alive and send us speeding away. Past Internment, past the stars and sun and moon, to whatever lies beyond.

9

All the cold weather has taken its toll on Basil. When he doesn't come to the breakfast table, I find him with the blanket pulled over his head. I peel it away, and his face is red.

"Basil?" I touch his forehead and his eyes open, glassy and dark.

"Are we home?" he asks.

"No." I run my hand down his face, feeling either cheek. "You've got a fever. I'm going to get a cold cloth."

"Don't leave," he says. "I dreamed all night that I was in a world of doors, and you were forever moving through them."

"That was only a dream," I say. "I'm here."

He sighs, closes his eyes. "You smell like tonic," he says.

"Are you angry?" I bite my lip. "Birdie took us to see the theme park last night and we shared a bottle of it."

"Pen was with you?" He opens his eyes.

I nod.

"Be careful, Morgan. She isn't as strong as you."

"Pen is one of the strongest people I know," I say.

"Not about that," he says. "You know what I mean."

Though I never speak of Pen's attraction to tonic if I can help it, it's not something that can be hidden from everyone. What began as a worrisome habit over time became a part of who she is.

I climb into the bed beside him, rest my chin on his shoulder. "I know," I say. "Don't worry. Just sleep."

He's in a thin and fitful sleep for much of the morning, and I begin to worry that this will prove to be more than just a cold. While he sleeps, I have hours to wonder about viruses that may be in this foreign air, or about our immune systems being ravaged without Internment's temperate climate.

But by midafternoon, he's awake and asking for something to eat. "What would you like?" I ask, and brush the sweaty hair from his forehead. His color is better now. Not so blotchy.

"Something close to familiar," he says. His smile is rueful, though I think he means to be reassuring. I know him, and I know that he's missing home.

"I'm so sorry, Basil," I say.

"There was nothing you could have done," he says.

Only a few weeks ago, we sat in the grass on a warm day and I confessed my curiosity about the edge. I thought it meant something was wrong with me. I worried about the king's specialist and remembering my pill so I wouldn't have to endure what Alice endured. I worried about my parents while I struggled to fill the emptiness my brother left us with when he jumped.

Those things all feel small and as faraway as a star. I couldn't have known about what was soon to happen.

"All I want to do is fix it," I say.

"The princess thinks aerial technology is advancing," he says. "Maybe one day."

"We might all be worse off for that," I say. "I've sort of begun to hope it doesn't happen." The weight of my sorrow and guilt is threatening to crush me, and I stand, as though that can rid me of it. "I'll go find some lunch for you," I say.

I'm happy to see Alice in the kitchen, helping the cook arrange a tray of pastries. She has been fastened to Lex's side since we arrived, but she can stay idle for only so long. She was out of their room for a bit yesterday, too, telling stories to the younger children and playing games with them.

"How's Basil feeling?" she asks me.

"Hungry. I came in to find something."

"I thought he might be," she says. "I've set aside some soup in the cold box. Give me a few minutes to heat it up."

"It's okay. I can do it," I say, even though I've no idea how to use this unfamiliar stove and was never much use even with the one I was familiar with back home.

And it is a peculiar stove, mint green with cabinets and six burners.

"Love, let me help you," Alice says.

"I'm his betrothed," I say, more snappily than I intended. "I should be able to at least boil soup if he's hungry." I have to believe these little gestures mean something, that this ring I wear still means we are to care for each other, whether or not there's a law down here that says we should.

I manage to heat the soup without burning down the hotel, and whether or not it's any good, Basil downs it without complaint while I sit on the window ledge, the portrait of a sullen girl against a world that is slowly prevailing beneath the snow.

"Something is on your mind," Basil says.

"Lots of things are on my mind," I say.

"Besides the obvious things, I mean. Is it something to do with last night?"

He's finished the soup now, and I set the bowl on the night table and climb onto the bed beside him. He wraps his arm around me and I close my eyes. There is still comfort in his touch. It gives me hope that we will find some normalcy in this world.

I tell him all about the telescope, and the planets, and the grand dream these people have of walking on the moon. I tell him all of this. But I don't betray the confidence of Internment's princess, or my best friend, who are at each other's throats, with me in the middle. I don't tell him how powerless I feel, and how very much to blame.

All I say at the end is, "I don't know what to do." It's become my mantra. My head is aching from that gin, and my mouth is dry. And what a mess I am. Not at all the one who can carry on my parents' legacy.

Basil can sense that there's more than I'm letting on. But he doesn't press, and I'm grateful for that. He's the only one on this planet who doesn't see me as a place to keep secrets, it seems. And he is always so patient with me.

"Rest," he says.

"Shouldn't I be telling you that?" I say.

He kisses the crown of my head. "You need to hear it more than I do."

It's the last thing that's spoken between us before we drift off. I'm able to pretend that the comfort of his arms is the only thing, and that when we both fall asleep, we're in a world of our own.

It's dark when I awaken, and I'm feeling worse for the sleep. My headache has doubled, and all I want is a hot bath and to go to bed, preferably without another spat between my roommates.

Basil's sleep is a heavy one, and it doesn't seem fitful anymore. His fever has gone down, but I bring a cold cloth for his forehead before I go upstairs. I want him to know that I am still here to care for him.

Celeste opens the bathroom door just as I was reaching for the handle. "Oh, Morgan, good," she says. "Just the one I wanted to talk to."

"Me?" I say.

She looks over my shoulder at the hallway of closed doors, any one of which can be filled with listening ears. She leads me into the bathroom, closes the door behind us.

"Tomorrow, I'm to see King Ingram," she says. "I wanted to invite you along. He's determined that the metal bird poses a risk. He doesn't want King Erasmus to realize we're here, so he's going to move it, whether or not the professor comes out."

"That should be a sight to see," I say.

"I suppose, if you're interested in that sort of thing," Celeste says. "That's not what I'm going for, really. I was hoping to speak with the king, is all."

I should go, if only to be aware of the king's plans. But I hate this role I've fallen into, in which I must watch the princess's futile attempts to save her mother while I'm to quietly try to sabotage it for the sake of keeping the entire city of Internment safe. "What are you speaking with him about?" I say.

"The truth is, I don't think he sees Internment as a substantial ally in this war. Nimble has spoken with him since our last visit, and it seems it would drain too many resources trying to focus all their attention into their aircrafts. Their technology is already ahead of King Erasmus's on that front."

"What about all that business of you being the heiress presumptive and him being a fool not to help?"

"All of that still stands," she says. "But it's taking a backseat to the war. He's spoken to his advisers since our meeting and now feels that his responsibility is solely to his own kingdom while it needs him the most."

I can't seem to look away from the tiles. "I don't see how I could change his mind," I say. "You hold more status than I do."

"I could use your support, as a fellow citizen of Internment," she says. The hope in her voice is too much.

"And—well. As someone who understands what it's like to have lost someone."

That gets my attention. Suddenly I'm finding it hard to breathe.

She goes on, "My father is very stubborn. He's afraid of the ground and afraid of advancement. And when my mother became ill with the sun disease, he implored every sort of treatment our doctors have to offer. But of course the treatments all did nothing. She grows weaker by the day."

"She has sun disease, then," I say. It's the same as a death sentence. It begins as a small boil and it multiplies until it has drawn all the color and all the life from a person.

Celeste grabs my hands, startling me. She holds them between our chests and I could swear I feel her pulse throbbing in her fingertips. "What Pen said isn't true. I had nothing to do with your parents. My brother and I have never had any say in my father's decisions, and while I'd like to deny that my father is to blame, I believe it."

I focus on the shiny gray flowers printed on the wall. Tears are threatening their way up.

"That's another part of it," Celeste says, her voice softening, the desperation becoming less prominent. "My father has made panicked, corrupt decisions to keep his kingdom from interacting with the ground. But if he could only see that there's an alliance to be made, all of that could stop."

I swallow something painful. "How can you be sure the alliance would turn out well?"

"How sure can one ever be of anything?" she asks. "But we have no other choice."

"You said you hoped we could be friends," I say. "As your friend, then, I think you should be prepared for your plan to fail. Have you given that a moment's consideration? You might be stuck in this world for the rest of your life. We all might." I say the words gently, but it doesn't take the edge from them.

She squeezes my hands. "That sort of thinking doesn't serve me," she says. "If I'm to accomplish something this big, I have to be certain I'll succeed, every second of every day."

She kidnapped me against my will, I remind myself. She threatened to kill me. I have no business pitying her. I have no business wanting to help her.

"I've invited you to come along tomorrow," she says. "The decision is yours, but I do hope you'll say yes."

She lets go of my hands and opens the door. "If you're going to have a bath, be sure to let the water run for a few seconds. It comes out cold."

With that, she's gone.

Before I go to bed, I check in on Lex and Alice, whose life in this world is parallel to their life on Internment. Lex mutters fiction to his transcriber while Alice patiently holds their marriage in place like a taut length of twine around a stack of old love letters.

"Good night," she says, and kisses my cheek and whispers, "He's grieving, and this is a strange place. He'll come around soon."

"Good night, Lex," I say. "You remember me, don't you? Your only sister?"

He raises his voice to the transcriber, drowning me out.

I used to worry when he behaved this way, but now it just makes me angry.

I am the only one in the hotel incapable of sleep tonight. Even Pen succumbed rather early, complaining of a headache. She blamed the princess for her headache and dragged the changing screen between their beds. Birdie, still hungover from the night before, spent the entire day feigning a stomach virus to ward off her father's suspicions. She doesn't come to our room and it's clear there will be no adventures tonight.

I listen to the clock ticking on the nightstand. Time is the same on the ground. Months and days, too. I had expected more differences between us and them, but all the differences are cultural. They have two eyes like us. They have a beating heart like us. And Birdie's friendship has been as easy and natural as it would have been had we met on Internment.

But when I look to the future, I'm not certain I see myself here. Nor am I certain I could see myself returning home. I feel very much that I am floating in a sky full of stars, with nothing to cling to.

And sleep will surely never come. When I can take it no longer, I climb out of bed and make sure the bedroom window isn't locked, in case I'll need it later. I quietly make my way to the kitchen and fold some apples and slices of bread into a cloth napkin, and I head for the metal bird.

I've taken these streets enough times now that I remember where the bird landed. It's far from the city proper, so there are no streetlamps to light the way. But that's no matter. The stars remember me; I was born and have lived my entire life beneath them, and they will always light the way.

The snow is beginning to melt, and it's as though Havalais has endured a flood. I see the night sky reflected in puddles, and I think I could get used to being here. Learn the history books and cast trinkets into the sea to make friends with the mermaids. Lex will come out of hiding and he and Alice will find an apartment, and they'll invite me for dinner sometimes. And there are no dispatch dates; Basil and I could live to be a hundred years old. We could travel all the way around the planet and never feel that we're standing upside down, and it will be a marvel for us.

Perhaps it's the silence of this night or the clarity of the stars. Perhaps I am disillusioned. But I am feeling brave enough to take on this world. And the moon as well, should there ever be a way for me to reach it.

When I reach the metal bird, it feels like a piece of some distant time.

I climb the ladder, knock on the metal door. "Professor Leander? It's me. Morgan Stockhour."

I hear rustling and clanging from within, then silence.

"I've brought food," I say.

No answer.

"The food here isn't very different if you know what to look for. They eat a lot of animals. And the strange thing is that they drink cow's milk. I can't say I care for it. It left me feeling a bit nauseous. Anyway, I've brought you an apple and some bread."

The door cracks open. "Oh, for the love of—will you stop talking? You're going to attract the animals."

I lean forward and try to see inside the bird. "Animals?"

"Yes, yes. Strange ones, at that. With beady red eyes and fangs."

"Can I come inside, then?" I say, holding the bundle up hopefully. "I'm alone. Promise."

The professor's arm reaches out for the food, but I hold it back. "First let me in."

"Oh, all right, all right. If there are eyes watching, they've already seen you." The door opens all the way, and there Professor Leander stands, holding a lantern. I make a note to bring candles the next time I visit; he must be running low.

"Nobody is watching," I tell him. "It's just an empty field."

"Nothing is what it seems here," he tells me as he climbs the ladder that leads to the kitchen. It's still filled with appliances that won't work without electricity. I'm not sure what he was planning for.

"They're going to run you out, you know. Tomorrow the king is coming to haul this bird away, whether you come out or not."

"Yes, yes." He bites into the apple with a loud crunch. "I've been expecting that. Judas and Amy tell me we're at war."

"Judas has been to see you?" I don't know why I should feel betrayed. It isn't as though I haven't been keeping secrets and sneaking away. "When?"

"Oh, now and again. Refuses to bring any food, though. He insists I come out."

"Why don't you?"

"Savages," he says. He raises the lantern and I can see all the creases in his face. "You're lucky to have your skin, the lot of you. Lucky they didn't take it away from you."

"They aren't scary," I say. "They're people, like us."

He finishes his apple and brushes past me and begins climbing the ladder. He takes the lantern with him, leaving me in the darkness. After a pause, he says, "Well, are you going to just stand there?"

I follow him up and through the hallway that leads to the helm, which is made up almost entirely of windows. He blows out the lantern, and starlight fills the space. For a moment it's like being home.

"See, there," he says, pointing across the water to where the lights of the capital city are glimmering. "That's the technology we copied. Copied their buildings and their trains, but tried not to copy their ways."

"It isn't very different," I say.

"It never sleeps." His voice is a hiss. "Always going. Always building, climbing an endless ladder until they make their way into the sky. It is only a matter of time."

"Before they reach Internment, you mean," I say, trying to understand.

"Internment, the moon, the bloody tributary so they can swim with the dead spirits."

Against all reason, I look to the sky and try to find that impalpable ribbon of light. "They don't believe in the tributary here," I say.

"Gardens of bodies," he mutters. "You learn all you need to know by how a people treats its dead." He looks at me, his face so close, I can smell the apple on his breath. "You mustn't die in this place."

I lean back. "I don't see how I should help that." He shakes his head, looks back to the city. It is a strange city, but I'm trying to make it seem familiar.

"What did you come for?" he asks, after a silence.

"To warn you about tomorrow," I say. But, now that he's asked, I wonder, "If you're appalled with the ground, and opposed to the way Internment is run, which would you prefer—to be here or to be there?"

"It's not about me," he says. "Not me. I'm not long for any world now. This trip was for my granddaughter. Those parents she's got were killing her with treatments. When Daphne was killed, they lost their perfect child. They forgot they still had another. They were going to declare Amy irrational soon. Lock her away."

I think of all those nights I found Amy hiding in the woods. She hid in the cavern and climbed trees and said that there was no one at home to notice she was gone. "They miss her, surely," I say.

"They're relieved," he says. "But, more importantly, so is she."

"She's sick," I blurt. "Judas is trying to hide it, but since he's been coming to visit and you have his ear, I think you should convince him to bring her to a hospital. From what I understand, the doctors here are more advanced."

"If you don't value your skin," the professor says.

He sits at the helm, and though the buttons and levers no longer work, he runs his fingers over them like a parent caressing its sleeping child. And in the apex between his forefinger and thumb I see a dark mass. The early sign of sun disease.

I feel as though I am being watched the entire way back to the hotel. The professor's paranoia is contagious, though when I strain my ears, all I hear is the roar of the tides turning. It has all that weight burdening it. It carries the reflection of the entire sky.

By the time I return to my bed, I feel as though I'm carrying the same weight.

"Wondered when you'd be back," Celeste whispers from the other side of the screen. "I'm surprised you went alone this time."

"I'm not sure what you're implying." I try to bury myself in the blankets, in the dark. "I only wanted to go for a walk without disturbing anyone."

"You don't need to lie to me," she says. "I don't feel excluded to miss the nightly parties. I need my eight hours."

"Then have them," I say. She's quiet, and I'm left with time to regret my sharpness. "I'm sorry," I say.

"Pen doesn't own you, you know," she says. Cool, practical. "You needn't include her in every moment of your life."

Now it's my turn to be offended. This from the girl whose brother finishes every sentence she begins in his presence.

Unlike me, she doesn't apologize for her candor. She lets it linger in the darkness, the last thing I hear before sleep.

10

There is something strange about the morning sky. Everyone in the hotel seems to sense it, except for Celeste, who is all energy and chatter about her meeting with the king. "It's right after breakfast," she says. "Have you decided whether you're coming?"

"Yes, have you?" Pen rolls her eyes. But when the princess isn't looking, Pen gives me a quick nod that says she wants me to go.

I've decided to, but not because it's what she wants. I'm going because I feel that the professor should have a friendly face in sight when he's dragged out of his life's work.

"I'd much like to go," I say, and mimic the sour face Pen gives while the princess is busy inspecting herself in the mirror. Pen throws a necklace at me.

Celeste smiles. "Excellent. See you at breakfast, then."

Once the princess is gone, Pen says, "You have to tell me everything."

"I don't *have* to," I say.

Pen pushes my shoulders down so that I sit on the edge of the bed. She climbs behind me and begins twisting and pinning my hair. She says it makes her anxious the way I let my hair just hang over my shoulders like a wet rag. Pen believes in a pristine appearance, always. It draws the line between living and giving in. Under the bloodshot eyes and ashen skin and frizzed hair her mother wears, traces of a pretty woman still linger, dying slowly.

"What has gotten into you?" she says. "You've been touchy. Is it Basil? Is he very sick?"

"I checked in on him earlier this morning," I say. "He's much better."

"What, then?"

"I'm only tired," I say.

She tugs a piece of my hair. "Hey, you know what I was thinking? When the war is over, we could get our own apartment in the city. Maybe Birdie would come, too."

"They cost money here," I say. "They aren't assigned."

"So we'll get jobs."

"What about Thomas and Basil?" I say.

"You're such a good girl," she teases. "Upholding the rules of betrothal when the law isn't looking."

"I'm still going to marry Basil," I say.

"So marry him, then. It doesn't have to be tomorrow." She pushes me toward the mirror so I can see what she's done. All my hair is off to one side and woven into a fish tail that winds into a bun.

"It looks nice," I say,

"Worthy of a day spent in the presence of royalty, if I do say so myself."

She rests her chin on my shoulder. We stare down our reflections as though they pose a threat. Who we are versus who we were supposed to be.

The clouds have become the color of mud. They are heavy and unreal, strokes in one of Pen's wild colorings when she's feeling fantastical and the look in her eyes says she is unreachable. I stare up with worry as the wind works at undoing my hair. Celeste holds her borrowed hat to her head. There's a violet flower with a blue stamen pinned to its side that complements the brightness of her eyes. If she's at all worried about the sky, she doesn't let on. She's watching the king's men in a circle around the metal bird. They've brought machines this time that look like giant metal monsters, one with two long fingers and another with teeth that are eager to tear the professor's invention apart.

"Stubborn, isn't he?" she says. "They're going to disassemble it whether he comes out or not." At the next gust of wind, she holds her skirt against her knees. "I wish they'd hurry up."

The machine with the long fingers rolls forward. I look away just as the metal begins to crunch. Voices shout into the megaphones for him to come out, and all I can think of is that mass on his hand that will be the death of him.

I run forward. Celeste calls after me but I run for the metal bird, past the men with guns and megaphones, up the ladder. Nobody stops me. The machine is still tearing at the helm. I hear the glass shatter.

"Professor Leander!" I call. I tug at the handle and find that it isn't locked. It isn't even latched.

He isn't on the main level and I climb the ladder up to the helm. Cold air fills the hall; the metal groans as it settles.

I find him sitting at the controls, staring at the open space that was once his windshield. The machine has stopped tearing at it, but only because I've run inside. They had no regard for his life at all.

"We have to go," I say.

He closes his eyes. "It ends here, then, does it?"

"It begins," I say.

He looks at me, unbelieving. We hold each other's gaze, and I see the moment when realization strikes him: I am it. I am the only one on this whole round, half-upside-down planet who is going to come for him. And I believe it's for me, not himself, that he stands.

He mutters complaints and curses the whole way to the door. I put my hand on the latch. "Ready?"

"Are they very barbaric out there?" he asks.

"Only slightly."

He clutches the book he grabbed on our way out, and then he holds it to me. *The History of Internment.* They are every-where to be found back home, but this must be the only copy the ground will ever see. Suddenly this book, a copy of which I handled and carried every day as a student, has become the last of its kind. "I'd like your friend to have this. The budding cartographer who drew me that lovely map."

"You can give it to her yourself," I say. "She'd love it."

He forces it into my hands and throws open the door.

A hush has fallen over the king's men. The princess stands among them, wringing her hands. She looks nervously at me.

"Ladies first," the professor says.

I climb down, and the moment I touch ground, all the men raise their guns to the professor. They are all wary of this bizarre and wild-haired man. I look up at him. There is nothing like sanity in his eyes. *Don't do anything stupid. Don't do anything stupid.*

He holds his hands up to show that he is not armed. Guns don't exist in our world; I know the proper name only from hearing Jack Piper boast about the king's artillery. But it's as though the professor knows all about them. It's as though he knows everything. What a terrible burden it must be.

He climbs slowly, shivering at the cold, under the scrutiny of a dozen men and a dozen guns. The king is not even present for this moment. He has sent his men and his permission and his blessing, but he hides in his castle for the dirty work of the demolition and the moving of the pieces.

The professor sets one foot on the ground, then the other. And then with a feeble grunt he collapses.

Celeste does not mind the intrusion on her time with the king. It gives her an opportunity to see the hospital of Havalais. And, as she is quick to remind me, she is all about finding the sunny side of things. The king's driver gives us a full tour.

"Isn't it astounding?" Celeste says.

"I don't much care for hospitals, actually," I say.

The driver boasts about the top-notch technology of the facility. Blood transfusions and burn units. Something called cancer. He's surprised that we've never heard of it. He says there are so many types, and surely we must have them on Internment but know them by another name.

Celeste begins describing her mother's symptoms.

I try to let the noises of the building drown out the words. I do not want to hear about illnesses or death or medicine. It's strange how this hospital seems to carry the same memories as the one back home.

I clutch the history book to my chest. The princess has yet to notice I'm even carrying it, so immersed is she in the workings of this place. That is another cruel thing hospitals bring—hope.

There are so many open doors revealing the sick and the dying. I focus on the tiles to keep myself occupied, and note all the differences between them and the floors back home. The architecture of these buildings isn't very different. Only newer and brighter. Jack Piper says they've already begun plans to rebuild the banks. There's no shortage of brick and mortar, even at wartime.

I can't help overhearing when the princess asks about fertility treatments. On Internment, this is the most important wing of a hospital. Genders are predetermined to make sure everyone has a match. We have little gray screens that can look inside the womb. But there's none of that here. Genders are left to chance. Health and growth can be foretold by drawing blood, but there is no way to visually see. Most parents are just happy if their children are healthy, the king's driver says. It matters only that they're born healthy, and the doctors see to that. As to the rest of their lives, they're on their own.

I'm grateful when we finally step outside the hospital. I don't know all of what Celeste has learned, but she's lost her cheer, and the meeting with the king is a solemn one. More warfare. He is not going to retaliate against King Erasmus's bombs. He would like to wait until the time is right before announcing the arrival of visitors from the magical floating island. When? Perhaps the spring. That's when all the snow is gone and flowers begin to bloom.

The king and Jack Piper have been working it out. For now, they'll tell anyone who inquires that we're relatives visiting from overseas, from a neutral island known as Norsup. And when the time is right, they'll announce who we really are. It will be a wonderful bright spot and just what Havalais will need after all this talk of war.

Celeste hates all the waiting. She speaks calmly and firmly as she proposes idea after idea for Havalais to ally with Internment now.

"It just isn't feasible right now, doll," the king says.

"There must be something Internment has that you would want," Celeste says. "Our electricity is a touch more advanced. You have moving picture shows, and we have something like that, but with sound."

"When Havalais and Internment meet, it will be a glorious thing," King Ingram says. "But it will take time."

Time. She hasn't got time. That's what she's thinking; a clock is always ticking in her brain. Time is what's killing her mother. Time will be the downfall of her floating kingdom.

The driver holds the car door open and we climb inside.

"Skin cancer," she whispers, after the door has closed. She looks at me. "That's what sun disease is, you know. At least, that's what it seems to be."

"Can it be cured, then?" I ask.

"There are treatments. But we don't have anything like them in the bloody sky, so a lot of good they'll do her from down here."

"I'm sorry," I say. "I truly am."

The driver gets behind the wheel and we begin to move. She doubles forward and hides her face in her knees. It's the first time she's lost her composure at all since we've arrived. "I didn't want to think you were right," she says, and sits up again. "When you said that my plan might fail, I thought, 'What does she know? She's only a girl, not a drop of nobility in her.' But the list of differences between us grows shorter every day we spend here." She nods to the shop windows we're passing. Luxurious fur coats in deep browns and smoky grays. Hats and bags to match. Shoes that would make us tall enough to pluck clouds from the sky and mold them how we pleased. "I have pages in my wallet," she says. "But they're useless here. Just paper. Everything I have is just pieces of paper."

That's a good way to put it.

I take her hand. It's a pathetic offering, but she squeezes

my fingers, and she just seems grateful to have something to cling to.

She's quiet for the rest of the ride. There was a time when I would have been glad for her silence, but now it only adds to the weight of those darkening clouds over our heads. Sadness filling up the sky.

"It sounds like the clouds are growling, doesn't it?" I say, as we step out of the car.

She looks upward, nods.

And then the sky makes a sound that is louder than a growl. A fierce boom that causes us both to flinch. *It must be another bomb,* I think. I wait for the smoke. I expect the hotel before us to go up in flames. But the driver isn't at all worried. A short distance away, he's coming out of the carriage house and walking for the back door that leads into the kitchen. "Better get inside, girls," he calls to us. "Looks like rain."

Celeste and I look at each other, confused. And then her mouth falls open in astonishment and she holds up her palm. I don't understand until I feel a drop of water land on my face. And then another. And then thousands, pouring all around us as though they're stampeding from the sky. There's another boom that shakes the earth.

I tuck the history book under my shirt to keep it dry. Celeste is laughing and she's got her arms spread out. What an unusual world.

Basil wants to go out and feel the rain for himself, but I stop him from putting on his coat. "You're still recovering," I say. "It's frigid outside. And those flashes of light—what if they're dangerous?"

We're standing at his bedroom window, and he smirks at me.

"What?" I say.

"You're worried about me."

"Of course I'm worried about you," I say. "Things don't just come falling out of the sky at random where I'm from. I don't want you standing under it, not with that cold."

"It's the same water as our lakes on Internment," he says. "Only Internment is above the storm clouds, so the soil must absorb it."

"Pen would lecture you and say our lakes were a gift from the god of the sky if she heard you talking like that." I stare at the city lights in the distance, the ocean leading the way. "I wish she and Thomas would come back. Did they say where they were going?"

"They didn't tell anyone. Just stole away somewhere after breakfast."

They must be so frightened. The water sounds like tapering applause. Another boom makes me gasp.

Basil stands behind me and holds my arms. "It's thunder," he says.

"What causes it? Is their god trying to tell them something?"

"It's only weather," he says. "Annette came to bring me tea when I was too sick to get out of bed. She told me all about the types of weather they have."

"I wonder what will fall from the sky next," I say.

"Some fish, perhaps, to swim in all this water."

Basil laughs. His breath tickles the back of my neck. He kisses under my ear. I close my eyes. "You're safe," he says. I believe him.

When he tries to kiss my skin again, I turn my head and catch it with my mouth. The world outside throbs with a flash of light.

"Be careful around Judas," he murmurs, and when he tries for another kiss, I lean away.

"What are you talking about?"

"We're in a different world now," he says. "It may seem that the rules have changed. But that doesn't change who we are or what we've done."

"He was accused of murder, you mean," I say. I take a step away from him. "What brought this on?"

"Thomas and I share a room with him," Basil says, nodding to one of the empty beds. "We're just not convinced he's all right. And I know that you're fond of him—"

"Fond?" I say. "I don't think he killed his betrothed. I think the king set him up. That's not the same as being fond."

"I just want you to be careful," he says. "That's all."

"Careful," I echo. "Why do I keep hearing that word? Why does no one trust me to be careful?"

"I trust you, Morgan. Of course I do. He's the one I don't trust. I worry that he's taking advantage of your kindness, is all."

"How would he take advantage?" I say. "I have nothing at all to offer."

He averts his eyes and a flush of color spreads across his cheeks, and he doesn't even have to say what he's thinking. I don't think that he can. I don't know whether I should be angry or try to reassure him. This mad world below the clouds has me constantly at odds with myself.

"I wouldn't, Basil," I say. "And I'm a little hurt by your implication."

Basil has only ever been right about me. He even knew I was daydreaming about the edge before I worked up the courage to tell him. But this time he's so wrong that it makes up for all of that.

"Like I said"—he's looking at the sky that swirls and grumbles like a ferocious animal, not at me—"he is the one I don't trust."

Alice has turned the thunder into a story. The fireplace is the only source of light in the living room and she makes shadows on the walls. The children are mesmerized. Even Birdie, slumped with her legs dangling over the armchair, has set down her book to hear the tale of the princess who fell in love with a ghost across the lake.

The children interrupt her to ask for more details— anything to keep the story going longer. What sorts of creatures are in the lake? What color is the princess's hair?

I linger in the doorway for a while and listen to the excitement in her voice. It's been a long time since I've heard it. It's been a long time since she could be this good at pretending to be happy.

Just as she's telling about the wind full of stardust that

obscures the princess's view of her beloved ghost, she meets my eyes. "Then what happens?" she asks me.

"Happily ever after?" I say.

"It can't be that easy!" Annette pouts.

"It isn't," Riles says with certainty.

"There was something the princess wanted," Alice tells her. "Something that the ghost couldn't give her."

I wish I didn't have to hear what she's going to say next.

"A child."

Annette and Marjorie are wide-eyed. They want desperately for this princess to have a proper romance, and what sort of happily-ever-after could lack such an important piece?

I don't stay to hear how the story ends. By the time I reach the top of the stairs, I'm so sad and angry, I don't know what to do with myself. It has given me just the bravery I need to confront my brother.

I don't knock. I just open the door. He stops murmuring to his transcriber. He knows it's me. He can listen for a person's footsteps. For breathing and the way a knob turns. He can listen for everything but words. He doesn't listen to a thing I say anymore.

"Why did you do it?" I say.

"What's that, Little Sister?"

"Why did you jump? You had to know that it would hurt you. That it would hurt Alice, and all of us."

He shakes his head, turns back to his transcriber. "Not now. I'm in the middle of a tragedy. A man's about to kill his sister for intruding on his masterpiece."

He reaches for the switch that will turn the transcriber on again, but I snatch it away. He reaches for the stream of paper as it moves just out of his reach.

"Tell me," I say.

Slowly, he stands, feeling along the wall. "Morgan, I absolutely will kill you if you do anything stupid with my novel."

"Yes, yes, wouldn't want anything to happen to some gears and some paper. After all, it isn't something trivial like a living person."

"You're being a brat."

"You're being a ghost," I say. "Can't you see that? You're acting like it's already over. Maybe you wanted to die when you jumped over the edge, but you didn't, did you? And it's no use pretending you did."

A flash of light fills the dreary room, but he doesn't know about it. I back myself into a corner. The transcriber is heavy in my hands. I feel that I am holding his heart and all his thoughts. Pieces. That's all I ever get of him.

Softly, he says, "I didn't go there to die."

"What, then?"

"I didn't even jump," he says. "I only wanted to see what was out there. That's all. Backfired a bit, didn't it?"

He sits on the edge of the bed. His knees are shaking. I hold the transcriber to my chest. Its wheels have left black trails on my arms. It's ruining this dress that belongs to a woman I've never met. "You worked in a hospital, Lex. You knew what the edge did to people."

He shrugs. "I wasn't thinking about that. Maybe what they say is true and the winds there really do make a person go mad.

I climbed over the train tracks, and I walked for paces and paces and paces. I thought about moments of my life, but the funny thing is, I did it in backward order. I thought about Alice in her wedding dress, and all those red flowers she was holding as she stepped toward me. I thought about opening my eyes underwater and making faces at the trout. I thought about the day you were born. You were too small, you know. I was only allowed to see you through a window. You looked at me, though, and you were so fearless; it was like you knew something I didn't. Something I'd forgotten because I didn't know I was supposed to remember. So I mouthed to you through the glass, 'Don't forget.' It's the first thing I ever said to you.

"That morning, before I walked to the edge, I came downstairs and I found you at Mom's dresser. Your face was covered in her cosmetics, and you looked at me in the mirror, and it was that same look."

I remember that morning perfectly. I was just barely thirteen, and I wanted to see how I would look when I was older. Only, I made a mess of myself. I scrubbed the cosmetics from my face before going to class, but I could still feel it in my pores, still taste the stain on my lips when they came for me and told me something had happened to my brother. I've never much cared for cosmetics since.

"I reached the edge," Lex says. "And then I looked up, and the world had stopped. There was no fence. No sound. The grass just . . . stopped. And I had this feeling like the solution to everything would be down there if only I could dig through all those clouds. So I leaned forward to look."

There are tears in my eyes. I'm awful for pushing for this. "The last thing you saw was a solution hiding under the clouds, then," I say.

"No," he says. "The last thing I saw was a dream that lasted for days. I dreamed of a gray thing on a screen. I was trapped in the last moment of its life, and I dreamed that I could hear its heart beating. Then one day I woke up, and the only heart beating was mine. It was gone, and there's been darkness ever since."

He lowers his head. His hands are open and empty in his lap.

Tentatively, I kneel on the bed beside him. I return the transcriber. He turns it about, smoothes the paper, but it doesn't seem to matter to him as much as it did a few minutes ago.

"Nimble Piper wears lenses that help his vision," I say. "He says he's nearly blind without them."

He shakes his head. "It isn't that simple, Little Sister. I don't even see images in my memories anymore. I don't think I'd know the difference between red and blue. It can't be returned like flipping a switch."

"It's worth a try," I say. "There are so many new things worth seeing. It's a new world."

He laughs without humor. "Is there not cruelty in this world too?"

I lean my head on his shoulder. He musses my hair, but hesitates when he feels the fish tail braid. He wasn't expecting anything to be different about me. I'm still thirteen years old, looking at him in a mirror.

"That's just a part of it, Lex," I say. "Things are terrible and then they get better, and back again."

I climb off the bed. I open the window, and the smell of wet earth fills the room. I grab my brother by the arm, and he actually lets go of his transcriber and doesn't fight me when I pull his hand out the window.

Rain fills our palms and splashes onto the window ledge.

"Storm clouds," he says. "They can look at them through the scopes."

"We haven't got a scope," I say. "We have a window, and that's so much better, don't you think?"

He raises his eyebrows at me. He's smiling and trying to hide it. He doesn't want anyone to see that he's still alive in there.

"Today it's an open window," I say. "Baby steps. We'll work our way to the door, and then we'll deal with what's on the other side of it."

Pen runs into our bedroom. Her hair is dripping onto the floor, black cosmetics running down her cheeks. At first I can't tell if she's distressed or excited, but then she bursts into laughter. "Have you been out there?" she says. "Isn't it incredible?"

"I was worried you'd be scared," I say.

"Oh, it was terrifying at first. Thomas and I were at the harbor, and we heard these loud snaps like the god of the sky was cracking a whip. I thought the world was going to end. But then nobody around us seemed to notice at all, and when the water started to fall, some of the people raised these funny canes they'd been holding, and the canes bloomed open over their heads."

She wrings out her hair, darkening the carpet. "It was wonderful. I'm in need of a hot bath, though, before I catch my death. It's so cold down here, I don't know how they get on. I feel like the cold is trapped inside my bones. Do you ever feel—"

She stops talking because I've pulled her into an embrace. She smells like wool and wet air and redolence she borrowed from one of the many dressers in this sprawling building.

Her arms wrap around me with uncertainty. "Is everything all right?" she asks.

"I'm just glad to see you so happy," I say.

She draws back and holds me at arm's length. "Is there anything you want to talk about?"

My betrothed thinks I'll be seduced by a murderer, and my brother is far too young to have given up, and Alice is inventing ghost children downstairs.

"No," I say. "Go have your bath. I've got a present for you after."

She nods to her bed. "Is it that lump under my blanket?"

I push her toward the door. "After," I say.

She takes the shortest bath in the history of this world and our own, I'm sure. As soon as she returns to our room, she makes a line for the bed and pulls back the covers.

I lean back on my elbows on my own bed, and I can't help smiling.

"Morgan," she gasps. "Where did you find it?"

"The professor gave it to me. He said it was a gift for my friend, the budding cartographer."

She holds it in both hands and stares at the cover. I have the thought that one day her great-grandchildren will have that book in their possession; it will be worn and yellowed by then, and it will be the most precious thing her family could ever own, because it will be the only piece left of that magical island hovering out of reach.

Pen throws her hand over her mouth to catch her sob. In an instant her eyes are red and wet.

"I thought you'd be happy," I say.

"I am," she says, and wipes her tears with the back of her hand. "I think this might be the greatest day of my life." She falls onto my bed beside me. "It's like the sky opened up and it sent this water to scrub away every bad thing that's ever happened to me." She bumps her shoulder against mine. "I love this day, and I love this book, and I love you more than life, Morgan Stockhour."

"I love you, too," I say. I don't even have to think about the words, they're that easy and I'm that sure of them. So why can't I say them to Basil? He's told me he loves me enough times.

"Pen?"

"Mm?"

"Do you ever tell Thomas that you love him?"

She crinkles her nose. "Why would I say a thing like that?" She lies back and holds the history book over her head and sighs happily. "What should I read first? Something with the stars, I think."

145

11

The rain turns into snow, and the snow into rain. For weeks the two weather patterns engage in a sort of dance with each other. It's much more than we're accustomed to, and one at a time we all fall victim to runny noses and fevers.

Jack Piper says we only need to get used to the cold, and then we'll be fine. Birdie sneaks gin into our tea. "It'll make you right as rain," she tells us. "That's what we say down here."

"It's the rain that made us this way," Pen says.

"I never thought of it that way," Birdie says.

Days blur by. One afternoon, while I'm feeling too sick to be up and about, I rest my head on Basil's knee as he reads to me in bed. The rain has become so normal to me that I forget I'm hearing it sometimes, but the thunder still makes me jump.

Basil doesn't miss a beat in his reading, but he runs his fingers through my hair.

"What's that part you just read?" I ask. "About throwing that girl into that thing."

"Volcano," he says. "I think it's a sort of mountain that has fire inside it. So to appease the volcano, they're making a sacrifice. Otherwise it'll flood the entire island with lava. I think lava is a sort of melted stone."

"So is the volcano a god, then?"

"Shh, just listen. It'll explain."

Pen, half-asleep in her bed and ravaged by fever, mumbles, "This story is the most ridiculous thing I've ever heard."

"I could find another one," Basil says.

"No, I want to see if they'll go through with it," she says.

"I don't understand why they're throwing her into the volcano," I say.

"Because she's a virgin," Basil says, and clears his throat.

"We could throw Morgan into the volcano," Pen says. "That ought to save at least ten islands."

"Hush, you." My face is burning. "Keep reading."

Pen doesn't make it to the end of the story. By the time the young girl is saved by the hero from someplace beyond the ocean, Pen's asleep and dreaming. Of some other girl in no need of any heroes, knowing her.

Basil sets the book on the nightstand, dabs at my face with the damp cloth that held an ice cube earlier. It's still cool, though; still a relief.

"I don't like seeing you this way," Basil says.

"It's only a cold," I say. "You had it, and you got better."

Thunder shakes the walls. I close my eyes and see the volcano erupting with liquid fire. The girl and the hero are drifting away on the sea. They aren't even looking back.

Basil says words that I can scarcely make out. Morgan, Morgan, love, here, the rain.

"Yes," I say, although I'm not sure what for.

I open my eyes and am greeted by Amy's blond hair strewn across my pillow. Her face is buried under the covers. "You were talking in your sleep," she says.

"What are you doing here?"

"Bad dream," she says. "You don't mind, do you?"

A flash of lightning fills the room. Shadows of raindrops curtain the walls. "What was your dream?"

She yawns. "Internment came crashing down. The sky was full of screaming, and the screaming was trapped in the clouds, like a net. I can still hear it."

She burrows herself against me. I don't mind the closeness; it makes me think of home. There is too much space on the ground; everyone is so far from everyone else.

I touch her forehead. She's under the spell of this weather, too. "Internment isn't going to fall," I say. "You're only delirious."

"If it fell, maybe it would fall into the ocean." Her voice is sleepy. "And float away and away."

Strange, strange girl.

"I worry about you sometimes," I say.

"I worry about you, too," she says.

"Why me?" So tired. I close my eyes and I am adrift on an ocean the color of her hair. Gold and yellow and white glittering under the sun.

"You had to hold everyone together. Your parents and your brother. Lex said it."

"When did he say that?"

"At jumper group. The king mandated as part of our therapy that we express at least one regret for jumping. One regret every week. He has lots of regrets, and many of them are about what happened to you."

This clears away my sleepiness. I open my eyes. Lex never talked about what went on in jumper group, not even with Alice. It wasn't allowed. But we're away from Internment's rules now. "What did he say?"

Amy's voice is fading; she's falling asleep, if she was truly awake to begin with. "He said that he had broken everything, and you were the only one trying to glue them back together. Only, you couldn't. Too many pieces were missing, cracked beyond repair."

It's true. I spent years trying to cheer my mother out of her melancholy, trying to get her to speak. I tried to hold myself together, didn't let them see me cry, so that they wouldn't have two broken children. When they couldn't bear the sight of what had become of their son, I went upstairs and delivered messages and food and money to my brother. I tried to stop needing them, when every second of every day, I resented it. Resented him.

I close my eyes, but it's too late. Tears squeeze their way out. They are silent. I don't want anyone to know.

"I didn't do a very good job," I say.

"No," Amy says. "They all let you down."

"Why are you saying all these things?"

"Because," she says. "Someone needed to. You still do it now. You try to hold everyone together. Sometimes you can't."

I dream of my mother. She's threading one of her samplers. Strange streams of light in the clouds.

Lightning.

She knew about lightning.

Celeste is the last of us to succumb to the weather. She fights it, getting dressed each morning and forcing herself down the stairs.

She stares at her breakfast plate with glassy eyes.

"Would you just go back to bed before you infect us all?" Pen says.

I kick her under the table.

"No meetings with the king lately, I've noticed," Thomas says.

Celeste shakes her head. Her voice is a whisper. "No. No meetings."

Guilt is a pain in my chest. I stare at my hands in my lap. My betrothal band is made of sunstone. Or phosane, as it's known here. It's a secret that could save her mother's life and destroy our home.

Basil tells me that I'm pale and he asks if I'm feeling sick again. I shake my head, force down breakfast even though all the Pipers are wrong, I haven't gotten used to the taste of eggs, and I don't understand how they can all go without fresh fruit until the weather gets warm.

But there will be no fresh strawberries today. There will be only rain and snow and clouds that hide Internment from view.

I hope that we won't all wilt waiting for the sunlight. I hope the secret about sunstone is the right one to keep.

12

The first day of spring smells like copper.

Spring. The word is everywhere. Annette fills the rooms with paper flowers and ribbons. Amy loves this. She follows Annette from room to room, both of them finishing the lines of each other's made-up songs.

"We can go fishing soon," Birdie says during lunch. She's gotten bolder now, hemming her skirts with ball pins and wearing red lipstick to the table, much to her father's displeasure. She says we've made her brave.

I worry we've all become reckless. Pen has become dependent on our almost nightly adventures, and some days she ventures out on her own with no word as to where she's been when she returns. She prefers gin to sleep. She laughs louder than she used to. She has good days and bad days, and on the bad days, she locks herself in the bathroom and runs the water to drown out the tears. She doesn't blame me. She says it's just the way it has to be, and she won't hear any talk of going back to the sky. She dabs under her eyes with the paisley hand towel, smiles at her reflection, tells me, "There. All better."

Now her voice is bright. "Sounds like fun."

"It's too cold for the fish," Nimble says. "But I'm going to uncover the boats today, if anyone would like to tag along."

Annette and Marjorie eagerly raise their hands.

"Anyone who is tall enough to reach the cereal boxes," he amends. They grumble.

After breakfast, Nimble and Birdie lead us to the docks. There are at least a dozen boats bobbing on ropes, covered up in blue blankets—tarps, Nimble calls them. They're for the hotel, he explains. The Pipers rent them to guests. Some of the boats are big enough to live in, I think.

Pen kneels at the edge of the dock and reaches into the water. "How deep is it?" she asks.

"Here?" Nimble says. "About ten feet, I think."

She stands. Her fingers are dripping water onto the boards. She nods to the horizon. "What about out there?"

Nimble laughs. "Much more than ten feet. Hundreds. Thousands."

She smiles over her shoulder at me. It's a mischievous but melancholy smile. "Want to swim for it?"

I can't tell if she's kidding. Thomas links his arm through hers; he isn't taking any chances. "It's too cold, heart."

"The cold probably wouldn't get you," Nimble says, pulling on the tarp, revealing another boat that's half the size of my apartment back home. Birdie helps him with the folding.

153

"No?" Pen says. "How would I die out there, then?"

"The mermaids could mistake you for a treasure, pull you down to their collection of trinkets," he says. "You could be swallowed up by a whale. Or you could have a limb bitten off by a shark and then bleed to death. But most likely, you'd get tired and drown."

She stares the ocean down like she is accepting its challenge.

As though to prove that there is a god in the sky looking out for her, the clouds break apart and create a distraction. "Look!" Birdie says, and we all follow her gaze. As small as a stone in the sky, for the first time we get a glimpse of home.

Basil hugs me to his side. We shield our eyes and stare for as long as we can stand it, before the sunlight becomes blinding.

"We should look through the telescope," I say to Pen. But she's gone. Not in the water, but down the pathway that will take her back to the hotel. Thomas goes after her, and when she realizes he's behind her, she runs. She was always the superior athlete of the pair and he can't keep up. I watch him double over to get his breath, and she is only just getting started. By the time he's regained himself, she's out of sight.

"Should we go after her?" Birdie says.

I shake my head. "She'll come back if she wants." The reminder of home was surely too painful.

Thomas is still trying to catch up. He's mad for her—always has been. I've recently begun to believe that love is synonymous with madness. It can't possibly be an act of sanity. It is restless and always in pursuit. It will fall from the sky to have what it wants.

Pen doesn't come out of hiding until dinnertime. I'm not sure where she's been all day, but she's got a crown of yellow flowers in her hair. "Buttercups!" Annette says. "Do you have those on the floating island?"

"Yes," Pen says. "But we call them raydrops. Like drops of the sun's rays."

"They aren't made of sun," Annette challenges.

"And they aren't made of butter," Pen says. "We don't even have butter on Internment. That's one of your strange inventions."

"Why don't you have butter?" Riles asks.

"Because we don't consume things that are extracted from udders." She's being snappy, but I can hear the sadness in her voice. She twirls her fork around the plate and stares at the unfamiliar food this world has to offer. If she's hungry enough, she'll force some of it down. But most nights she just pushes it around and says "Thank you; it was delicious."

She's quiet for the rest of the meal, except for when Nimble mentions a moonlit boat ride, and she says it sounds like an adventure.

After dinner, I follow her upstairs and we pick out hats and coats to wear on the boat.

"Where were you all day?" I ask, placing a cloche hat on her head; we have a similar sort of thing on Internment that we call a shell hat. She studies it a moment before deciding it doesn't go with her dress.

"Theme park," she says. "I didn't have any money for the telescope, so I just sort of . . . wandered about."

"Were you at the restaurant bar?"

She shrugs.

"Pen. We had a pact."

She stares over my shoulder a moment before looking straight into my eyes. "I don't need another Thomas to talk to me like I'm a child; one is more than adequate," she says. "I am going to step past you now, and go downstairs, and have a moonlit boat ride." She retrieves her buttercup crown from where she'd tossed it on the bed, and places it in my hair. "You are welcome to join me."

She leaves the room, and she doesn't look back to see if I'll follow.

It's a warm night, and I shed my coat as we're walking for the docks.

"Let me carry that for you," Thomas says. Somehow I've straggled behind Basil, Pen, Birdie, Nimble, and the princess, whose vivacious chatter seems to be filling up the night air.

"I'm all right," I say, hugging my coat to my chest.

"Are you?" he says. "You seem troubled."

"No," I lie.

"I thought Pen might have confided in you what she was doing today," he says.

I am immediately uncomfortable at the thought of being caught between the two of them. I don't think it's right for Pen to keep secrets, but I've kept secrets from Basil myself, and I know that she must have her reasons. Whether or not I agree, it isn't my place.

"You might try asking her yourself."

"Well, that won't do any good, will it?" Thomas says, and for the first time in all the years I've known him, I hear an edge to his tone, like he's challenging me. "She doesn't tell me all the things she tells you."

"I'm sure that isn't true," I say.

"Isn't it?" he says. "She tells me that she loves it here. That's clearly a lie. Says she wants to forge a new identity and live in the city. But the city is loud and filthy and nothing like home. She's trapped here—we all are—and she won't just say what she's thinking, that she wants to go home."

"I can't speak to her thoughts," I say, feeling just brave enough. "But she has said nothing of the sort to me, and this is a conversation you should be having with Pen. Excuse me." I push forward and catch up to Basil and the others.

Pen doesn't notice that Thomas and I were talking at all. She's walking apart from the group, looking at the stars as she goes, pointing and mouthing their names. There is a chapter in the history book devoted to the spirit of every animal that has been immortalized in the constellations. When I look up, all I see are stars, but Pen knows their names. She knows more than anyone else I've ever met. The gods and the glasslands and the archipelago that's caused this war. Every time she opens her mouth to speak, there's the chance she'll say something great.

Lately, though, she hides that greatness away, as though she believes it would be wasted here.

She doesn't look away from the sky until her feet are on the dock.

Nimble helps us climb onto the boat, one at a time. Celeste lingers at his side. The two of them have become inseparable of late, and I wonder if she considers at all the boy she's betrothed to. I wonder if she's accepted that she will never see him again.

"This is a boat?" Pen says. "It's enormous. Where does that door lead to?"

"Downstairs," Nimble says. "Don't worry; there'll be a tour."

"Another one?" Celeste whispers to him, giggling. I suppose she thinks I couldn't hear that, and I intend to perpetuate that belief.

So Nimble gives us a tour of the boat, which he calls a yacht. There's a helm with a wooden wheel, and a rack of tonic bottles with price tags hanging from the corks.

"That's the spirit bar," he says. "We charge by the glass."

"It's pricey," Birdie says, snatching a bottle off the rack. "But it would seem one has been stolen. Huh. Pity."

"My kid sister's gone corrupt," Nimble says. "You couldn't at least go for the cheap stuff, Birds?"

She hugs the bottle. "We have guests."

Pen moves up the stairs and stares out at the water. "Are we going to leave the dock?" she asks.

"Can't," Nimble says. He lights the lantern hanging over the top of the stairs, and the yacht is swathed in its dim glow.

"Father would kill us." Birdie rolls her eyes. "We're expected to stay on top of the upkeep, but we can't go anywhere in the yachts unless he's here to supervise."

"Why not?" Pen asks. "Afraid you'll sink and drown? He'd still have three spare children left."

"Pen, what a horrible thing to say," I tell her.

"I was only kidding."

"He's worried about the boats getting harmed," Birdie says. "We can still have fun. No worries." She waves the bottle over her head. "Nim, get the glasses."

I've never seen a boat like this, with seats and room to lounge about. At home we have rowboats that can seat two, but they're for fishing, not leisure. And our lakes are small enough that we can see one side from the other.

I find all the space dizzying. Birdie pours a glass of sparkling tonic and hands it to me. "Champagne," she says. "For celebrating."

"What are we celebrating?" Pen sits next to me.

"True love," Birdie says. She points the bottle at Nimble and Celeste, who let go of each other's hands the moment they realize we're all watching.

Pen nudges me, but I'm still too wounded by her betrayal to delight in this bit of gossip. I lean against Basil.

Celeste pointedly sits as far from Nimble as she can. "Full moon," she says, nodding at the sky.

"No, it isn't," Pen says. "It's waxing gibbous. It'll be full tomorrow."

"Did I tell all of you?" Celeste says cheerily. "Our Pen knows absolutely everything."

"You should know more about the sky," Pen fires back. "You are named for it, after all. Celeste the Uncorrupted."

"The who?" Birdie asks.

"Uncorrupteds are martyrs," Pen says.

"Like saints?" Birdie asks.

"That's one of your words," Pen says. "But yes, if you like. Celeste was what you'd call a saint. She slit her wrists to escape her tormentors that wanted her to speak out against the god of the sky." She regards each of us as though telling a fireplace tale. "She died and was rewarded for her sacrifice by becoming a permanent star in the sky. Bit of a raw deal, if you ask me. Only a star."

"I love all your stories," Birdie says, brilliantly breaking the tension with another round of champagne. "Which star is it?"

Pen throws her head back to look at the sky. "Oh, you know," she says. "One of them. It's not important."

Thomas frowns at the fresh champagne in Pen's glass.

The conversation goes to the stars, Birdie explaining the constellations and what they're all supposed to mean.

Thomas is talking to Pen with words that are only murmurs to the rest of us. She nods, but when he tries to put his arm around her, she scoots away from him. "I want to go swimming," she announces.

"Not in this water, you don't," Nimble says. "Lots of things lurk around here at night."

"Like sharks?" Pen asks, delighted. She wraps her arms around me. "Tell us about those. They sound so menacing, don't they, Morgan? Just the word alone. 'Sharks.' You have to grit your teeth when you say it."

"What do they look like?" I ask.

"Really? You've never seen one?" Nimble says. "What *do* you have in your water?"

"Trout," we all answer in unison.

"Imagine a very large trout, then, with a dorsal fin and a taste for blood."

Pen shivers excitedly. "As large as a person?"

"You'd fit in the stomach of one, easy."

Thomas moves the bottle away when Pen reaches for it. We can all see that she's had more than enough. I suspect that she had enough even before the champagne, but she's gotten so good at hiding it, I can't be sure.

"I'm not afraid of your overgrown fish," Pen says, letting go of me and falling back into her seat. "To be eaten by a fish, you'd have to be a special breed of daft. Do I look daft to you?"

Pen is one of the brightest people I know, but since leaving the sky, she has lost her head a bit.

"Let's not challenge it, dear," Thomas says. Normally he enjoys fantastic notions, such as being eaten by a carnivorous fish, but I think he and I have the same fear that Pen will do something rash with even the smallest bit of encouragement. There weren't many threats on Internment, but here on the ground the people live among them. It isn't safe for someone who sees things the way Pen does—as though every corner of the world must be conquered.

"I should like to see what's in these waters," Celeste says, looking over her shoulder at the moonlight breaking and rematerializing on the surface. "But in the daylight."

Pen sheds her coat. "Everything seems safer in the daylight," Pen murmurs to me. "Should we go for a swim? Just us. No princesses."

Unlike her mother, she is still articulate when she's drunk, but there's a quality to her voice that tells me I'm not speaking with the normal Pen. Something is off. I've learned not to say anything she'd perceive as combative. "We can't go in now," I say. "Tomorrow maybe."

Thomas catches us whispering to each other, and he puts his hand on Pen's shoulder. "I think we should all go back inside," he says.

She wrests away. "You go on if you want to," she says. "I have a previous engagement with the fish. And I want to see this Ehco I've heard so much about, that holds all the world's anger and sorrow."

Before he can stop her, she has kicked off her shoes and dived over the railing. She shrieks when she hits the cold water.

"Pen!" Thomas calls. We all run to the edge of the boat.

Pen is laughing, fanning her arms in the water to keep herself afloat. "I don't see your sharks, Nimble," she says. "The only thing biting me is the cold."

Thomas reaches his arms out for her. "Come up before you make yourself ill."

"At least the water ought to sober her up," I say to Basil.

Pen starts paddling back toward the yacht, but then she stops, staring at the back of her hand in the moonlight. "My betrothal band is missing."

Thomas's tone goes deadpan. "What?"

"It must have come off when I jumped." She stares into the dark water, but all that's visible are glimpses of her own clothes as she moves.

"Just come out of there," Thomas says. "You aren't going to find it now."

I make a fist to protect my own band. The thought of it being irretrievably lost in these strange waters full of odd creatures is too much to bear. "Pen, we can look for it tomorrow when there's light."

"There's something shining down there," Pen says. "I think the water's shallow here. I can get it."

"Pen!" Thomas says, but she's already gone. Basil claps his hand on Thomas's shoulder to reassure him, but Thomas's spirits are as lost as that ring. "I suppose I should go after her before she hurts herself," he sighs, kicking off his shoes.

I wince when his body hits the water. I can smell the cold of it from here.

"Ah, true love," Nimble says. "There's no one in this world I'd catch hypothermia for."

"Not even me?" Celeste says, nudging him.

I stare into the water, trying to find a trace of either of them.

Basil retrieves a stack of folded towels from under the seats. "Can you see anything?" he asks me.

"They've been gone a long time," I say.

"They're probably bickering down there," Nimble says. "That seems to be all they ever do."

The water breaks, but my relief is short-lived when Thomas surfaces alone. He takes a breath and disappears again.

Something is wrong. He can't find her.

Now it's my turn to kick off my shoes. The chilly air hardly registers when I unpeel myself from my coat, and Basil is trying to hold me back. "No," he says. I slip out of his hands and dive headfirst into the sea.

This water is far more abrasive than that of the lakes back home. It burns my eyes and nose, and even in the darkness, I can see that it's murkier. For an instant I have no sense of up or down, and I bob to the surface just long enough to note where I am and take a breath.

Underwater, I look for any trace of movement. There's a flicker of something light. I kick toward it, but something hinders my path. I press my hand against the shadowy wall—the side of the boat. Every instinct is telling me to return to the surface. My lungs burn. My already limited vision is tunneling. I fight my way down the side of the boat, toward that light little something. My fingers close around it, and I think I must have found a dead mermaid before I recognize it as Pen's hair. I grab her arm, and my heart is pounding. She doesn't resist. She comes away from the bottom of the boat like a piece of kelp. "Kelp" isn't a word either of us had reason to know before we came here.

I tuck her to my side and kick my way back up, at last granting my body's pleas for oxygen.

A small distance away, Thomas has also surfaced. "I've got her!" I cry, before he can go under again. He's at my side immediately, taking her limp body from my arms, holding her head above the surface.

"Pen!" I never knew him capable of such fear. He's pressing into her neck, trying to find a pulse. I can tell by his desperate fumbling that he can't get one.

I don't allow myself to think she isn't breathing. The cold water has gone thick around me, and I'm sure it's freezing me in place. I can't move but to keep myself afloat.

"Bring her here!" Nim calls. He's on the dock now. Basil is leaping from the boat after him. They kneel at the dock's edge, and it takes both of them to hoist Pen up. She was weightless in the water, but now her body is heavy and uncooperative. Thomas is already up beside her, and Basil reaches his hands out for me. He has to pull me most of the way; my legs don't want to work.

Basil tries to keep me from seeing her, but I push him aside.

She's lying in a strip of moonlight, as still as the bodies awaiting the tributary. Only there is no tributary on the ground. If any of us were to die down here, I fear we'd be lost forever, interred in a garden of stones.

Basil is pulling me into his arms, trying to soothe me even before I'm able to panic. But the panic comes a moment later, and I'm shaking my head, saying, "No, no, no." I see her eyes rolled back, and I can't bear to think they will never again brighten when she's happened upon a new idea.

Nimble is telling Thomas that they can try to revive her. I've heard of this. Somewhere in Lex's medical texts there are many pages devoted to the art of last-hope desperation. But the illustrations make it seem so matter-of-fact; there's nothing on any of the pages about what truly stands to be lost.

I watch, helpless, as Thomas holds her nose shut and breathes into her mouth, and Nimble presses into her ribs. They take turns, like it's some school-yard game, and they can't mess up, they can't do a single thing out of time.

Basil wraps a towel around my icy shoulders, and he's holding me so tightly, as though I am the one who is slipping away. It doesn't matter that I've made it out of the water. If Pen is lost, I'll spend the rest of my life trying to claw my way to the surface in time to save her.

Thomas murmurs some desperate words before he brings his lips to hers again. Her chest rises with the air he gives her, automatically, mechanically. But then she convulses, and water spills from her mouth and she comes alive with a round of violent coughs and gasps.

"Attagirl," Nimble says.

I let out the breath I'd been holding.

The stars above me reemerge from the darkness, and I feel as though I, too, am returning from death.

Pen pushes herself up, retching.

Thomas's relief is palpable. He seems at once years older, and he's shaking as he hunches forward to see her face. "Have you come back to me now? Margaret?"

She splutters a mouthful of water. "You know I hate that name."

"She's okay," Thomas announces.

He wraps her in a towel and scoops her into his arms. It's the sort of display she would normally protest, but she's dazed and still a bit drunk.

"Home now?" she says.

"Not quite, my love." He kisses her forehead as he carries her away through the sand. "If only I could."

Nimble runs ahead of them, shouting directives to his parade of siblings, who are filing out of the hotel to see what's happened. Celeste and Birdie are at his heels.

Basil wipes the water from my shuddering jaw.

"Are you hurt anywhere?" he asks.

"I don't—think so. I can't feel my body, though."

I look at the hotel in the distance. Figures move within the windows.

"Hey," Basil says. I look at him. "I want you to know I'm proud of you."

"I didn't do anything," I say. My teeth are chattering. "Just went for a little swim, is all."

"This water is not like the water back home," he says. "It was the unknown. And you dove right in. That was extraordinarily brave."

I think my cheeks have thawed enough that my smile comes through.

"But never do anything like that again, do you hear me?"

"She's on her own if she goes over a second time," I say.

"Come on. Let's get you out of this cold." Basil helps me up, righting me when I stumble.

He drapes his coat over me and I lean against him. "Basil, I don't know what to do about Pen."

"You're a good friend to her." He rubs my arm. "But let Thomas look after her. It's what he's meant to do. It's what they both need."

As we grew up, Thomas and Basil teased Pen and me about the way we cared for each other. I've always suspected there was a bit of jealousy under all of it, that each of the boys knew they had to share the girl they loved. What Pen and I have for each other isn't a threat to our betrothals, but we have each other's hearts just the same.

But all I say is, "I know."

We've reached the front door to the hotel.

"Promise you'll go right to bed after you've dried

off," Basil says. "This cold could be lethal."

"I promise." There will be no adventures in the city tonight. "You should sleep, too."

In the warmth of the lobby, the feeling returns to my limbs. My head is aching and my left hip is sore. I have some vague recollection of hitting it on the dock as I climbed up.

Annette runs to us, bright-eyed. "Is it true you were nearly swallowed by a killer whale?"

Sharks. Killer whales. This place is enough to put me off swimming for the rest of time.

"Who told you such a thing?" I ask.

"No one. I just assumed. Everyone was dripping wet. Nimble said you were right behind them, so I already drew a bath for you."

"Annie, words are too small for my gratitude right now." I kiss Basil's cheek and I let the smallest Piper lead me upstairs.

I stay in the water until it's gone from hot to cold, and despite persistent lathering and wringing out, my hair still smells of salt.

When I return to the hallway, I hear voices from around the fireplace. Nimble and Birdie are diverting the children's questions and replacing them with fantasies about sea creatures that will devour them if they don't pipe down and go to bed. I don't want to hear any of it. I want only to go to sleep and forget this horrible night happened.

The door to my bedroom is closed. I try the handle. Locked. "Pen?"

"Are you alone?" she says.

"Yes."

"Are you certain? You haven't brought along a lecture, have you?"

"Not for tonight," I say. "Miraculously."

There's a pause before the lock is undone and the door opens.

Pen is already making her way back to the bed, a cup of tea cradled in both hands. "I was hoping to keep Her Royal Highness out of my hair this evening."

She sits with her back to the headboard and draws her knees to her chest. There's color in her face again, and her hair is plaited to set her curls. Her eyes are red, irritated by the salt water. There's a bruise on her forehead, which solves the mystery of why she never surfaced from under the boat. Normally she is all grace—a strong swimmer and a brilliant athlete, but enough tonic will make her another girl entirely.

She smirks demurely at me, quite aware of her pathetic appearance.

"Oh, Pen," I say. "Where have you hidden that strong girl I so adore?"

"I killed her," she says, and smirks into her tea.

I take the cup away and set it on the nightstand. "I worry you'll catch a fever from that icy water," I say, and fit the blanket that's wrapped around her shoulders.

She raises her arm so that I can climb in with her.

"Be careful," she says. "I keep a knife in that pillowcase."

"Why?"

"Because I would be a fool not to."

I peel back the edge of the pillowcase, and sure enough I

see the hilt of a kitchen knife under the pillow. She's taken every precaution against this world, but none against her greatest threat—herself.

She can sense my frown and she fixes her eyes on me.

"You scared me half to death, I'll have you know," I say. "I can't have you swallowed up by the sea."

"Or a shark," she says, resting her head on my shoulder.

"Not without warning the shark you're coming for it first," I say, and she gives a small laugh.

"Every time I blink, I see water," she says. "Can you stay with me? I feel I'll drift away if I have nothing to hold on to."

"Of course," I say. She wriggles her fingers between mine. "But I am furious with you. You'll never make it up to me."

"You won't hold me to it. Your heart's too good for that."

"I'm not the one you should worry about," I say. "You ought to console your betrothed."

She drapes her arm over her eyes. "He was a fool to follow me," she says. "And I have no ring to show I was ever his. He could leave me anytime it strikes his fancy."

"I won't hear this kind of talk tonight," I say. "I can still smell the tonic on you."

"They don't call it tonic here," she says, adding a flourish when she says, "It's alcohol. Or absinthe, or gin."

"Whatever you call it. We agreed, Pen. And you could have drowned."

"You're starting to bore me," she says.

"Fine." I untangle myself from the blanket. "Sleep alone, then."

She grabs my wrist. "Don't be that way," she says.

"Come on. If you leave, Thomas will come in, and I feel just awful about my ring."

"He doesn't care about the ring." I let her tug me back down to her side. "You didn't see that look in his eyes when you were pulled from the water."

I don't know if the magnitude of my words reaches her, but for the first time all evening, she looks truly sorry. "I can't face him. Not tonight. You're the only one I can stand to be around. Please just stay."

I ease her back against the mattress and I tuck the blanket around her.

She closes her eyes. "It was an accident," she says. "I know that I'm forever giving him a hard time about things, but I've never once removed that ring. I wouldn't."

"He knows that," I say. "We'll find it, Pen."

She yawns. "Turn out the light, would you?"

I do as she asks, and I lie beside her.

The moon burns through the curtains. Waxing gibbous. An unblinking eye.

"The day that my mother told me your whole family was dead, I ran upstairs to your apartment," Pen says. "The door was open. She might have tried to stop me—I scarcely remember—but she couldn't. I went to your bedroom and I saw all of your things just as you'd placed them, and I couldn't breathe. My parents had to drag me away, and I remember I was screaming all the while."

"Pen, let's not—"

"I know you feel guilty that I was brought along. But I want to tell you that it's for the best that I was. Internment or Havalais, or the dark spaces between the stars, I couldn't face any world without you."

I close my eyes, but I can still see that moon in my eyelids. This world nearly killed Pen tonight, and here she's trying to console me.

"We've both scared each other, then, and now we're even," I say. "That's why we must both be more careful."

"So we can live to be a hundred," she says.

"And see men walk on the moon."

"Morgan?" she says. Her voice is hoarse and tired. "Have you asked anything at all of the god in the sky since we left Internment?"

"Only that we wouldn't die as we were spiraling away from it," I say. "Do you think the god of the sky would hear us from down here?"

"Lately I wonder if the god of the sky even heard us when we were in the sky," she says.

The words are so unlike her. Our belief systems no longer aligned after Lex's incident, and I would often find myself wishing she could at least be curious about the world beyond our own, to question the things I questioned, but now it breaks my heart to see her losing the faith she's always been able to hold on to.

"I was reading the tourism book in the lobby," I say. "There's something called a church, where people down here go when they need to feel close to their god. Supposedly there's one nearby that's historical. We could go, if you'd like."

"I read about it, too," she says. "I just don't know, Morgan. I think I'd like to sleep now. I'm quite tired."

We say nothing more. After a while, her breaths come rhythmically. I stare at the ceiling and I hope the god in the sky can hear me asking for her safety. In this whole great world, and in all the space between here and Internment, I can think of no one who needs him more. Not even the princess, who has descended forever from her kingdom.

What feels like hours later, the door creaks. A sliver of light widens; it stretches just far enough to reach Pen's pale hair.

Thomas whispers her name.

"She's asleep," I say.

"In that case, Morgan, a word. If you don't mind."

This doesn't bode well. Thomas rarely has cause to speak to me unless Pen is between us. But she's in a sleep so heavy, she may as well be gone; she doesn't stir as I climb away and move out to the hall.

Thomas closes the bedroom door, taking care to hold the knob so it doesn't make much noise.

The low light exaggerates the shadows under his eyes. His hair is still damp, and it hangs heavy on his face. Heavy like his shoulders and the breath he draws before he speaks. "Don't you think these games have gone on long enough?"

"Games?" I say.

"The sneaking out until all hours. The drinking. Did you think my silence meant I was unaware? I know Pen like I know the back of my hand."

I've barely had anything to drink this evening, but my stomach is churning as though I've downed a bottle of gin. "It isn't a game." It isn't much of an argument, and my voice falters. "We've only needed to cope—"

"What you need," he interrupts, "is to stop behaving like children. What Pen needs is to be away from this wretched place. It's slowly draining the life out of her. Surely you can see that."

I open my mouth, but I have no words. He's right; I've been denying it for some time. He isn't the only one who knows Pen well; he's always been betrothed to her, but she and I were born the same week, in the same ward of the hospital, and the longest distance between us has only ever been a flight of stairs.

And to really know Pen, to understand her fears, all one has to do is meet her mother when she's inebriated, which is always.

"What happened to her this evening is on you," Thomas says. "You dragged us all down here." He presses his finger between his brows, closes his eyes. "She could have died, and it would have been your fault. And we wouldn't have even been able to send her off properly to the tributary. She would have been gone forever, just gone."

It's a bomb to the chest, the truth. Her blue, parted mouth. My fault. "I'm sorry," I say.

"You've lost your parents, and I'm sorry for that. I know you don't mean anyone harm. But my betrothed's life is not a price I'm willing to pay for this pilgrimage you're on. If you care about her at all, you will find a way to get her home."

This is a strikingly intimate side of him. He has always doted on Pen, endured her jabs, flicked her hair and prattled on and on to her about his favorite novels while she rolled her eyes. But tonight he pulled her lifeless body from an ocean of mermaids and sharks, and it ignited the love he's had for her all his life—a love that is brutal in its sincerity.

"Thomas, I didn't want her dragged into this world with me."

"Yes, but she was," he says. He's looking at me, and in his eyes I see some mix of anger and sympathy. "Wherever you go, she follows you, one way or another. Even if it isn't what she wants."

I have also followed Pen to places I didn't want to go, but I don't say that.

He leaves me alone, fist to my chest, heart hammering beneath it. He's said aloud my darkest fear, that I have made the wrong decision to keep what I know about the glasslands a secret.

My parents died to get away from King Furlow's domain. That was their choice. They understood the risks and they took them.

But Pen asked for none of this. She is still alive. I can still bring her home.

I wake several times in the night to be sure Pen hasn't drifted away in the sea.

Safe, I tell myself. She's safe.

Unconsciously she rolls her head toward mine. We have always looked after each other, Pen and me.

Thomas is right. There's no fighting it. Away from Internment, she's like one of the flowers in the lobby. Snipped from its roots, it can only die.

13

When I awaken, the princess's bed is empty and still neatly made. In an act of mercy, she found someplace else to sleep and granted Pen a much needed night free of aggravation. Though it could be that she needed a break from Pen as well. I'm more mediator than roommate to those two.

The hotel is silent as I make my way down the stairs. Everyone is asleep.

I open the front door, letting in a draft and the chirping of insects. Hopping songstresses. Down here they call them crickets. And paces are miles, and lengths are feet, and pages are dollars, and colors are paints.

But wind is still wind, and the moon is still the moon, bright in the sky even as morning adds bits of gold under the clouds.

I step outside, and though this world isn't mine, it greets

me just the same. I shall miss it if I'm forced to go. I'm not a fugitive here, or a fugitive's daughter. If I were to return to the sky, I wonder what the king would do to me. The princess likes me, so that's something, and once I tell her about the phosane, she'll be so happy to go home that she'll tell her father to show mercy. I like to think we're becoming friends.

But then there are the others to consider. Judas can never go back. Lex would be furious if he knew what I'm planning. But Pen would be livid, not for her own sake, but for the sake of the city. She would hate me. She will hate me.

A rustle overhead makes me look up. A bird flutters away from its branch. I hear a little giggle in the leaves.

"You've picked a good one," I call up. "I've never seen a tree this high on Internment."

"Quite limitless down here, isn't it?" Amy peeks forward, revealing her face.

"Do you think Daphne would have liked it here, then?" I ask.

She retreats back into the leaves, only to reemerge in another spot moments later. "Yes," she says. "Thank you for asking. No one ever asks about my sister anymore."

I watch a rodent scurry across the grass. Birdie says they all start coming out once the snow is gone. The warmth has done a world of good for Amy, too. She hasn't had a fit in days.

"How's your friend?" she asks.

"Pen? She's better now."

"I like her," Amy says. "She says things most people aren't brave enough to say, doesn't she?"

Light is beginning to touch the water. From here it's an endless trove of clear gems, as though the mermaids have released their treasures and they're all floating on the surface. Though, I have learned that beautiful things can be dangerous in this place.

"The sea to the people down here is like the sky to us," I say. "Every world must have something that seems infinite."

"Every world has its own gods." Amy is scaling the branches on her way down. "That's what Daphne would say. She'd find that part fascinating." She hops to the ground. "But you didn't come here to talk to me about the sea or my sister, did you?"

"I didn't know you'd be out here at all," I say. "I only came to think."

"Think about what?" She sits beside me and leans against the tree. "I'm a great listener. I'm nothing at all like Judas."

She's right about that. If Judas knew what I was planning, he would have my head.

"I'm about to do something that can't be undone," I say. "I was always going to make this decision. I see that now. I was only waiting for the proper moment, when it became a matter of life and death."

"Life and death?" she says.

I hesitate. "What do you think would happen if we were to return to the sky?" I say.

"I don't know," she says. "I don't think it would be as though we never left it. The king has surely covered for our disappearances now. Told everyone we were killed, made an example of us to keep people afraid of the ground."

I roll the back of my head against the tree so that I'm looking at her. "It would really shake things up if we returned, wouldn't it?"

"Very much." I can't tell if that's a smile on her face. She looks concerned. "You know a way back, don't you?"

"King Ingram says that they'll develop the right sort of plane that can reach Internment eventually. Perhaps years from now, assuming it ever becomes a priority. But I might know a way to speed things along."

I've begun to twist my betrothal band around my finger. Sunstone. Phosane. In one world, it's as mundane as glass. In another world, it's precious enough to start a war.

Amy hugs her knees. "You can't tell Judas. He'd try to stop you."

"So would just about everyone else," I say. "Basil would say it's too dangerous. Lex would say there's nothing left for us there. Pen would say that this world would destroy Internment. The professor would, too. With the exception of the princess and Thomas, everyone would try to stop me."

"I wouldn't," Amy says.

"Do you miss home?" I say.

"Oh yes. I hadn't expected to. I miss my parents, even if they aren't the affectionate sort, really. And I miss Wesley. Quite much, actually. We were to be together for the rest of our lives." She tugs at the betrothal band still hanging from a chain around her neck. She slides her finger through it, and it doesn't fit, not yet, but soon it will. "I'm beginning to understand what that means now. I didn't before."

I cant my head to the sky. I can see Internment as a shadow behind a cloud. "I fear what's to become of us all," I say. "We may be doomed whether we stay here or return."

"We were cursed, remember," Amy says. "We were meant to stay interned in the sky, and we broke the deal."

Cursed, yes. Even if I mean well, like Thomas said, there is the promise that we'll all be doomed somehow. It's in our history book.

I lean against Amy, and she puts her arm around my shoulder and pats my head, like I'm a child.

"What would Daphne have me do?" I say.

"The boldest thing imaginable," she says. "Always."

Bold. Yes.

So strange, the way a dead girl's voice is carried on the breeze of a world she has never seen.

Pen sleeps through breakfast. I keep my head down to avoid Thomas's glances from across the table. Basil frets. Annette asks if I saw any whales and Riles tells her not to be so dense.

The plates are collected and everyone scatters off in different directions. Birdie and Nimble invite me to go fishing with them, but I've had enough sea for a lifetime. Basil asks if I'd like to go for a walk into the city, but I'm afraid I'll end up telling him about the phosane and he'll try to stop me, so I tell him I'm going to read in bed, which of course makes him worry even more. "Or maybe I'll take my book outside," I say. "I haven't decided."

We're standing in the hallway outside his room, and for the moment we're alone. "Are you certain you're all right?" he says. "Nothing you'd like to tell me?"

My mouth is dry. "Like what?"

"You've got that look about you," he says. "You had it for days after your brother jumped."

"Pen scared me about as much as my brother did," I say. It isn't the whole truth, but at least it is the truth.

"She's all right now," Basil says. "Isn't she?"

It isn't true, and I sense that he knows it. The water isn't the only thing that threatens to pull Pen below the surface.

"She's not the only one I'm worried about," I say. "This place is doing something to all of us. I'll never understand why you followed me here. You don't even seem angry about it."

"I am angry," he says. "I'm angry about a lot of things."

"But not with me?"

"Never with you."

He's staring at my open mouth and I know he's waiting for me to tell my secrets. I think he's the loveliest creature to have ever been born, the way he cares for me.

"Do you suppose there's anything I could do that would make you change your mind?" I say. "About not being mad at me."

"I'm certain there isn't."

"There's something I have to do now." I take a deep breath and exhale the words, "Trust me?"

"Yes," he says. He doesn't try to stop me as I hurry down the hall.

When I get to the lobby, I find Pen curled on the couch, that heavy black book from the nightstand open across her knees. The people of the ground call it *The Text*.

"Are you all right?" she says. "You're all red."

"Just a little warm," I say. "I'm about to go out for air. How's your book?"

"It starts off reasonably enough," she says. "Their god creates light, and the earth and things. I was beginning to see it as a prequel to our history book." She flips back and forth through the pages, gesturing. "And then this god of theirs creates the first man and woman, and a page or two later their children are throwing stones and murdering each other. It doesn't bode well for the dawn of humanity, does it?"

"Maybe it will get better," I say.

"I'm only on the first chapter, and already there's talk of flooding the world and drowning everyone. It can't possibly get worse, I should think."

From the kitchen, Nimble laughs pointedly.

"Fantastic," Pen grumbles. She shoots me a bitter smile. "Lovely place we've fallen to, Morgan. I can't thank you enough for forcing me along."

I stare at my shoes. I can't meet her eyes.

"I didn't mean to say it like that," she says.

The words hurt, but not as much as it hurts seeing what this place is doing to her.

"No matter," I say. "I'll be back in a bit."

"Careful," Pen says, studying the open book. "There are spying divinities and floods out there."

Celeste is nowhere to be found in the hotel, and since the weather has turned more agreeable, she's taken to spending her days outside.

It doesn't take me long to find her. She's on a bench in the manicured garden between the hotel and the theme park. The shrubbery here is quite strange, fashioned into the shapes of animals and spires.

Celeste could still be a princess, the way she sits among them. Her posture is exact, her hair long and full of daylight. And though the passage of time here has begun to darken her spirits, there's still a glimmer to her eyes—hope she was born with.

I stand several paces away for a long time, watching her, trying to convince myself that it isn't too late to change my mind about telling her. I could turn around before she sees me. I could run. But run where? For all its space, the ground holds no solutions. Bravery is still the thing that sets change in motion.

Be brave, I tell myself.

I step forward.

Celeste leans forward to pluck a skeletal flower from the grass. She looks at me for a moment, then she blows on the flower, causing its white starlike plumes to float apart from the seed head. "Skeletal flowers," she says. "They call them dandelion puffs down here. Did you know that? Nim told me."

"Why?" I say.

She shrugs. "Colloquialisms." She pats the space beside her on the bench, inviting me to sit. "I hope Pen is feeling better. I've thought it best to stay out of her way until she's feeling more herself."

At the mention of her name, I feel the weight of Internment on my chest again. I am about to betray my best friend, and the words are caught in my throat. *I have something to tell you. I have something to tell you.* My knees are shaking; I wrap my skirt around my thighs to keep them still.

"I have something to tell you," I say. "I'd intended to keep it from you, but it isn't my decision to make."

"You're speaking in riddles," she says.

"I'm sorry." I close my eyes for a long moment. "I wasn't prepared for how difficult this is."

She raises an eyebrow at me.

"I know Pen hurt your brother," I say. "But before I say a word of what I've come to tell you, I need you to promise me that she'd be safe. And Judas. All of us. If we were to return to the sky, I need you to promise that everyone would be safe."

Now she is the one who looks shaken. "Do you know a way back?"

"I need your word."

"You have it, then." She shows a row of perfect white teeth, a smile she can't hold back. Her face is alight.

"The first time you were to meet with King Ingram, you asked Pen and me about the glasslands," I say. "They're powered by a substance called sunstone. It's fairly common on Internment; the soil produces it. Pen and I did a little research. She thinks Internment may have once been a part of the archipelago King Ingram and King Erasmus are fighting for, and that the sunstone that powers the glasslands is phosane."

The princess is tearing the dandelion stem to ribbons.

"Actually, she's quite sure of it," I go on. "Her father brings home bits of sunstone now and then, and she recognized it immediately when we looked up phosane at the library. And if King Ingram knows about it, perhaps he'd be more eager to ally with your father."

"Which would mean we get to go home," Celeste says. But her smile falters. "But we can't prove it. King Ingram might think we're just making this up to speed things along. I don't suppose Pen has an image of the glasslands to present."

"There's something better," I say.

She realizes I'm staring at her betrothal band, and she stares at it too. Confusion turns to realization, and then there are tears in her eyes. "These are made of . . ."

I nod.

She hugs me.

I've never hated myself more.

14

Amy sits at the top of the stairs and watches me through the railing posts. I can't read her expression, but she's watching Celeste button her coat, and I am sure that she knows what I've done.

Pen looks up from her reading. "I should like to meet this king you're forever running off to see."

Celeste hooks her elbow through mine. "You will," she says. "Just not today. Private conference."

Pen mimics her under her breath and makes a face at her book.

"I am so glad to see you well again," Celeste says, and her sincerity startles Pen, who looks quizzically at me.

"We'll be back before dinner," Celeste says.

"Can I come?" Annette asks, bouncing at our feet.

Nimble puts his hand on her forehead. "Nope."

Celeste opens the door. She can't get moving fast enough. "Are you coming, Morgan?"

"No," I say. I know that I should, but I've used up all my courage telling her about the phosane, and I have none left to see what will happen next.

"But you have to," she insists.

"I thought this kingdom practiced free will," Pen says.

"We do," Annette says. "Stay, Morgan. We'll make brownies."

Celeste stares me down until I look at her. "You're sure?" she says.

I nod.

Once they're gone, I go to the harbor. The water is especially clear today, and I pretend the sea is the sky, and that the clouds are as close as their reflections.

"You belong to the sky," a voice says. I didn't hear Judas approach, but now he's beside me. "There isn't any fighting it."

"What makes you say that?"

"I feel it, too," he says. "I miss a city that blames me for my betrothed's murder; how backward is that?"

"'Would the people of the ground think Internment is a paradise, or a punishment?'" I say, quoting Daphne's essay.

Judas gives a rare smile. "You read it, then?"

"All of it," I say. "Lines of it appear in my head sometimes. Lines I didn't realize I'd memorized. They're strangely relevant much of the time."

"She was filled with things like that," he says. "She'll haunt me for the rest of my life."

"I'm sorry she couldn't be here," I say. I truly mean it. "Judas," I say. "If she were here, what would she have to say about returning to Internment?"

"If she were here, things wouldn't be what they are," he says.

That's true. If she were alive, I would still be up there, fretting over my silly fascination with the ground, all the while knowing I'd never see it. The train wouldn't have gone backward that day; it would have taken me straight home.

"But I think she'd be for it," he says. "She was curious and she'd have wanted to see this, but she was loyal, too."

"What about you?" I say. "You miss it, but do you want to go back?"

"I can't," he says. He looks back at the hotel. "I'm surprised your betrothed isn't running out here to make sure I don't try to kill you."

"He's just protective," I say. "It isn't anything personal."

"Yes it is," Judas says. "Even here, I can't escape that stigma."

"Don't worry about what Basil thinks, then," I say. "You know the truth, and it just so happens I believe you."

"You're a little bit of a rebel," he says.

"No one's ever called me that, I'm sure," I say.

"There are worse things to be called."

"Yes." I stare into the sea, past the broken reflection of the sky, until I can see nothing but murky darkness. I see no trace of Pen's ring; the most precious thing she owns, and it's as though it never existed now that it's fallen here. Something that's always been there, just gone.

"Never thought I'd be so afraid of the water," I say. "I thought at least water would be the same thing on the ground as it is in the sky, but everything here is so much more daunting. Everything. I fear that if I took a step down, I'd fall into a chasm."

"That's apt," he says. "And everything costs money. Even hospital stays. I heard Jack Piper talking about the professor's bill. Once this war is over, I think we're all going to have to get jobs if we ever expect to be in charge of our own lives here."

"Were we in charge of our own lives back home?" I say. "Instead of money, maybe we were paying with our freedom. What would happen if we didn't want to marry our betrotheds, or we wanted to talk about the ground, or we wanted—I don't know—more?"

In unison, we say the answer: "Declared irrational."

On Internment you could be questioned for so little as having messy hair too many days in a row, or for wearing too much cosmetic, or for having a dress that is hemmed too short, a shirt that is too wrinkled. It always made sense to me back home—a messy appearance implies a troubled home life, a troubled mind—but here the king has more important things to worry about. It isn't so strict. The individual isn't as important as the masses. I'm still not sure which I prefer.

"So we are better off here," Judas says.

"I took offense when you told me to be careful," I say. "But you were right."

"I shouldn't have talked down to you," he says. "I have trust issues, you could say."

"Understandable," I say.

"It's just that you seemed the sort that always follows rules. You look like you've never done a thing wrong in your life, and people like that lack common sense."

"Is this part of your apology for offending me?" I say.

"Yes."

"Anyway, I've done plenty of things wrong. When Pen and I were kids, we stole her mother's tonic and we had to replace it by pouring a little from each bottle and filling them up the rest of the way with water. We were sick for days."

"The two of you are as close as betrotheds, aren't you?" he says.

"Closer, probably," I say. "Because nobody told us we belonged together. We just always knew somehow that we were meant to be friends."

"Everyone needs someone they care for like that," he says. "Life's too lonely if you're only living it for yourself."

"I have Basil, too," I say, though whether I'm reminding him or me, I'm not sure.

"Basil looks out for you," he says. "Pen sounds like a terrible influence."

"She's still a genius," I say.

"There are different sorts of geniuses," he says. "You're one too. I've never met a person with your ability to make peace. Everyone in that hotel is at odds with someone, but not you. It's a little bit charming."

"That may be the nicest thing anyone has said to me since we landed."

"I said 'a little bit charming.' That's all."

"It's a nice thought, but isn't true," I say.

"I may be a fugitive," he says, "but I always tell the truth. Mostly."

I steal a glance at him, but look away before he notices. I hope I haven't just ruined his chance to have a life here, and that he won't hate me when he finds out what I've done.

We both stare at the horizon, as though it will open for us, as though there is a world between the sea and the sky, and it will be perfect there.

Judas is the first to look away. "I'm going back," he says. "Are you coming?"

"In a bit," I say. I'd like to stand here and enjoy the notion that nobody in that hotel is at odds with me. If it's true, it surely won't be for much longer.

The sun sets the sky on fire as it goes down. I lie in a giant metal teacup, my legs draped over its brim. Annette says they spin when the ride is turned on. Spin until some people laugh and others throw up. When she told me about them, I was appalled. Something like this would never be permitted back home. But now I think I understand; people want a thrill simply because they're allowed. They want to go as far as they dare.

"Morgan!" a voice is singing. The princess could have a promising career in theater, the way she projects.

My evening of solitude is coming to an end now. I don't answer, but I can hear her footsteps running, and I know she's found me. She rattles the gate as she tries to open it. "It's locked," she says. "How did you get in?"

"Climbed over," I say. I look over my shoulder at her. The fashions of the ground are much simpler than the billowing skirts, laces, and bell sleeves that were her trademark back home, but she still manages to look like royalty in brown gingham and a cloche hat. She places one foot on the base of the gate, gives a halfhearted leap, and huffs.

"There are spikes at the top," she calls. "What if I impale myself?"

"You shall have to be careful," I say.

"You didn't ruin your skirt?"

I run my hands over the fabric, inspecting. "I may have snagged it a bit."

I should do the decent thing and help her, but I'm finding her attempts greatly amusing, and I'm in need of cheering up.

"Didn't you say that you and your brother were experts at sneaking out?" I ask.

"There weren't spikes involved," she says.

"You left your kingdom and glided thirty-five thousand feet to the ground," I say. "You can conquer the fence."

"Conquer it." She shakes the hat from her hair, lets it fall. "Right." With renewed fervor, she tries again. She wedges herself between the spikes atop the gate's bars, takes a breath, and drops to her feet.

I clap. She curtsies and then dusts herself off. "What are you doing out here?"

"Trying to stop time," I say. A flock of birds cuts through the sky, spread apart like eyelashes.

She climbs beside me into the teacup. She fiddles curiously with the small round table in the center. The cup groans and rotates clockwise.

"Well?" she says.

"Well?" I look at her.

"Aren't you going to ask how it went? What the king had to say?"

I look at the sky. "I can see the moon while there's still daylight," I say. "The long season is starting. But they call it spring here."

Celeste pats my hand. She knows this isn't easy for me. "Come on," she says gently. "Ask me."

"What did the king have to say? Morbid curiosity begs to know."

"I used to think there was only one sort of plane," she says. "But there are just so many, Morgan, did you know that? Biplanes and passenger planes and all sorts that are built for specific purposes." She twists the table again. The gears are stiff, but she puts muscle into it, and the cup spins very slowly. "None of them are capable of flying above the troposphere. And even if they could, they would be no match for Internment's wind barrier."

I know all of this already, but I let her explain it again because I'm dreading whatever point she's getting to.

"But the king's engineers are working on a new plane that isn't really a plane at all," she says. "A jet."

It's a sharp word. Jet.

"It sounds like something that could slice the sky open," I say.

"Precisely," she says. The teacup goes still. "I wanted to say thank you," she says. "I really do think this will speed things along, and that we'll be returning to the sky soon. King Ingram says that if my ring proves to contain real phosane, his engineers and mechanics may be able to use it for fuel."

I sit up straight, look at her hands folded on the table. "You gave him your betrothal band? So he can ruin it?"

"Not ruin it," she says. "Use it. It wasn't doing any good on my hand."

"But it's your *ring*," I say. "Doesn't it mean something to you?"

She laughs. "I don't think my ring means to me what yours means to you. What everyone else's means to them. I hardly even know the boy; I can count on one hand the times we've spoken."

Every generation has its prince and princess, and they are traditionally sheltered. Everyone knows this. But still, I thought they must know their betrotheds. "How are you expected to be in love if you rarely see each other?"

"Love doesn't have anything to do with it," she says. "Not for my brother and me, anyway. It's all business. But I believe I have quite a talent for it. Papa will be pleased with how I've handled King Ingram. I've set the foundation for a good relationship between Havalais and Internment, one that will last for generations."

I don't know whether she's boasting or dreaming.

"That's a nice thought," I say.

"This is a war, remember," she says. "After King

Erasmus bombed us, we bombed back. But King Ingram doesn't make that public knowledge. He wants to present an image of peace."

"An illusion of peace," I say. Even more reason for me not to trust him.

Amy dreamed that Internment fell to the ground and everyone's screams were caught in the clouds. It was the week we all succumbed to the weather, so it may have been her fever, or it may have been a premonition.

"You look like you're cold," she says. "It's getting dark. Let's get you back inside."

I shake my head. "I don't want to go back there," I say.

"I'm not going to breathe a word about this to anyone," she says. "Nimble won't either. It's too soon. So you've no need to worry."

This does nothing to ease the guilt. I've been outside all day. "I'd like to sleep out here," I say.

"It gets chilly at night," Celeste says. "Besides, that would be terrible for your back."

"Go inside if you want," I say. "It shouldn't matter to you what my back and I do."

"Of course it matters. I'm your friend."

"We aren't friends," I say. "You don't want me for one, anyway. I'm not a very good one."

"What are you talking about?" she says. "You dove into a frigid ocean to rescue Pen."

"And then I told you her secrets. The last thing she wants is for this kingdom to reach Internment. She thinks they'll destroy it, and she's probably right, and I'll be to blame."

"Hey," Celeste says. "If I thought for a second that were true, I wouldn't have told King Ingram about the glass-lands. Internment is my home, too. My kingdom. I would sooner grow old and die down here than see it destroyed."

I look at the moon.

"You're putting too much on your shoulders," Celeste says. "Let me bear some of the burden. Diplomacy is in my blood."

"Pen hates you," I remind her.

"Pen hates everyone. She doesn't count."

I suppress a laugh.

"You're more cautious and discerning, and you like me," Celeste says.

"I never said that."

"You do. And I like you, too, and I don't want you to catch a chill, so let's go inside."

"Pass," I say.

She rests her forearms on the table and leans toward me. "Very well," she says. "You trusted me with Pen's secret, and it's only fair that I trust you with a secret I've been keeping as well. Maybe it will even things out."

I should tell her that this isn't necessary. When I came to her about the phosane, it wasn't because I expected anything in return. But I can't help being curious; she has spent her life in that clock tower high above the city, and nobody on Internment gets an opportunity to hear about what that's like.

"My brother and I have had betrothals since birth, like everyone else," Celeste says. "Mine is . . . well, he isn't the kindest boy, to be certain. I've never much cared for him, and he sees me as nothing more than a way to boost his social status. He'll be a prince once we're married; if my brother predeceases him, he may even become king, and all I am is the property that makes this so."

"That sounds awful," I admit.

She waves her hand, brushing the thought away. "I've always seen him as an annoying obligation, but my brother has had a worse go of things. The girl to whom he's betrothed is quite beautiful." She looks away from me, to the hotel in the distance. She seems uncomfortable. "But Azure doesn't have any interest in beautiful girls," she says. "He keeps it a secret from Mother and Papa, of course. What would they do with a prince who dreams of falling in love with another prince? He even tried to keep it from me, but it was always just the two of us growing up away from the rest of the city; we were each the other's only friend. Of course I figured it out."

I remember the glib joke she made while I was their prisoner, about her brother being attracted to her betrothed. An attraction to the same sex could mean being declared irrational if an attraction camp provided no solution.

"When did you realize something was wrong with him?" I ask.

She looks sharply at me. "I've known about it since we were children," she says. "But there is nothing *wrong* with my brother. It's our world, our rules. I—" She cuts herself off, flustered. "You couldn't know what those camps do, Morgan. Papa has shown my brother and me many things we'll need to know when Azure inherits the city. There are tonics involved, and surgeries that are worse than death. You wouldn't ever want to see for yourself, much less send someone you love there. I've feared for my brother's life every day. If Papa were ever to find out, I truly worry that Az would end himself." She struggles with her next breath like the words were strangling her.

There's a lot of ugliness behind what keeps Internment going, I've realized. Even its prince and princess live in fear. I was certain the princess looked down on my family for having a jumper, but in truth she's had a similar fear for her own brother.

"You're right," I say. "I haven't seen, and I wouldn't want to. But my father and brother did, and it changed them." I meet her eyes. "I'm sorry I accused you of not knowing what goes on outside your clock tower. It appears you know more than most."

She tries to smile, but can't quite manage. "Az says that once he's king, he'll do away with betrothals, and stop the drug that keeps eggs from splitting into a double birth and things like that. But that's only talk, of course. It wouldn't be that easy. The city would fall apart without its rules."

"'Rules,'" I sigh. "I've come to hate that word."

"I've come up with a plan or two of my own," she says. "My brother will be king one day, but he's all whimsy and little logic. He needs me. I truly believe that a union between Internment and Havalais will change things. Internment needn't stay the same forever. The ugly things needn't be the mortar that keeps the pretty things in check. So you see, Pen's secret will not be wasted."

I want desperately for her to be right.

"So that's my biggest secret. My own phosane, if you like. Now will you please come inside before we catch our deaths?"

She grabs my hands and pulls me out of the teacup. My feet are heavy. Celeste won't tell anyone what I've done. Not yet. But still, the guilt of it waits for me in that sprawling building whose lights stretch across the grass.

After I've climbed the fence, I realize how far the hotel seems. A lifetime away. Celeste doesn't mind my slow pace. She keeps beside me. She puts her arm around my shoulders. I suppose she thinks that our secrets have forged a bond between us.

"How is your brother faring?" she asks. "I don't think I've seen him at all since we've landed."

I'm immediately on the defensive. Even though she has just shared her family secrets with me, my instinct is to be protective of my brother. Even on the ground, I feel that it's important to prove his sanity. "He just likes his privacy. He isn't irrational."

"I know that," Celeste says. She stoops to pick up a dandelion puff, but rather than blowing on it, she twists it in her fingers. "I'm not my father's spy, you know. I'm not going to write a report on everything everyone says and submit it to him so he knows who to punish."

The dandelion puff is slowly coming apart. "I used to think everyone in the kingdom loved my father," she says. "But you came all this way to get away from him, didn't you?"

He killed my parents, but I can't remind her, because it's become impossible to say. Killed. Dead. I am sick of such miserable words. I only nod.

"Well, you needn't worry," she says. "You can stay here if you'd like. I'll go back alone."

I'm not worried only about what's to become of us. I'm worried for the entire city.

I say nothing the rest of the way to the hotel. Celeste fills the silence with chatter about the stars and the smell of the grass and how she wishes Internment knew the wonder that is rain.

Basil is on me the second we walk through the door. "I've been looking for you everywhere," he says.

"I went into the city," I say. I've told so many lies since we've come here, I don't see the harm in one more. With each one, the stigma fades a bit more.

I don't know how I manage to get through dinner. I force down just enough of it to ward off Basil's suspicions. Annette's chatter fills the room, and I'm grateful.

Birdie takes a sip of milk. "How are you finding *The Text*?" she asks Pen. "You've been reading it all day, haven't you?"

"Fascinating," Pen says.

"Ah yes," Nimble says. "The world's greatest work of fiction."

Jack Piper shoots him a venomous stare. "You may excuse yourself," he says.

Nimble sets down his fork, gives us a cheery salute, and leaves.

"You'll have to forgive him," Jack says. "I don't know where this side of him comes from."

"From Mother," Birdie says. The other children stop chewing. It was bold of her to say, but now she looks at her plate, her hair curtaining her face from her father. Jack Piper lets this slide with little more than a clearing of his throat. Fathers are more forgiving of daughters than of sons.

I'm grateful when the plates are cleared and I'm able to leave.

Pen catches up to me halfway up the stairs. "Where were you all day?" she says.

"Just out. Around."

I can't look at her. I move quickly, but she keeps pace. "Do you know what Her Royal Whatsit went to speak with the king about?"

"More of the same," I say. "She wanted me to go along because she'd like us to be friends, but I'm not interested."

"Not interested in the king's politics, or being her friend?"

"Either."

She's suspicious. I'm quite sure it isn't merely my guilt that's telling me so. But she doesn't push me any further. She lets me go ahead into the bedroom and she doesn't follow me. Moments later I hear water filling the tub as she draws a bath for herself.

I climb into bed and try to read the latest of Birdie's novels. But I only find myself envying the protagonist her problems. Her parents have sent her to something called a boarding school to keep her from the boy she loves. But she hasn't destroyed any cities. In two hundred pages, all will be well again.

I begin to think of Prince Azure, up in his sky, ailing from the wound Pen inflicted upon him. I've hoped for him to survive, out of common decency and regard for human life, but for the first time I truly hope Celeste can return home and find him safe and well. Even the prince and princess, dressed in their white furs as they squander their days as they please, are not immune to the horrors of Internment's king.

As a medical student, my brother was needed more than once at the attraction camps. They're set far from the residential sections, near the remote fields where food animals are bred. Even the trains don't stop near them. He never spoke of what he saw there—I'm certain he was sworn to silence. Any time I asked about his work, he called me a pest and sent me away. Now I wonder if he was trying to protect me, or if he was trying to forget.

I used to think attraction camps were meant to help. I thought those declared irrational had done something wrong or were broken somehow. I felt so much love for my city, grew up feeling lucky to have been spared by the god of the sky. I don't know what to believe anymore, and against all reason I am starting to hope that whatever the princess has planned will fix things.

Pen returns from her bath, and I pretend to be asleep. I feel her shadow covering my eyelids. "Morgan?" She pushes on my shoulder. "Are you asleep? Really? It's only seven thirty."

When I don't respond, she leaves me. I hear the brittle pages of *The Text* turning as she picks up where she left off.

"The bit about the ark was interesting," she says. "Their god flooded the world to start over again. So when their god doesn't like someone, he tries to drown them."

I think she's talking to me, but then I hear Thomas say, "That wasn't an act of god last night, Pen. That was gin."

"Well, maybe gin is an act of god, then."

"Not likely." The mattress creaking. Soft laughter. "Morgan's asleep already?"

"Yes," Pen says. "She's no fun."

"You could do with less fun," Thomas says.

"How unfortunate for you," she teases. A kiss. "I—" Pen begins, hesitates. "I really am sorry, Thomas."

Murmurs too soft to hear; a side of her I'm not permitted to know. Every couple on Internment seems to achieve this degree of intimacy but Basil and me. I try to love him the way he loves me, and rather than passion, all I can feel is myself trying.

Pen has spurned Thomas's advances since they were toddlers, and she never runs out of insults. He looks like composted broccoli or she'd sooner marry a toad.

But now that she thinks no one else can hear, she tells him, as clear as anything, "I love you."

Why would I say a thing like that? she told me.

So we're both liars, then.

15

Thomas leaves, and Pen reads for what seems like hours. I don't sleep, not even when the princess comes in and turns out the lights.

Back home, Lex pacing the floorboards above my bedroom used to comfort me, and whatever was troubling me would seem much smaller. But here there's the chirping of hopping songstresses that go by some other name, and the breathing of my roommates, who only stop arguing when they're asleep, and the kind of silence that's a net for too many thoughts.

After my tossing and turning has made enough noise, Pen whispers, "Do you need an anchor?"

"I just can't get comfortable," I say. "I think the mattress needs to be flipped."

"Switch beds with me, then," she says.

"I'm fine."

"If you're angry with me, just come out and say it," she says.

"I'm not angry with anyone," I say. "I'm just uncomfortable."

"You're full of it, is what you are," she says.

I turn away and pull the blankets tighter around me. The ticking of the grandfather clock in the lobby adds itself to the silence.

"Whatever I did, I'm sorry," Pen says. "Is it what I said earlier about you dragging me to this place?"

"It isn't you."

"Well, it isn't the mattress."

In an act of great mercy, we're interrupted by a soft knock at the door. The door creaks open. "There's a Tony Valencia double feature at the cinema," Birdie whispers. "Anyone interested?"

"Who's Tony Valencia?" I ask.

"Haven't I shown you his picture in the magazines?" Birdie says. "He's the berries." I don't know what this means, but her dreamy sigh gives me a good guess.

"Just what I need." Pen throws back the blankets. "Another man in my life. At least this one doesn't speak."

"Part of his charm," Birdie says. After we've changed, Birdie throws beads and pearls around our necks and hustles us for the window.

The air is brilliant and cool. Before I came here, I'd never been outside of a city and its tiny parks and gardens. I didn't know grass and flowers could go on and on farther than the eye can see.

We walk to the dock and board the ferry, and Pen kneels at the railing and reaches her hand into the water, letting her fingers slice through it as we move.

I keep her in my line of vision as I ask Birdie, "Does your father tell you much about the war?"

"Oh, no," she says, and glances over her shoulder at the water. "He doesn't think girls should be bothered. He'd rather confide in my brother, even though Nim would sooner end a war than be a part of one. They can't see eye to eye, but Father keeps forcing it. He's already polishing Riles to follow suit. He's twelve; he isn't meant to care about politics, but he wants so badly to make Father proud of him."

"Is that why your mother left?" Pen asks. "All the pressure of living up to his standards?"

"Pen," I snap.

"What?" She turns to Birdie. "You're the one who brought her up at dinner. You don't mind if we talk about her, do you?"

Birdie shakes her head. Her hair bounces around her shoulders. "It's true." She leans back on her elbows against the railing. "She wanted to see the world, and Father didn't understand. She was starting to dress differently. He said she'd changed, but she was the same as she'd always been, if you ask me. She was just getting bolder about what she said aloud. She's the one who gave Nim his nickname; I suppose she thought being named after our father would make Nim turn out like him. But he would never be like him; she told him he was all soul inside, no fight."

"Nicknames are a rebirth, where I come from," Pen

says. "A lot of people have them on Internment. They're a way to cheat the system."

"All of our given names have to be from an approved list," I say.

Birdie crinkles her nose. "Sounds like something my father would enjoy. He does love his lists."

"So—what? Your father made her leave?" Pen asks.

"No," Birdie says. "I don't know what happened exactly. One morning she was gone."

"Gone?" Pen and I say.

"Yep. She sends telegrams and postcards, though. The last time I heard from her, she was studying to learn twelve languages and had become a nude model for some painter halfway across the world. That was a year or so ago."

I can't decide whether this is romantic or insane. This must be why betrothals are mandatory back home, to prevent such flighty behavior. Not that a woman who left her family would be able to go very far on Internment.

"But you don't have arranged betrothals here," I say. "If your parents were so incompatible, why did they marry at all?"

Birdie smirks. "Nim is the reason they got married. He was completely accidental, and there isn't a day that goes by that our father lets him forget it. Though, Father isn't really one to talk, if you know what I mean."

Alice and Lex come immediately to mind, the injustice of having to lose their own child simply because it wasn't planned. I force myself to push the thought away.

"You couldn't make that up if you tried," Pen says.

"Father tells people that Mother's in the country caring for her ailing mother. When he's all tied up in knots about something, he'll say I look just like her, like he's accusing me. He's paranoid that I'll turn out the same way."

"Will you?" Pen asks.

"Maybe," she says. "I don't see anything wrong with wanting to see the world. And I have no interest in typewriters or childbearing, which is all that's expected of me here."

"Typewriters and childbearing are miserable options," Pen says.

"I don't see anything wrong with them," I say.

"Morgan's a good girl," Pen says, by way of explanation.

"I wish you'd stop saying that," I say. I lean around her to look at Birdie. "I think you should be able to do whatever you want. All I meant is that you don't have to be like one parent or the other."

"I've never had friends like the two of you," Birdie says. Her smile is an indication of a slow awakening. She is a woman slowly being realized. Her father is afraid of that, and I'd like to tell her so, but I don't know how to say the words in a way that would make sense. I don't know how to explain that we have more power than we know. We are young and bright and waiting to see what we are capable of.

The ocean's mist has caused our hair to frizz around our faces, and I wish that I could hold this moment still, because it is perfect.

The ferry reaches the city. I'm finding that the vertigo I experienced in the transition from the water to the ground has lessened. I'm becoming used to this place.

Birdie walks ahead of us, and she begins to say something, but she hears someone call her name and she spins around. "Nim?" she says, unbelieving. "Riles?" Her brothers are stepping off the ferry. "Were you both there the whole time?"

"Of course we were," Riles says. "We didn't swim."

"Why didn't you say something?" Birdie says. She groans. "Don't tell me Father sent you after me."

"Don't be stupid," Nim says. "We didn't see you until a second ago. There's a brass concert in the center that Riles wants to see." He regards Pen and me. "Our father doesn't allow brass in the house."

"Devil's music," Riles adds cheerfully. "He thinks it'll hypnotize me."

"We don't have brass on Internment, but I can't see why it would be banned," I say.

"We only ban talk of the ground," Pen says. "Music should be fine as long as it entices people to stay."

"Internment is weird," Riles says, and tugs on Nimble's sleeve. "We're going to be late."

Birdie nudges Riles's backside with her shoe. "Get outta here, kid. You bug me."

"That's because you're bug-eyed," he says.

"Come over here and say that." She stoops to his height and they wave their fists at each other in a mock fight until she pulls him into a headlock and he tries in vain to free himself, but he's laughing.

I tell myself it does no good to be envious, that my

brother and I still communicate in our own peculiar way, but I find myself missing the years before he jumped, when he was full of life like this.

"You're crushing my larynx," he croaks.

"Fine, you big baby." She lets him go. "Enjoy your concert."

Nimble tips his hat to us. "See you at breakfast, ladies."

Birdie waves. We watch them disappear into the crowd.

"A lot of people tonight," Pen says.

"This week is the spring festival," Birdie says. "Everyone in Havalais flocks to the city, it seems. Most of it will begin tomorrow, but a few concerts and carts will be set up tonight."

"I don't know anything about war," Pen says. "But isn't it a bit of a mockery to have a festival?"

"In a way, that's what King Ingram wants," Birdie says. "We have to seem unaffected. From what I understand, Havalais is doing much better than Dastor right now."

She hasn't even finished with the words when I hear it. That faraway whistling in the air. My body understands before my mind can catch up. My blood is cold and I'm grabbing Birdie and Pen by the arms, pulling them against me. If they know what I know, they don't get a chance to say it. We can only stand frozen as the whistling turns into a crash, and the ground shakes under us, and the city turns to smoke and flame.

Screams are everywhere. How they have the energy to scream, I don't understand. Sound is caught in my throat.

My feet are stuck here. My breaths are shallow and loud.

Birdie, wound around my arm, begins to shake. It's slight at first, and then it overtakes her, and she screams too.

She tries to run, not away from the flames and toward the harbor like everyone else, but into the heart of it. Pen and I hold her back, but she is no longer the mild-mannered girl who apologizes for rolling her stockings or daring to speak of her mother at the dinner table. She is wild, stronger than both of us. She's screaming for her brothers.

"You can't!" Pen says.

But Birdie is beyond logic. And I can't fault her for that, but I also can't let her kill herself.

"They're together," I tell her. "Nimble will get Riles out safely."

I've got her wrist, and she digs her nails into my skin, trying to free herself. She's slipping away. She isn't going to hear any of my logic, and if she runs into this frenzy, we'll never get her back.

"I'll go with you!" I lock my fingers in hers. If I can't stop her, at least I can try to keep her safe. "Okay? We'll find them."

"Excuse me?" Pen's voice is shrill.

"Go back and wait for us at the harbor," I tell her.

She mutters curses and takes my hand. "You know I won't leave you."

We run against a stampede of humans who have become animals; they have no faces; they are round mouths and round eyes and horrible noises. And then, as the smoke thickens, the bodies are lying on the ground, crawling, gaping. I don't know where the bomb hit, but we're surely getting closer to it.

The smoke makes water flood my eyes, but Birdie's tears are real. I can hear her sobbing, gasping, unrelenting. She tries to call for her brothers, but a cough fills her mouth instead. It's impossible to see anything, understand anything. Pen tugs me, and I tug Birdie. She tries to resist, but she's out of oxygen, out of fight.

My knees are buckling, and Pen has moved between Birdie and me, and she's the one holding both of us up. She pulls our collars over our mouths, but it does no good.

I don't realize we've reached the harbor until I see the ocean for myself. It's unrecognizable here, shrouded in ash that's overtaking Havalais like a disease.

We've arrived just in time to see the ferry departing.

Birdie falls to her knees, and I spill after her, gagging.

"It's coming back, right?" Pen says, kneeling in front of us. "It has to come back."

Through her coughs, Birdie nods.

There are hundreds here. Perhaps thousands, all in the same state as us—if they're lucky. I can hardly see anything but gray and black and smears of red. Pen's sleeve is gone, her arm raw and bloody. I can't get the breath to ask her if she's in pain. She is as stoic as stone. She wipes at Birdie's watery eyes.

"They're gone," Birdie moans.

"Don't talk like that," Pen says. "Maybe they got on the ferry."

"Nim wouldn't leave me," she says. "I know he wouldn't. And they wouldn't have made it back to the harbor in time. They were all the way at the center." Birdie turns onto her back, stares into the city that is a gradient of black and deeper black.

"Okay," Pen says. "So where is the center?"

"Gone," Birdie says. She closes her eyes, shudders with what may be a cough or a sob.

I flinch and realize I closed my eyes. I force them open. I can't imagine what overtook me that I should be tired at a time like this.

Pen turns me to face the water. "Watch for the ferry," she says. "It's got to be coming back soon."

Birdie shakes her head. "My god," she says. I have never heard her call upon her god before. She has never needed one so much as she does now. "My god, my god." Her voice is creaky. I can't stand to see her so broken.

The screams have all faded to whimpers and groans; Birdie is one sobbing girl among hundreds.

"Look," Pen says. "The moon is full."

But I am in no state to be taunted by the sky and its wonders. I am beyond my nightmares, and I want to go home.

Birdie sits up. She coughs before she's able to call out, "Nim? Nim!"

I try to follow her gaze, but I can't see anything but ashy air.

"There's no one there," Pen tells her.

"I see him," Birdie says. "He's got Riles—something is wrong. Nim!"

213

She stumbles to her feet, and I start to say, "Birdie, no," but she's already gone, running over and between bodies that may be living or dead, toward something that I can't see.

"We have to go after her," I say.

Pen winds her arm around me, and even with that red wound, she is strong. "Don't you dare."

She's just said the words, and then the ground shakes again, and the city is overtaken anew by flames.

16

The ferry doesn't come back.

Pen keeps saying, "Morgan, Morgan, Morgan," and the words turn to birds. Lovely blue ones that soar up and up until they are black lines. I want to tell her to look at the sky. The flames have burnt through the troposphere, and there is Internment through a scorched hole in the sky. It's so close, I'd touch it if only I had the strength to reach. There are the roots of trees I used to climb, and soft white clouds.

Look, Pen, look; you're missing it.

I wish she'd stop calling my name, for the urgency in her voice is making clouds appear, and it's getting harder to see the city.

She hits me across the face, and I open my eyes to realize I was dreaming. There is no Internment to be seen—only smoke. Pen is knelt over me, trembling. Or maybe the ground is trembling—I don't know. The city burns behind her.

"Don't leave me now," she says.

I struggle to sit up, but I can't, and I don't understand why my leg is burning.

"Is anyone coming?" I say.

"I don't know."

"Where's Birdie?"

"I don't know."

"Did she find her brothers?"

She places my head in her lap. "I don't know."

She was right. She was right about everything. King Ingram and King Erasmus are cheerfully ripping each other's kingdoms apart, and they'll bring this ugliness to Internment. There will be no peaceful alliance; Celeste's mother won't recover; things can only get worse and worse.

I close my eyes to ward off the tears, but Pen says, "Hey," and shakes me. She will grant me no rest. But she might not be so eager for my company if she knew what I'd done. And I'd like to tell her now, if for no reason but to clear my conscience. But these may well be our last moments, and at the very least she should spend them thinking that the city she has loved all her life is safe. That it will be hovering in the sky long after these fools who run the ground have destroyed their own kingdoms.

Pen plays with the beads around my neck. They are a part of another world, a thousand miles and an hour behind us.

I feel for the strip of fabric tied around my wrist, a

memory that I belonged somewhere once. Annette asked me about it one evening at dinner, calling it a strange bracelet, and I didn't want to tell her. It would feel too strange to bring my parents' names into this bizarre world that astonishes at one turn and destroys at another. I don't believe my mother would have been strong enough to know suffering like the kind that happens here, and my father would have driven himself mad trying to fix it.

"The first bomb was just to get everyone to the harbor," Pen says now. "All the survivors would come here and be like caged animals."

There are such horrible things in her head, and what's worse is that she's right. She almost always is.

A voice shouts our names, and I'm not sure if I'm imagining things. A shadow in the smog is running for us. "We're here!" Pen says.

Nimble is still wearing his lenses. That's my first thought when I see him. I don't know how many things these bombs have destroyed—buildings, bones—but two tiny circles of glass on one boy's face are still intact. It makes me laugh, and the laugh turns into a cough.

"She's hurt," Pen says. "I think I've stopped the bleeding."

"I'm fine," I say. "Where's Birdie?"

He doesn't answer. His left arm is dead weight at his side. "Where's Riles?" I ask.

"My father is coming for us," he says. "Stay right here so I'll be able to find you."

"Wait," Pen says, but he's already gone.

"He's probably got Riles and Birdie someplace safe," I say.

"There is no 'someplace safe,' Morgan," she says.

"Yes, there is," I say. "And I've destroyed it."

If she heard me, she doesn't acknowledge it. "Do you suppose Jack Piper will be able to get to us through the melee?" she asks.

"I don't know," I say. "Pen?"

"Mm?"

"What story from *The History of Internment* would you compare this to?" I think it would comfort me to hear a story from our home.

She runs her fingers over the beads around her neck. "There isn't one," she says. "There is nothing like this in our history."

It feels like ages, but cars come. The smoke begins to settle. I don't see Jack Piper, but there's a man who kneels before Pen and me, and he asks if we're the ones who have been staying with the Pipers, and he gives us a ride in his ambulance, which is like Nimble's car, but just a bit longer, and I'm carried to it rather than allowed to walk.

And somewhere on the way to the hospital, I see the red mess that my leg has become, wound with the remains of Pen's sweater, which really belongs to Mrs. Piper. And all I can think to say is, "Lex is going to murder me."

Pen gives a small laugh. "Thomas is going to murder me," she says.

"Nobody in this car is going to die today," the driver says.

It's a nice thought, and one that many people in Havalais can no longer have.

There are rules, so many rules the hospital has. I've heard Judas and Amy complain about sometimes being turned away when they try to visit the professor. But it's immediately clear that rules do not apply in a time of mass crisis. Pen and I are herded to a room where she's treated for her arm and I'm treated for my leg. And now, under the unnaturally bright lights, wearing a white gown so thin it lets in a chill, breathing in the smell of abrasive chemicals, I begin to feel the pain in my leg. I smell the soot in my hair. I see Birdie running into the cloud of screams and I'm unable to stop her. Over and over she runs, and a moment before the air explodes, the moment begins again.

But it isn't until Basil appears in the doorway, out of breath, that I break into tears.

Thomas is right behind him, and he runs to Pen as Basil runs to me. The nurse is too busy to pay any mind, and she leaves us. Outside the door I hear a mess of noise and desperation.

"How did you find us?" Pen asks.

"We've been running from room to room," Thomas says.

Basil is dabbing at my runny nose and eyes, but I wrap my arms around him. All I want in the world is for him to hold me steady. The ground is forever shaking. I am seeing this moment and also the moments in the city between the bombs.

"Basil," I whimper.

"I'm here," he says. Kisses my shoulder. Smoothes my hair. "I'm here. I won't leave you."

"I don't know where Birdie is." I grab his shirt in my fists. "Or Riles and Nim."

I want him to tell me that they're okay, but he can't.

"How did you know we'd be at the hospital?" Pen asks. And her tone turns worried. "Did something happen at the hotel?"

"Everyone there is safe," Thomas says. "We were woken by news of the attack, and when your beds were empty, the princess said she'd overheard you talking about going to the cinema, and Nimble had told her he would be taking Riles to some concert."

Basil eases me against the mattress. "Your eyes are dilated," he says.

"She probably has a concussion," Pen says. "She took a piece of shrapnel to the head after the second explosion."

"I don't remember that," I say.

"No, I don't suppose you would. You were too busy muttering about tree roots in the sky and trying to get me to look at them."

Basil frowns and brushes his thumb across my brow. "I've been so worried about you," he says.

"Is Nim here?" I ask.

"Somewhere, yes."

"Good," I say. He'll be looking for his brother and sister, and he'll find them, the way Basil and Thomas found us. We'll go back to the hotel, and we'll endure a lecture for our actions, but we'll be okay.

Despite persistent evidence to the contrary, there is something in me that believes we'll be okay.

"I have something for you," Thomas tells Pen.

He holds her betrothal band up to the light before he places it on her finger. "Annette found it while she and Riles were cleaning the yacht yesterday."

Pen stares at it for a long while, as though she is trying to remember the girl she was just hours before, who would have thought a betrothal band to be among the most important things in her world.

Dreams are indistinguishable from truth. I know I'm awake only because in all my waking moments I am calling for Basil, because I worry he'll leave my side, and calling for Pen, because I worry her survival was a fever dream and that she was lost at the harbor. Across the room, Pen isn't much better off. I hear her sobbing, Thomas whispering.

When Nimble appears in the doorway, his left arm in a sling, I'm not sure if he's really there at first.

"Everyone alive and accounted for?" he asks. There is something wrong with his voice.

"They'll be okay," Basil says.

Nimble nods. "Good," he says. "That's good."

"Birdie?" is the first thing I'm able to get out.

He looks at me, and his face softens. His eyes are shining with tears. I think of what his mother said, about him being all soul inside.

"It doesn't look good, kiddo," he tells me.

"But she's alive?"

He rubs at his eyes under the lenses and nods.

"Riles?" I say.

Across the room, Pen sits up, listening.

Nimble turns away from us, and I think he's going to leave. He takes a step. But then he turns back around. "Riles is dead."

I don't understand. My body won't let me understand; it is so bruised and tired and shocked, it can't make room for this news. My vision clouds and I smell ashes.

Nimble's mouth is a wobbly line. He looks to Basil and then Thomas. "Take good care of them, boys. We already have more fatalities than this kingdom will be able to stand."

It could be days, or hours. Nobody will tell me what's happening outside the hospital. The nurses force Basil and Thomas to leave because it's too crowded to accommodate the well in addition to the wounded. But they don't want to go. They tell us they will stand outside if they have to. They say, "Don't worry; we'll be here."

"We'll worry less if you go to the hotel, where we know you'll be safe," Pen says. What she doesn't say is that the hospital may be another target.

A nurse says she loves our accents and asks if we're from someplace called Norsup. Pen says that we are, and I hope it isn't another kingdom that King Ingram has angered. We get new roommates in the three empty beds. The nurses curtain us off so that I can hear only the other patients' groaning and whimpering and snoring, but Pen and I leave the curtain open between us, always.

She recovers quickly in the coming hours, and doesn't seem to notice the layers of gauze wrapped around her forearm. Several times she leaves the room, only to later return, escorted by impatient nurses who tell her she needs her rest.

She sits on the foot of my bed. "I found Birdie," she says.

I prop myself on my elbows. My leg is throbbing through the numbing salve they've applied to it. Sliced open by some airborne sharp object, but not broken. I could force myself to walk on it if it means seeing Birdie alive. "How is she? Can you take me to her?"

Pen shakes her head, looks at the ground. "This is bad," she says. "All of this is just . . . unimaginable. Nobody even died in the bank explosion; it was a weekend, everything was closed. That was meant to be a warning. King Ingram ignored it."

"Jack Piper is his first and only adviser," I say. "I'm sure he had something to do with that."

"Well, hooray for him," Pen says. "He just got one of his own children killed, and maybe another."

"You said Birdie is still alive," I insist.

She strokes the back of her hand against my face. "It isn't good, Morgan," she says.

"I have to see her," I say. "Pen, you have to show me where she is."

"You can't walk," she says. "Do you propose I carry you?"

"I can walk if I lean on you for support," I say. She hesitates. "Pen, if she isn't going to make it, I should be able to see her. Time is a factor."

Pen leans back to peer into the hallway. "It's chaos out there," she says. "We might be able to get by unnoticed." She helps me get to my feet.

The instant I put weight on my leg, it ignites with new pain. I bite down on my lip to stifle my scream. That's all it takes to make Pen change her mind. She pushes me back against the pillow. "I'm not going to let you hurt yourself," she says. "Just—just stay there, all right? I'll be back."

She's been in and out of our room so many times, she's gotten quite good at getting around the nurses. I've always known her to be clever, but even I am impressed when she returns with a wheelchair. She seems quite pleased with herself.

"I've memorized the building's layout as best I can," she says, wheeling me out into the hall. That's the mapmaker in her. "We're in the east wing, which is where they seem to be keeping all of the cases that aren't life-threatening. Burns and breaks and things. Birdie is across the building. There's a sign that says it's the burn unit, but there's a whole mess of patients everywhere. No one even noticed me."

These are the halls I walked after the professor collapsed, and the driver took Celeste and me on a tour. The halls were nearly empty then, voices soft and calm, patients quiet in their beds. But now there are burns and tears and trays of bloody bandages everywhere we go.

We round several corners before my wheelchair collides with the white skirt of a nurse who looks positively undone. Her hat has come unpinned on one side, and it's flapping like a dog's ear against her severe ponytail.

"What are you doing out of your beds?" she says.

"Hang on," Pen tells me, and with a lurch, she runs down the hall, pushing me so fast, my hair is blown from my shoulders. I claw at the armrests. The nurse's high heels clack against the polished floor as she chases us, but her insensible shoes are no match for Pen, and Pen knows it, which is why she's laughing. It's absurd enough that I laugh, too, and call back, "We're sorry, truly," as we disappear around another corner.

Pen slows to catch her breath, but there are still traces of laughter even as she coughs.

That is, until we come to a stop before an open door. Unlike the other hallways, it's quiet here. There are many doors, and I would like to think Pen has made a mistake stopping before this one. The body in that bed could not possibly belong to anyone we know.

Slowly, Pen wheels me through the door, bringing me close enough to the bed that I can have a better look. The body in the bed has one leg elevated on a rope that hangs from a pulley on the ceiling, and the leg is wrapped in bandages that are soaked through with brown splotches, blood; the mouth is parted open, held that way by a thick hose that disappears down the throat. The eyes are swollen and pink, smeared with some greasy salve. The face is scratched, scraped, patched by white strips of bandages. The hair is matted with blood, but, strangely, it's the first part of Birdie that I recognize. It still has a bit of a wave to it, and it rests over one shoulder, the way it always has.

"Birdie?" I whisper.

But she doesn't hear. Her chest rises and falls in tandem with some sighing machine, which, along with the ropes and bandages, is holding together what's left of her.

Pen touches my shoulder. She wanted to protect me from this, but I insisted. Up until this moment, I thought that whatever state Birdie was in couldn't be worse than Lex after he went over the edge. But Lex, at least, still looked something like Lex. I didn't have to stare at him, trying to find traces.

This is— I don't know what I am supposed to make of this.

"My brother was right," I say. "There's cruelty here, too."

"I've been thinking the same thing," Pen says.

I look over my shoulder at her. "Why isn't anyone with her? She shouldn't be here all alone."

"They aren't allowing visitors," Pen says.

"But her father is the king's adviser," I say. "That's got to mean something."

"On the contrary, it means less than nothing," Nimble says. I turn in my chair and see him standing in the doorway. "Everyone hates the king right now. It's been only a day, and already there's talk that he planned for this to happen. And that's just in this one building. Imagine what the rest of the kingdom must be saying."

I can't bring myself to look at Birdie again, and so I focus on her brother. There are purple shadows under his eyes, and he's whiter than the walls and bedding in this place. I see the veins in his good hand as he clenches and unclenches his fist.

"I'm sorry," is all I can say.

"It's my fault," he says. "When our mother left, Birdie developed a habit of sneaking away at night. I thought it would be good for her, maybe she'd make some friends for a change, take her mind off things. None of us gets much freedom."

"It sounds like you were only looking out for her," Pen says.

He nods. "The city has always been safe, you see. Safe enough that I wouldn't think twice about her going off alone, or bringing one of the kids with me when I go." His voice gets congested and his eyes become inflamed. All of the Piper children have those light blue eyes I've always found so beautiful. "I neglected to take it seriously that we're at war. I found it all sort of funny, the way King Ingram and King Erasmus exchanged threats over a bunch of rocks out in the ocean."

"You can't have known," I say.

"I should have. Even Celeste tried to warn me, and I laughed. I laughed. I told her that this sort of cold war baloney had been going on for decades."

"To be fair, she is rarely ever right about anything," Pen says. I'm not sure if she was making a joke, but Nimble laughs anyway, bitterly.

"Has your father been here?" I say.

"It wouldn't be safe for him out here, and anyway, he'll be busy right about now. The king needs him."

"You and Birdie need him more," I say.

Nimble shakes his head. "No we don't," he says. "Our father is the last person we need. Next to our mother, that is."

He watches Birdie, who doesn't blink or move. I wonder if she is dreaming, or if she has moved past that by now. I wonder if she's dying, or if in a way she's already dead.

"We're here for you," Pen offers. I can see in his expression that her kindness has startled him. "If you need us, that is. We're here."

"Thank you," he says. He is still watching his sister. I don't know how he has the bravery. Hours ago she was smirking at him in the glow of a streetlamp. "She came after me, didn't she? After the explosion."

He doesn't need us to answer.

"We made a promise. Our father has always kept us sheltered, insisting on private tutors, having us live in seclusion so that the political discussions in schools and on the streets wouldn't conflict with what he'd have us believe.

"After our mother left, he tightened the reins. Birdie and I would talk about getting rich somehow, running away. One of us would unearth another phosane mine or write the next timeless novel and make millions. At first it was just talk, but the more we talked, the more it became fact. One of us would make it, and then we'd be able to get away. But we wouldn't leave each other behind the way our mother did."

When Pen suggested that Nimble and Riles might have taken the ferry after the bomb hit, Birdie was certain they hadn't, and now I understand why. And suddenly I have the courage to look at her again, to see what I think Nimble sees: traces of her soft, timid expressions under all the blood and burns; a girl whose life is unfinished, plans and intentions suspended somewhere in the smoke and rubble. A sister, a daughter, a friend.

I take her hand. In the novels, this is all it takes for a girl in peril to awaken from her trance. But her fingers are slack in my palm, and her skin is cold, and I don't know where she is, only that I can't bring her back.

"She told you, didn't she?" Nim says. "About our family and who we are to the king."

"Yes," I say, but it had been during one long silly night we shared while we had too much to drink. She never mentioned it again.

"We used to joke about it," he says. "But with all the hatred everyone has for the king right now, I don't know what kind of danger we'd all be in if anyone found out."

"No one will find out," Pen says. "It's been a secret this long, right?"

"You're bleeding," Nimble says.

"Oh," Pen says. "So I am." Her bandages are soaked through with it, probably from the adrenaline when she ran from the nurse. She presses her fingers against the stain and it comes off on her skin.

"You should go back to your room and rest," Nimble says. "Both of you."

"We're okay," Pen says. "It's nothing very serious."

"Let's keep it that way," he says. "Please. Birdie would want me to look after you. You both mean a lot to her."

I lay her hand back on the mattress. A comatose princess in a burning kingdom. "She means a lot to us, too," I say.

Pen grabs the handles of my chair and steers me forward. "We're in the east wing," she says. "Come and find us if you get lonely. We're surely not going anywhere for a while."

He offers something like a smile as we pass by.

We make it back to our room, and after Pen helps me into my bed, she returns the wheelchair to the hallway. Someone will need it more than I do.

After the energy Pen has put forth this afternoon, she is asleep seconds after climbing into her bed. Her breathing is uneasy; she mumbles and stirs. I hear her as I drift into a sleep of my own. I don't know that it can even be called sleep. It is only moments I've already lived, bolder and more vivid now that they've had time to grow. The bomb wakes me over and over. Birdie runs into the haze. Nimble and Riles walk into the crowd, their lips moving as they say words that I can't hear. The ground shakes. I wake clawing at the mattress.

". . . His victims are crushed, they collapse." Pen is sitting beside me, a book open across her knees. "They fall under his strength. He says to himself, 'God has forgotten; he covers his face and never sees.'"

"What are you reading?" I ask.

"Verses," she says, struggling to pronounce the peculiar name. "*The Text* breaks off into this sort of poetry."

"Where did you get a copy of *The Text* here?"

She laughs. "They're everywhere. It's like they mortar the walls with them down here. I thought you wouldn't mind if I read aloud."

"I don't mind." I close my eyes. I don't have to believe the words to take comfort in them. There's comfort, also, in the cadence of her speech, the subtle inflections and emphases that I took for granted back home, where everyone spoke the same way.

"I'm trying to skip around to the nice parts," she says. "But sometimes it sounds nice, and then it goes somewhere ugly."

"They like that down here, don't they?" I say.

"Are you from the north somewhere?" a voice says through the curtain.

"Norsup," we say in unison, and we say no more about the differences between the sky and the ground. Pen reads, and I coast in and out of sleep. This time it is dreamless. And then, when Pen's voice has faded so far into the distance that it is scarcely there, I relive another moment. I'm standing with Celeste, behind the gold curtain in the lobby, and we're watching the smoke rise from where the bank was bombed. She smiles at me. "We've come just in time to save them," she tells me. "Wouldn't you say?"

I wake with a gasp.

I am sure I will never again have a night of uninterrupted sleep.

A nurse is standing in our doorway with a wheelchair. "You're being released," she says. "Someone has come to collect you."

231

"Both of us?" Pen asks.

"Yes, doll." The nurse is clearly in a hurry, judging by the speed with which she changes our bandages and moves me into the wheelchair. I suppose there's no shortage of people in need of our beds.

As we head down the hallway, I wonder if Jack Piper has risked his safety to collect his only remaining son, and to see what's become of his eldest daughter.

But his driver is the one waiting for us at the door. Nimble is already there, and he looks as though he needs this chair more than I do. The nurse touches his good arm and he flinches. He looks down the hallway, until it forks into different directions, one of which begins the labyrinth that leads to his sister, and I can see that he doesn't want to leave her.

Outside, the smell of damp earth and the singing of crickets go on uninterrupted. The basics of nature see no cause to be still for the likes of us.

Once I'm in the car, I look back at the hospital. It is made of squares of light against a black and starless sky.

"I've never had a friend like you either," I whisper to Birdie as we drive away.

17

The youngest Pipers are uncertain what to do with themselves when there is no routine. It's just Marjorie and Annette now. No Riles to tell them which things are too selfish to mention in their prayers, or to reach the crackers when they're hungry after lunch. And no father telling them to sit straight, eat their boiled carrots, and don't fidget. They sob all day; it's one long sound that begins in the morning and never really stops as the sun changes its position in the sky. They don't speak. Something irreparable has happened; they understand that much.

Alice reads to them, and they sit still but don't listen.

Nimble isn't faring any better than his little sisters. He sits in a wing chair in the lobby, saying nothing as Celeste fusses over him, bringing him food he doesn't eat and tea he doesn't drink. She tells him to please, please talk to her, he's got her scared, she wants to understand what's in his mind.

But she can't understand, and it's that simple. She didn't see the things we did. When he falls into a frail sleep and wakes kicking his foot like he needs to run away, she has no idea what he might have dreamed, but Pen and I do. The three of us seem to have formed an unspoken agreement to stay near one another. Touching shoulders, touching hands as we pass by, smiling wearily, speaking little if at all.

Celeste, Basil, and Thomas have formed a sort of bond as well. They are on the outside trying desperately to see through the wall that's been built between them and the ones they love. And when they can't console us, they console each other.

Alice reads on. Fairy tales and novels and plays. No one really pays attention, but I'm grateful to have a familiar voice filling the silence.

Amy and Judas hover on the outskirts of the room, not daring to approach any of us. It's as if they know there's a delicate balance, and one misstep will cause everyone in the house to collapse into a sort of chaos that can't be undone.

Pen reads *The Text of All Things*, and she tries to draw the divinities. She sketches Ehco in many forms, but most prominently as a water monster with human fingers, and screaming mouths for scales. And I begin to think Ehco is real, and that Pen has captured him exactly.

The sun goes down. Jack Piper doesn't return, and, uncertain what else to do, everyone goes to bed. Basil carries me up the stairs and feeds me a spoonful of that awful medicine the hospital has given me in a brown glass bottle. "Would you like me to stay until you fall asleep?" he asks.

"No," I say. I don't mean to sound so sharp about it, but I am too drained to bring myself to say I'm sorry.

He tucks the blankets around me. "I'll check on you through the night," he says.

I close my eyes, hoping that he won't kiss me good night or say more nice things to me. I have no room in me for affection. I can't bear to be touched by anyone right now. But my betrothed knows me well, and he leaves.

I hear footsteps in the hall moments later, and I think he's come back already, but when I open my eyes, my brother is the one standing in the doorway.

"Lex?" I say, unbelieving. He has hardly left his room since we arrived.

"I have the right room, then," he says. "How cluttered is the floor?"

"No clutter," I say. "There's a bed on the left, and two beds on the right. I'm in the farthest one. I'd guide you, but—"

"Alice told me you hurt your leg," he says. "Is it serious?"

"No. They wrapped it in gauze and sent me home with something in a brown bottle. It'll be fine." I'm astounded that he's here, making his way to me. And without Alice, at that. I have always been the one going to him.

He feels for the first bed, Pen's, and then mine, and he sits beside me. I take his hands.

"You were right, you know," I say. "This world is miserable and I hate it. The only things I've liked about this world are the things Gertrude Piper showed me." I can't go on telling him what's happened to her.

"You don't hate it," he says. "You don't hate anything. Not truly. You only say that you do sometimes out of anger."

"I hate when you tell me what I'm feeling, too," I say.

"Don't confuse my philosophies for yours, Little Sister. I'll go on hating everything, and you'll go on finding the good in things that don't deserve it. And we'll never agree, but we'll both be right."

"Is that what you've come to tell me?" I say.

"No," he says. "I came to yell at you for sneaking off in the middle of the night and scaring Alice out of her mind."

"Tell Alice that I am most sorry," I say.

"I don't know what you've seen, Morgan, but I—"

"I'd rather not talk about it," I say.

"I've also, maybe, come to tell you that I'm sorry that it's come to this. When Mom and Dad and I talked about coming to the ground, we thought it best to shelter you from it, but then, you have to understand that none of us really thought we'd pull it off. We didn't expect that Daphne Leander would be murdered or that the professor would get the bird running in our lifetime."

"What's done is done," I say. "Why bring it up now?"

"Because, after the other night, waiting until dawn to hear whether you were among the casualties in the city, I began to think you might have been safer on Internment. Even with the king's specialist trying to poison you. I knew Internment had its horrors, but they are nothing compared to this."

"How is it that there are two worlds — one in the sky and one on the ground — and I forever feel that I have nowhere to go?" I ask.

"Internment is still your home," he says.

"But there's nothing left for me there," I say. "You and everyone else are here. Mom and Dad are dead."

"Dad isn't dead," he blurts. And immediately I can see that he regrets it. His skin pales and he cannot seem to comfortably place his hands anywhere. For a moment he touches the scrap of cloth around his wrist, nearly identical to mine. A sign that we're both in mourning.

Through the haze of shock and grief and utter exhaustion that has numbed me these few days, something within me begins to stir. Something frightening. "What?" I say.

He has gone as still as a statue.

"Lex." My voice is soft because it's all I can manage. I pull my hands away from his. My bones are shaking. "What are you saying?"

"He's not dead for certain, at least," Lex says. "After Daphne's murder, when it began to look like we'd really try to get away, Mom and Dad told me that if things went from bad to worse, I was to get you to the bird. Alice and I weren't to go searching for them. If they didn't make it back to us in time, I should do whatever was necessary to protect you."

"What's all this talk of *you* protecting *me*?" I snap. "I've been the one looking after you for the last four years. Who would make sure that you were eating? Who would sit with you when Alice had to run errands all day? Who carried dinner and messages up and down the stairs like a bloody mailboy day and night when Mom was too sad and Dad was too stubborn to deliver them themselves?"

"You would have tried to find him," Lex says.

"Of course I would have tried to find him!" I say. I want to say more, but the words are a frenzy inside me and they're moving too quickly to make sense.

"Morgan, try to understand," he says. For once he isn't being condescending; he sounds contrite.

He reaches for my shoulder, but I move away. "No," I say. "You try to understand. Why should you be the one to decide that we leave him behind? Why shouldn't I have decided for myself whether to go after him? It's like you think you are more entitled to them just because you're older, and you've seen the edge, and you were left with scars. I have scars from that day too, Lex. You didn't take a plunge off Internment's edge alone, you know. You took us all with you. Mom, Dad, Alice, and me. We've all had to watch as it took over our lives. That day you crossed the tracks, you didn't think about what would happen to us, not at all. You didn't need Mom and Dad anymore, but I still needed them." My voice has gotten louder, but it cracks. "*I* needed them."

My breathing is rapid. "You took our parents from me once before. How could you do that to me again?" I would like to run away now, but my leg wouldn't oblige.

My reaction has Lex afraid, and I wonder at what he expected. "Morgan, please," he says. He tries to touch me and I move away and I hit him, push him, say such awful, hateful things that it's as though something has taken over my tongue and I am powerless to stop it. I scarcely know what I'm saying. The words get louder until my voice becomes a scream. He won't leave me. Why won't he leave? He's trying to find and hold my hands—the only pieces of me that are still familiar to him.

I hear footsteps running up the stairs, and then Alice and Basil and Pen are in the room. Alice pulls Lex off the bed, and Pen wraps her arms around me, rocking me and whispering, "Shh, shh, Morgan, shh." After what happened to us at the harbor, she can't stand the thought of seeing any more pain. She looks at my brother. "What in the world did you do to her?"

Neither of us answers. I've broken into tears. I see explosions, explosions, explosions, Birdie fighting feebly for her life, my father's sad eyes, the creases in his patrol-man's uniform. My brother was the selfish one, he said, but not me. Never me.

I'm choking on the memory of smoke, and the tears and the saliva that's pooling around my teeth. I make the most hideous sobbing sounds. They surely aren't human.

I see Lex with his head down, Alice's arm around him, and I can't be certain, but I think he's crying too. I've never spoken to him this way. The way Alice frowns at me tells me that she knows what's happened. Has she known this whole time? I can't stand the thought that she would betray me, too.

"Morgan, you have to calm down," Pen says. "You're going to make yourself sick."

"I needed them," I murmur through my sobs.

"Shh, shh."

Basil brings a wet cloth, and he dabs at my face and the sides of my neck. "What happened?" he says, once Lex is gone and I've settled some.

"I'll never forgive him," I say. "Not for this."

"Yes you will," Basil says. "He's still your brother. You've just had a fight, is all."

"Some fight," Pen says. "What did he do, Morgan?"

"He lied," I say. I don't tell them any more than that; I have no idea what to do with what I've just learned.

My brother tells me that I don't know how to truly hate, but I can't think of a person in this world or the next that I hate more than him. It's ugly and dark, and it scares me the way that the explosions at the harbor scared me.

Basil and Pen sit with me while my body calms. My face loses its heat; my lungs take up a gentler rhythm; my tears dry and the gurgling coughs die away. But the hatred stays. It is inside me and around me.

Nimble knocks on the doorframe. He could be a ghost. A ghost in a sling and pin-striped pajamas. He's got a bottle and a spoon in his hand. "This will put you to sleep," he tells me. "I thought you might need it." He sets them on the night table beside *The Text* that's bookmarked by a pencil and pad, which Pen has been using to take copious notes. He leaves without another word.

The liquid is amber, and it tastes like every bitter thing combined, but before long my eyelids are heavy. "On Internment we have pills, but on the ground they have bottles and spoons," I say. "It isn't very different."

"Good night," Basil whispers. I see light against my eyelids as his shadow leaves me, and I reach out and grab his arm.

"Stay," I murmur. I move to make room for him on the mattress. "Please stay."

"Okay." He's still whispering, trying to keep the tentative calm the medicine has caused me. "I'm here."

He climbs in beside me, and I wrap myself around his arm, pressing my cheek to his shoulder so hard, it starts to hurt. I'm so grateful for him, grateful that if I had to fall through the sky, he chose to fall from it too. I want to tell him, but the words dissolve along with consciousness, and everything is beautifully, peacefully, medicinally dark.

Rather than dreaming, I relive another memory.

I'm small, and I'm thinking of how big Lex is getting, and how like our father he is. So serious at thirteen. He's starting to get bulging veins in his hands; he says it's because he's taken to running. He likes to do things that get his heart racing. He likes to feel the throb in his throat and to lose his breath and know that his body is working. I like to run, too, and he says that when children do it, it's not the same, but he can teach me when I'm older.

My father picks me up over his head, and I laugh as all my thoughts break like the sunlight on the water. Internment is on fire in the minutes before the stars start coming through.

My father's uniform is crisp; it whispers as he reaches up to steady me on his shoulders.

We're watching the fire in the water, and he tells me, "You're getting too big for this."

"I'm not bigger than I was yesterday," I say.

"A bit," he says. "A fraction every day."

"I don't want veins in my hands," I say.

He laughs. I don't think he knows what I mean.

I begin to worry for what the stars will bring as they appear, one at a time, in the darkening sky.

Jack Piper returns in the morning. The cooks, restless by the lack of routine, are serving breakfast. A few of us are even sitting down to humor the idea.

We all turn at the gust of wind Jack Piper has brought in with him.

He does not look as bereft as I think he should. "Everyone, get changed into your dress clothes," he says. "Meet at the cars in twenty minutes."

"Where are we going?" Marjorie asks.

"We're going to bury your brother," he says.

Annette's eyes are wide and they fill with tears. "Without a church funeral?" she says. "The priest has to say the burial prayer. If he doesn't say the prayer, how will Riles be able to get to heaven?"

"You can ask Nimble," Jack Piper says, as he steps outside again. "This is his fault."

It is the most horrible thing I have ever heard anyone say. Annette runs from the table, sobbing. Nimble puts his face in his hand. Celeste grabs his chin, forcing him to look at her, and she stares at him, hard. She kisses him, and it's no matter who sees it. The rules of decorum have died along with the casualties of the explosions. "It's not your fault," she says. "It's not."

He shakes his head, pushes himself away from the table. "I'd better get changed," he says. "He'll leave in twenty minutes whether we're ready or not."

We all leave the table. Basil helps me up the steps, and then I try to situate myself using the crutches that the hospital gave me. I'm a little wobbly, but I'm able to move about, at least.

Pen and Celeste and I change into dresses that Mrs. Piper left behind along with her children.

"He doesn't want their mother here," Celeste says, helping me with my zipper. "That's probably why the burial is today. He doesn't know how long it will take for her to hear what's happened to Riles. That's what Nim said."

"This family doesn't make any sense," Pen says. She watches Celeste brush her hair in the mirror. "Where's your betrothal band?" she asks.

"I removed it," Celeste says coolly. "It was about time."

Pen narrows her eyes, but says nothing. She holds my crutches and wraps her arm around me as we make our way down the stairs. It doesn't seem fair that my only discomfort is an injured leg, while Birdie clings to life all alone in a bed somewhere, and Riles is to spend eternity in the dirt.

Marjorie and Annette have buttoned the wrong buttons on their dresses, and the hair on their heads is a mess. They looked pristine every morning by the time the tutor came around, and I now suspect that was Birdie's doing.

I fix their dresses while Pen brushes their hair, and they begin to resemble something like themselves, but with droopy eyes and gray faces.

Annette looks at me as I straighten her collar. "Is my sister going to come home?" she asks.

"I know that she wants to come home more than anything else," I tell her. "But right now she needs to be near the doctors so that they can make her better."

Annette looks at her shoes and nods. I don't know whether she believes me, but I seem to have brought her no comfort.

"Is there anything that would make you smile, Annie? Even for just a teensy second?" I ask. "I've always thought your smiles have real sunlight in them."

"Really?" she says.

"Yes."

"A kiss, then," she says, tapping her cheek. "Right here. But when you do it, you have to make a funny noise like Birdie does."

"A funny noise, huh?" I say.

Marjorie, standing a pace away, peeks through her haze of grief with a bit of curiosity on her face.

"Like this?" I say. I kiss Annette's cheek, and when I do, I purse my lips and exhale from one cheek until a loud and bizarre sound comes out.

Annette's shoulders convulse with giggles. "Yes," she says.

"Are you sure it isn't more like this?" I say, and this time I make a different sound. She wraps her arms around my neck and gives me the same sort of kiss. She's laughing, and so are Marjorie and Pen; even Nimble smirks from where he's standing in the doorway. And I could swear the room gets a little brighter, as though we've invited the sunlight through the windows.

The sunlight is a skittish thing, though, and it flees when Jack Piper comes through the front door. The giggling stops and the youngest Pipers straighten their skirts, feel their hair to be sure it is perfect.

Jack Piper doesn't have to say anything. The girls know to follow their brother. They have always moved according to height, and now there's a gap where Birdie, followed by Riles, should march for the door.

Celeste follows after them, frowning at the back of Nimble's head. Pen helps me manage my crutches and get into the car.

I wind up wedged between Judas and Basil. "Where's Amy?" I ask Judas.

"She thought the graveyard might trigger a fit," he says, at a volume only I'm meant to hear. "She didn't want to cause an interruption."

With all that's happened, I haven't had a chance to check on Amy. She's got an extra sense about death, and I wonder if she felt it when the first bomb hit the harbor. When she told me of her dream about Internment falling from the sky, perhaps she had her facts confused, and what she was seeing was that attack.

"Feeling okay?" Basil asks me.

"It's impossible to be in high spirits on the way to something like this."

245

"I meant about last night," he says.

"I've put it aside for now."

"I could talk to him, if you'd like," Basil says. "I hate to see the two of you at odds."

"There's nothing left to talk about," I say. "Let it go." I feel guilty enough harboring so much anger for my brother when the Piper children are about to bury theirs. When I see the cemetery gates, a heaviness settles on my chest.

The sun cannot decide whether it wants to stay. It hides behind clouds, peeking out only enough to put light in the trees, throw a glimmer on some of the stones. The Pipers march ahead in their familiar order, and the rest of us straggle a few paces behind.

Thomas holds Pen's hand, a gesture she can neither reject nor embrace; she looks away from him, her lips moving as she reads the names on the stones we pass.

Basil walks beside me, our arms not quite touching. If there was tension as our affections for each other began to bloom on Internment, there is tension now as our affections seem to be waning, and we cannot decide whether to cling to them or let them go. All I can know for certain is that I care for him, that if he'd been lost that night at the harbor, a part of me would have been lost as well, just as a part of me is still halfway between life and death since the explosions, like Birdie in her hospital bed fighting to survive.

"I think that's the priest," Judas whispers from behind me. He's looking at a man dressed all in black, but for a white strip at his collar.

On Internment, we have officiates to bear the ashes, read about the tributary, and throw the ashes into the wind.

Rather than ashes, there's a glossy wooden box just the right size to hold a child, and a gaping hole in the ground. Annette and Marjorie break into a new round of tears. Jack Piper glances at them, and his tense jaw softens a bit, and he tells the priest, "The girls would like you to read the burial prayer."

It may be the only kindness his children can expect from him today.

The priest thumbs through his *Text*. Up until now it has been a source of entertainment for us, a bit of mythology to help us learn about this place. But now I see that it is as real to the people of the ground as our history book is to us. Whether the tributary exists, or whether the words in that black book are true, the idea of them is equally important. There is a need, in every world, to believe in things that cannot be seen.

The priest begins, in a theatrical, almost musical tone, to recite the prayer the girls have requested. It's unfamiliar to me, but Pen whispers as he goes on. She has already read this one.

I look at Nimble. His hair is parted and slicked, and he's much older in his plaid suit. Celeste is wound around his arm. But he doesn't hold her the way that she is holding on to him. If they were beginning to fall in love before this happened, she has advanced, while he's become frozen in time. He's still standing at the harbor, waiting for Riles and Birdie to emerge from the smoke so he can bring them safely home.

I hope that she'll be patient with him. He needs her, and when he is ready to rejoin the living, he'll see that.

The priest finishes his reading. There are two men in dirty clothes, and they manipulate a series of ropes and pulleys to get the box into the ground. It jerks with the motion, as though the boy inside has come alive again.

The hole in the ground seems infinite, and I'm surprised when the box reaches the bottom and it's still in sight. The Pipers grab handfuls of dirt, and, according to height, they take turns dropping it onto the final resting spot of their son and brother.

There is a moment of hesitation, and when a wind moves through, I feel that it has severed something that cannot ever be repaired.

I hope that Annette was right, and that the burial prayer will guide Riles where he needs to go.

Basil nudges me, and when I look at him, he nods off into the distance. Beyond the cemetery fence, half-hidden by trees, is a tall woman in a low-waisted dress. Nimble sees her too, and the numbness in his gaze turns to worry. He steers his sisters around so that their backs are to her. "Come on," he tells them. "Back to the cars."

"Are we going home?" Marjorie asks.

"No," Jack Piper says. I don't think he's seen the woman in the trees. "I've got a surprise for all of you. We're going to see the king. He's going to announce something special on the radio."

Celeste turns her head sharply to me.

I begin to understand. Now. King Ingram means to

announce to his kingdom the news about the jets, now that the country is war-torn and broken and the people are most likely to cling to the hope that there is something in the sky to save them.

A thousand horrified apologies are in Celeste's eyes.

Those murmurings that King Ingram was to blame for the harbor were right. He meant to announce Internment when the opportunity arose, and the bombings were just what he had in mind. Maybe it was even Jack Piper's idea: Ignore the warning bomb at the bank, wait for the real ones to come. He didn't expect that any of his own children would be there, but he was not above sacrificing someone else's children, someone else's parents and siblings and friends. And the funeral of his youngest son is not going to stop him. Things were set in motion the very instant I told the princess about the glasslands.

18

The stone of King Ingram's castle shimmers in the sun. Judas stares on in disgust as we approach. He has a bias against hierarchy, but at least the king who murdered his betrothed had the decency to live with some modesty.

Pen is too distracted to notice the castle at all. "Morgan?" she says. "At the harbor, I said there was no such thing as someplace safe, and you said yes there was, and you've destroyed it. What were you on about?"

I don't answer.

"I won't be angry," she says. "I don't think I could manage anger just now. I only want the truth."

"What are you accusing her of, exactly?" Judas says.

"She hasn't done anything wrong," Basil says. I don't think he believes that; he just can't stand Judas Hensley being the one to come to my defense.

But Pen is looking right at me, no matter how firmly I

stare at my lap. "Morgan knows exactly what I'm asking," she says.

"Then you don't need me to tell you," I say.

"You promised," she says. "You promised me you wouldn't tell anyone what we found at the library."

"This world made liars of us both, then," I say.

Basil touches my shoulder, and I flinch.

"I didn't mean for it to happen this way," I say. "I didn't know the bombs were coming."

"Of course not," Pen says. "You can never know what to expect when you deal with kings, or people from a strange land. That's why, when you discover something valuable, you keep your mouth shut." She speaks calmly, but there's enough fire in that last word to burn Internment from the sky.

"What did you do?" Judas is looking at me.

The car has stopped, and the driver opens the door for us. Basil helps me with my crutches. "Whatever it is, we'll fix it," he says.

I shake my head. "We can't. It's done."

Pen is already ahead of us, fastened to Thomas's side. It's what he's wanted ever since Lex jumped—for the girl he loves to distance herself from me. It's Celeste who's beside me now. "I'm sure that the rumors aren't true," she says. "The king didn't know that the bombs at the harbor were coming."

"If you really believe that, then you aren't as well versed in politics as you believe," I say.

She stares ahead at the castle doors that have opened for us. Her dread is palpable.

We enter the castle and walk past the parlor, down hallways and into depths I've never seen. I feel as though this place is swallowing us whole.

Basil offers to carry me, but I have no right to make this walk any easier on myself.

Pen glances back at me, and there's no anger in her face, but no warmth either. Thomas says something and she turns her attention back to him.

Celeste is ever at my side. We did this. Together we'll face whatever may come. She is poised and pristine, but I can feel her hope dying. She is the heiress presumptive of a floating kingdom, and she may have just been its undoing.

Judas walks behind us, glaring at the back of my head. I see his reflection in windows and polished vases and picture frames we pass.

At last this ominous march comes to an end. Jack Piper has led us to a heavy-looking door just beyond the reach of the window light. And as he turns to face his youngest children, I see how tired he's become in the trip from the cemetery to the king's castle. In his daughters he sees at once more life than he can bear, and he clears his throat before he's able to speak to them.

"King Ingram is going to speak into his radio, and it picks up every voice in the room, so you have to be as silent as mice."

They nod and begin to step behind their brother. As young as they are, even they know there is something to be feared on the other side of that door.

Jack Piper knocks three times, pauses, two times, pauses,

three times. There's the sound of latches coming undone, and then the door swings open.

I have never seen so many wires in my life. They're strung from the ceiling, dripping down one wall and across the floor in thick black rivers and routes, as though we have stepped inside a life-size map. The king sits at a table against the wall, where all the wires connect to brassy machines, one of which appears to be a sort of horn into which one might speak. The king's men stand guard at every corner of the tiny room, and they arrange us so that we're standing against the wall. The door closes. Pen looks nervously at me, and in her eyes I'm not sure whether I see blame or contrition.

"Welcome," King Ingram says, not looking at us. He is arranging wires into a panel of plugs. "I've been waiting."

From either side of our group, Nimble and Celeste lean forward to look at each other.

"Our sky princess has told me many interesting things about her floating city," the king goes on. "I was especially interested in your broadcast screens. She tells me they're something like our moving picture shows, but they can give a live broadcast like our radio waves. She tells me there are no radios on Internment, and that the screens are controlled by your king. I got to thinking that the reason for that must be so the signals wouldn't cross with ours. Your king really didn't want to open any communications with us, did he?"

He looks at Celeste, who flattens herself against the wall. She has lost all the shine and sparkle of her lineage.

The hopes she placed in the ground are as dead and buried as Jack Piper's youngest son.

King Ingram is a small man unremarkable in appearance, but now that I know his family secret, I see a bit of brightness in his eyes. I see that his grandchildren look something like him. I wonder if the throne would strip them of their souls the way it has this king.

The king says, "But for those screens to work, there must be radio waves. It's just that only your King Furlow and his men have access to them."

He turns back to his machines. I rest my weight against one crutch, and with my free arm I grab Celeste's hand. She squeezes it in gratitude.

"I had the great privilege of speaking with your king last evening," he says. "He was understandably reluctant to grant our jets access to his city. Because, you see, we would need a place to land. If our jet were to crash into a building and send the whole floating island up in smoke that would destroy all its phosane, that wouldn't do any good. And if he refuses to build us a tarmac, this could end badly for all of us."

Celeste squeezes her eyes shut for a long moment, collecting herself.

"He asked why he should help us. He's seen through those scopes of his how destructive we are. He doesn't want to displease his god of the sky." The king reaches for a chain fastened to his pocket. Rather than his eye lens, he has a clock. "I told him that I had a compelling reason, if he cared to listen, at noon today. We're coming up on that now." He twists at the knobs and rattles the wires, a maestro of this horrific organ. "Hello?" he says. "Hello, hello?"

There's a roar of static and something like a voice.

"How do you do!" King Ingram says. "Is this King Furlow?"

Whirring and swishing, and then a faraway, "It is."

"I'll cut right to the chase," King Ingram says. He looks over his shoulder to wink at us. "I have someone here who wants to say hello."

One of the king's men pulls Celeste forward. She lets go of my hand. She stands straight, fists balled. The king holds the metal horn in front of her face, whispers, "Say something, sweetheart."

"Pa—" Her voice hitches. "Papa?"

Static. Agonizing moments of static. And then, "—leste? Celeste! You're alive?"

Her shoulders shake, but to her credit she doesn't cry. "Yes," she says. "Yes. I'm here."

King Furlow hesitates up in his sky. Thirty-five thousand feet above us, he has just revealed his great weakness—that he loves his children, and one of them is held at King Ingram's mercy.

Celeste says, "Is Az—"

King Ingram takes the horn away from her, and with a dismissive wave, he beckons one of his men to push her back against the wall.

She holds her hands over her mouth, but through her skin and bones I hear the words she's whispering to the god in the sky.

King Furlow's voice is broken, scattered in the airspace between the two kingdoms. Negotiations are made. He says, over and over, the word "yes." He will build what needs to be built. He will prepare what needs to be prepared. He will gather the men to pave the field beyond the train tracks. All he asks is that his daughter is safely returned.

There is no mention of doing a thing to help the ailing queen.

No one says a word on the drive home. We sit still in our fancy clothes, and our eyes don't meet. And when we get inside the hotel, the radio in the kitchen is announcing what I already know.

Hello, yes, hello, this is your king.

Don't despair.

There is hope.

Help is coming soon.

I move for the stairs as fast as my crutches will allow. Arms go around me to hold me steady. Pen and Celeste. No matter what tensions exist between us, we still belong to the same world. We'll still band together when we need to.

We say nothing as we make our way up the stairs. In our room, we sit on the edges of our beds, forming a sort of triangle.

Celeste is the first to speak. "I didn't get to ask Papa about Azure. He seemed barely alive when I last saw him. I don't even know if he's woken up."

Pen shakes her head. "You shouldn't have come," she

says. "You're the reason Internment is going to let Havalais in. Everything is going to fall to ruin."

"Pen, don't," I say.

"Don't you dare," Pen says. Her voice is dangerous and low. "You don't get to tell me what to say. Not after what you just did. I don't even know who you are since we've come here."

She stares at me, and I don't look away, because she's right and I must face it: I betrayed her, and I betrayed our kingdom, and I'm not sorry. To keep her safe, I would betray a thousand kingdoms.

"Why must you always be so awful?" Celeste says to Pen. "We've all lost something, and here we are coping. You're the only one determined to make things more miserable than they already are. What's happened in your life to damage you so much?"

Pen flinches as though some invisible demon is blowing on her hair. "I don't have the head for this," she says, and leaves the room.

I fall back against my mattress. "Another fantastic mess," I say.

"My father has something up his sleeve," Celeste says, but she doesn't sound too sure. "If King Ingram really does intend to harm Internment in some way—and I'm not saying he does—my father and his men will have ways of preventing that from happening."

"You said King Ingram's engineers were working on getting the jets to fly," I say. "How soon will they be ready?"

"I don't know," she says. "They may be ready now, if he's announcing it on the radio. He said that if my ring was made of real phosane, it would be enough to fuel them." I feel her eyes watching me. "You don't look well," she says. "You're sweating."

"I'm all right," I say. "Today has just been taxing, and it's barely past noon."

She sits on my bed, touches my forehead. "Can I get you anything? Some water?"

"You wouldn't have a time machine, would you?"

She laughs. "If only."

If only. I'd push Riles and Nimble and Birdie and Pen back onto the ferry. I would say, I have a funny feeling we shouldn't be here.

Celeste pats my knee and stands. "You should have a nap," she says. "I'm going to find Nim."

"Hey," I say.

She's already in the doorway and she turns to face me. "Be patient with him," I say. "He's hurting and he's afraid."

She smiles, sadness in her eyes. "I know that." And then she's gone.

When I close my eyes, I see Riles and Birdie crouched together and pointing at the stars. They're laughing. They don't see me.

The pain wakes me.

"Sorry," Pen says. Celeste is gone, and I hear evening crickets through the open window. Pen is sitting at the foot of my bed; she has undressed my wound and is dabbing at it with some liquid from a glass bottle. She frowns. "I can't tell whether it's infected."

"Where did you run off to earlier?" I ask. My voice sounds far away.

"The hospital to check on Birdie, if you must know. I had a dream last night that she disappeared. I looked everywhere I could think of, and it turned out that she had become queen, and her throne was a thousand paces high, and when I looked up to see her, I was blinded by the sun."

"It sounds like a wonderful dream," I say. "All I've had are nightmares."

"How can you think what I had wasn't a nightmare?" she says. "To dream of someone who is most certainly gone and to be tricked into thinking she's still here."

She dabs at my wound again and I suck air through my teeth.

"Has this been hurting?" she asks.

"Not very much until you started doing that. Could you stop?"

She tears the gauze with her teeth and sets about wrapping my leg. "Thomas told me what he said to you the night I nearly drowned," she says. "He said the reason you told King Ingram about the phosane was because of me. Is that true?"

"I did it for a lot of reasons," I say.

"Thomas is an idiot," she says. "He had no business blaming you for anything I've done."

"You want to go home, Pen. You can't tell me otherwise. And so do I." Even if there's no home left for me to return to.

"I'm still mad at you," she says, pinning down the end

of the gauze. "But I didn't mean what I said about not knowing who you are. I know who you are." She gathers the soiled bandages, and she kisses my forehead before she leaves.

I close my eyes. Riles is waiting for me with a fistful of dirt; the dead are patient and will wait for us to sleep so they can speak to us.

"We have to bury them," he says. The harbor is burning behind him. I want to take him away from it, but he does not have the luxury of waking. He is all out of mornings.

I let him lead me into the smoke of this dream. I keep him company for a while, though I'm frightened. It is the very least I can do for him.

19

After I've followed him through paces of smoky rubble, Riles disappears, and I'm staring at the ceiling light. The crickets outside have turned to the sound of rain. It rains all spring. Birdie told me that.

"She's burning up. I'm going to get Lex," Pen says. I heard her voice calling me as I dreamed.

Basil is sitting over me with a damp towel. "Morgan?"

"Don't get Lex," I croak.

"We have to. He'll know what to do for your fever."

"I don't want him," I say. "I don't want him near me. Get Alice instead."

"I'm here," Alice says, moving through the doorway. "What's going on, love? Not feeling well?"

"Pen says she's been crying out in her sleep," Basil says.

Pen is wringing her hands anxiously.

"I just can't get a proper rest," I say. "Every time I

close my eyes, I relive moments. I see the dead."

Alice brushes her fingers across my forehead.

"That's to be expected," she says, and frowns. "You've been sufficiently traumatized."

I close my eyes, and Birdie is smiling at me an instant before the explosion comes.

"Morgan?" Alice says. I already know what she's going to say. "I think you should let Lex help you. He won't talk to you if you don't want him to. I'll tell him."

"I'd rather die," I say.

"Oh, stop it," Pen says. "Whatever he did couldn't have been as bad as all that."

There's a part of Pen that is still on Internment, where fights and squabbles can last only so long before all is forgiven. I wish I could still hold on to this way of thinking. But my brother has betrayed me in a way I wouldn't have thought possible. He has shown me that we no longer belong to that world we left behind.

Alice pats my cheek. "He'll only be a minute." She leaves the room and returns moments later, Lex in tow. He doesn't utter so much as a word. I stare out the window. The curtains are parted and I can see the rain streaking the glass.

He feels the sides of my neck, along my jaw, and touches my forehead. He's being especially gentle.

He asks Alice to unwrap my leg and describe the wound to him. "Have you been dressing it yourself?" Alice asks me.

I shake my head. "Pen."

"You've done a great job," Alice tells her. "Expert, even."

Pen gives a small smile.

"There aren't any pink lines or sores," Alice says. "But it's a little bit swollen."

"It's better than it was this afternoon," Pen offers.

"Good. That's good."

Alice, under Lex's direction, applies the medication that sizzles and burns, and wraps my leg. "From what you describe, it sounds like it isn't infected," Lex says, talking to her, not to me. "Tell my sister that she needs to stop hobbling about so much. The hospital let her go only because it was overcrowded; that doesn't mean she's better. She needs to sleep as much as she can."

Alice looks at me. "Got that?"

I nod. Lex pats my good ankle. He's still here for me, he's saying, and he knows I'll come around, even if right now I'm tempted to kick him.

Alice leads Lex away. Pen follows after them. I hope she's going to find more of that sleeping aid Nimble gave us last night. From the hallway, I hear Lex asking about her arm, Pen saying it's nothing. They say more to each other, but their voices are too soft for me to understand.

It's just Basil and me. Celeste's bed is empty, though the clock tells me it's well after midnight. Perhaps she and Nim are together somewhere.

"Do you know what I think?" Basil says.

"What?"

"I think you are utterly unbreakable."

"I can't imagine what has given you that impression."

"As long as you're still alive, I'm right," he says.

I laugh. I don't know how in the world he has managed

263

to make me laugh, but he revels in it. I see the triumph in his quirked lip.

Basil.

I look at him now and do not see the boy I'm to marry, but rather the boy who will always belong to me, just as I'll always belong to him. Maybe the decision makers were wrong when they paired us together, because we are not ever going to be like Alice and Lex, or Judas and Daphne. There is a plan for us, but it isn't what anyone thought.

He pulls the covers up to my chin. "You know what I think? I think you're making yourself sick because you feel guilty that you made it out of the explosions when Riles and Birdie didn't."

Sounds about right.

"You're loved, Morgan," he says. "A lot of people would be broken if you hadn't come back from that night. I would be broken."

"A lot of people are broken because a lot of people are gone," I say. I want to say more, but he puts his finger to my lips.

"You're here," he says. "And you still have kingdoms to conquer and wonders to see."

I smooth my hands over his collar. "I've never fancied you a poet," I say.

He taps his knuckle against my cheek. "Get some sleep," he says.

"You'll be nearby?" I ask.

"Always," he says.

20

Rain turns to sun turns to rain. I barely get out of bed for days. Loath as I am to admit it, Lex was right. My leg has begun to heal now that I'm resting. I'm able to walk without the crutches as long as I move slowly.

In tandem with a clap of thunder, Pen sets the transistor radio on my night table and plugs it in. She sits cross-legged on my bed and looks at me as the voice comes through the static.

"—society inhabiting the floating island has offered their support. The king is to send representatives sometime this week. The details of the floating island's support have yet to be decided. More details as they come."

The announcer's voice turns into the burst of trumpet music that is the kingdom's anthem. Pen turns the radio off.

"I think Internment is officially at war," she says.

"Has there been any mention of us?" I ask.

"No," Pen says. "I'm a little surprised they aren't using us as proof that Internment is a real city. I thought they'd be making us sing and dance about now."

"People wouldn't buy that," Nimble says from the doorframe. "You know how many people have donned a phony accent and pretended to be from the floating island or from outer space? Thousands. King Ingram would look like some kind of weirdo if he tried to pass you guys off as proof."

"What's to happen to us, then?" Pen says.

"Anyone's guess," Nimble says. "I don't think my father even knows. That is, if it's even been decided. The point of this broadcast was just to tease the kingdom enough to have faith that our fine king will ride in on a white horse and save us."

His arm is out of its sling, and all that remains of his injury is some gauze around his wrist. I wonder how long I've been in bed.

"Isn't it dangerous to announce that he's going to Internment?" Pen says. "Won't King Erasmus hear the broadcast?"

"He will," Nimble says. "But Internment is in Havalais's airspace. There's nothing King Erasmus can do, unless he means to invade our territory completely, and his kingdom doesn't have the resources to do that. Right about now he's probably dismissing this as lunacy and hoping that's all it is." He shifts his weight. I don't think he came here to discuss politics. It must be awful and lonely for him, trying to hold his family together without his sister.

"You can come in, you know," I say.

He sits on the end of Celeste's perfectly made bed. "Thanks."

"Are you all right?" Pen asks.

"Yes— I— Maybe." He stares at his bandaged wrist. The last of his outward scars are fleeting. "They were allowing visitors at the hospital today. I got to see her."

"Is there any change?" Pen asks.

"A little, maybe. Some of the burns seem to be healing, and they've cleaned her up a bit. It's a wonder how much that can do. She looks more like herself. But that's all. She hasn't come out of it."

He looks so exhausted.

"She's going to get better," Pen says. It's a risky promise. "She's got a lot of fight. After the first explosion, Morgan and I tried to hold her back, and she overpowered us both." I envy Pen's confidence. I thought that looking at Birdie in that hospital bed was like looking at death itself.

"Has your father been to see her?" I ask.

He shakes his head. "I don't know. It's probably best if he doesn't. It'll only make him angry."

"Angry?" Pen says. "He should be angry. We're all angry. Look at what's happening to your kingdom, and what's about to happen to mine."

"I didn't mean that he'd be angry about that," Nimble says. "It's just, she reminds him so much of . . ." He struggles and can't say the word, but I understand.

"That woman I saw in the trees at the cemetery is your mother," I say, "isn't she?"

"Not so much these days," he says. "But yes. And our

father's great fear was that Birdie would leave the way that our mother left. I don't know what it would do to him if he saw Birdie now. He might do something desperate—take her to a fancy clinic overseas, try some radical surgery that'd sooner kill her than cure her. He wouldn't be able to accept that she's gone."

"She isn't gone," Pen says.

"You don't have to—"

"No," Pen says. "Listen to me. I wouldn't tell you that she's going to pull through if I didn't believe it. And you have to believe it, too, because she can surely feel all this negativity right now, and she needs for us to have faith in her."

Nimble looks at her. "You really believe that, don't you?"

"I really do. And right now, it doesn't matter to her that there's a war going on. She doesn't care about how high the jets can fly, or what's going to happen to the magical floating island. She can't be troubled with where her mother is, or how her father feels about it. All that she can do is try to survive. She needs you to go in and talk to her, even if she doesn't always hear all the words you say. She needs us to believe in her."

She stares Nimble down the same way she stared the ocean down before and after it tried to drown her. Unafraid. There she is, the Pen I thought I'd lost to this place. I've missed her desperately.

Nimble is looking at her, and he surprises me with a smile.

"I'm glad we saved your life, kid," he says.

"I'm not all evil," Pen says. "No matter what the princess tells you."

Nim gives a weak smile, but it's short-lived. "Did Birdie . . . Did she say anything before she ran off?"

Pen and I hesitate. Because we don't want to relive our failure to keep her safe. Because the memory of her running beyond our reach is too much to stand.

"Please," Nimble says. "I want to know. I have to know."

"She called out to you just before the second explosion," I blurt. "Pen told her that no one was there, but she was certain she saw you. She said something was wrong with Riles."

"We couldn't stop her," Pen says. "I'm sorry."

"She did see us then," Nimble says. "I was trying to carry Riles to the harbor. After the first explosion, I knew he was hurt, but I didn't know how bad it was. I just knew we had to get away from there."

I don't want to hear this, but I let him speak. We may be the only ones who will listen. His sisters are too small, his father too unreachable. Celeste has been pleading for him to speak, but he loves her, and he can't put these ugly images in her head.

"There was blood coming—coming out of his stomach, and the harbor was in sight, but I stopped running when I realized he wasn't crying out anymore. People were pushing around me, and there was life and death everywhere. And I knew that Riles was gone. There wasn't even a proper moment to react. Another explosion came, and I thought—I hoped—that it would just be the end of the world. It felt like it was.

"That's the illusion of war," he says. "You think the world is over when your city comes down. But then you realize that you're just one city on a planet the size of ten million cities."

He's the only living son of a corrupt politician, but he is soft-spoken and kind. And I see what Celeste, the only daughter of a broken king, loves him for; they both want peace in their worlds. It breaks every rule, but they're meant to be together.

"I found Birdie a few yards away. I was afraid to turn her over. I thought for sure she was gone. But there was a little bit left in her, wasn't there? Just enough."

"I thought my brother was going to die once," I say. "I don't know if he held on because he wanted to, or because the doctors made him. At the time, I thought it was hopeless. But he got better. He's still here to drive me absolutely mad. Birdie can get better, too."

"Was there an accident?" Nim asks.

"You could say that."

"Did it ever go back to the way it was before?" he says.

"Well, no," I say. "But that didn't matter. When someone you care about is suffering, you don't care if the whole world burns down around them, or they're covered in scars, or blind. You just want them back. And you'll accept whatever conditions come along with it."

I think of Birdie's smile in the glow of a streetlamp the night we came out of the brass club; the streetlamp and the brass club are gone, but still I hope Birdie can be that girl when she comes back. If she comes back.

"You seem young to speak with such certainty," Nimble says.

I don't point out that he's only two years older than me. If I'm too young to have such experience with grief, so is he.

The trilling of a bell downstairs makes me jump. I've heard it a few times, but I cannot get used to there being a call box in a house.

Nimble looks worriedly at the door. His father's voice answers. I can't make out any of the words; Pen and Nimble are straining to hear him too. Minutes pass before there's the click of the receiver.

"How often are there calls?" Pen asks.

"Before the tourism season? Almost never." All the color has drained from Nimble's face. It could have been about his sister, or the war, or anything at all, but chances are that it wasn't anything good.

We don't talk. And, several minutes later, when footsteps start climbing toward us, I can hear my heart pounding.

Celeste stands in the doorway, her hands folded in front of her. She takes one look at the three of us, and breaks into tears.

Nim runs to her. "What is it?" he says. "What's happened?"

"It's now," she says. "I'm leaving tonight."

"Leaving?" Pen stands. "As in, going home?"

Celeste rubs at her eyes, nods. "King Ingram is sending his men around to collect me, and we're going straight to his jet."

"I'm confused," Pen says. "What are you crying about? It's what you wanted, isn't it?"

"Everything is going wrong," Celeste says. "King Ingram has been planning to use me as a bargaining chip this whole time. My father will do anything King Ingram says as long as I'm his hostage."

"You aren't a hostage," Nim says, but I can hear in his voice that he knows she's right.

Celeste looks at him. "I don't know when I'll be back. I don't know *if* I'll be back."

"Of course you'll be back," I say. "King Ingram wants an alliance between our kingdoms. There will be a lot of traveling back and forth." There has to be. I still have to get Pen home, and I still have to find my father.

But if Celeste hears me, she doesn't acknowledge it. "I don't even know if King Ingram will help my mother," she says miserably. "If my mother is still alive."

Nim holds her shoulders, but he has no words of comfort. He has already lost too much, and he's about to lose her, too. He rests his chin on the top of her head, amid her hair that's braided into a crown; she wraps her arms around him and whispers through her sobs, something about a last-resort plan. He shushes her, sways with her.

"Why wouldn't her mother be alive?" Pen asks me. I take her wrist and pull her from the room.

"We should leave them alone," I say.

"So, this is it?" Pen says, as we walk down the stairs. "She goes home and we all get left behind?"

"She's being used as a bargaining tool," I say. "It isn't what she wanted, and it isn't something we should envy."

Pen glances sideways at me. "I suspect we'll be used as

well," she says. "Once it's proven that King Furlow really exists and is going to help Havalais in the war effort, we'll be a commodity." She sweeps her arms out theatrically. "The residents of the magical floating island. Get a glimpse for a penny, snap an image for a nickel."

"Maybe not," I say.

"Maybe not," she mimics. "Oh, Morgan. Do you never tire of this delusional optimism about your poor decision making?"

"Don't take this out on her," Judas says. I have no idea how long he's been standing at the bottom of the stairs listening to us. "If I recall, you've done your share of things to contribute to this mess. The reason you're here at all is because you attempted to murder Prince Azure with a rock."

"I wasn't trying to kill the prince," Pen says.

It's a weak argument and Judas ignores it. "You're the one who figured it out about the phosane and the glasslands to begin with. So you must be smart enough to see that if you hadn't nearly gotten yourself killed, Morgan probably would have kept your secret. But you were too intoxicated out of your mind to see what was happening to yourself, much less what was happening to the rest of us."

"Judas, that's enough," I say.

"She dove in after you, you know," Judas tells Pen. "She saved your life. There aren't a whole lot of people in either world who would do that. If words must come out of your mouth at all, they should be 'Thank you.'"

Pen's arms are folded, and she can't seem to raise her eyes, and she mutters, "You weren't even there," before she hurries off in the direction of the kitchen, hitting his shoulder with hers as she goes.

"Judas," I hiss. I try to go after Pen, but he grabs my arm.

"I've been wanting to talk to you," he says. The anger in his voice is lessening now that we're alone.

I pull myself out of his grip. "So talk."

He glances into the lobby, where Marjorie and Annette are snuggled against Alice, who is reading aloud from a storybook.

"Can we go someplace?" he says. "Outside?"

"That depends on whether you're going to snap at me, too."

"Not at you. I don't know what it is about your friend," he says. "She irks me."

"We're all caught in trying times," I say.

"I know," he says. He holds the door open for me, and the doorway frames a painting of a day that is rain-dampened but bright with greens and whites, and everywhere flowers sneaking up from the dirt. It's irresistible. I follow Judas away from the house, to a tree whose trunk is wrapped in vines and leaves.

I fold my legs in the grass. It's wet but I don't mind. Judas fidgets before he sits next to me.

"When Amy told me what you'd done, I thought you'd lost your mind," he says. "Trying to go back to Internment after all that city has put you through—put all of us through. I was all set to write you off as irrational."

He wouldn't be the first, I'm sure.

"But I saw what was happening to your friend Pen,

and how it affected you. And I didn't know what exactly the princess hoped to gain from her trip here, but I suspected that you were trying to help her, too."

I run my fingertip over a yellow flower that grows wild among the grass. "If you're going to tell me what a mess I've made of everything, I already know," I say.

"Just let me talk," he says. "I don't give a lot of compliments. This is weird for me."

I look at him. Compliments?

"That night you pushed me into the lake to hide me from the patrolmen, I wondered what your game was. And ever since that night, I've been waiting for you to collect on that favor. But you aren't going to, are you? You just wanted to help me."

I shrug. "They were after you. You were innocent. It was the right thing to do."

"You're the only one who believes I'm innocent," he says. "Besides Amy and the professor, that is."

I fall back against the grass. "Unfortunately for you, nobody takes me seriously," I say.

"I do." He props himself on his elbow. His shadow shields my eyes from the sun.

"Why?" I say. Every nerve stands to attention as I watch him rub his chin and the side of his neck. There's sunlight through his fingers, long shadows are ovals that cling to his knuckles, and I want him to touch me.

"You are a rare spirit," he tells me.

"I'm not anything special," I say. The words float up into the sunlight, where they burn away. Everything burns away, and all I see is him, all angles like a prism held to the light.

"You don't even know what you are," Judas says. The words hum in my ears. He's closer, and I reach for his shoulder. It's jagged with bone, and I've wanted to touch it since the night he pinned me against that tree in the moonlight. Now I'm finally brave enough.

He leans closer, and my eyes close, and he kisses me. My heart is like this world's rain hitting against the window. I can't breathe. I had thought all kisses were like the ones I've shared with Basil, that they started out timid and uncertain. But this one goes through the skin. He's so confident, a different boy from who he was a moment ago.

Yes. Daphne's voice. The words she wrote on paper that led to her death. *My betrothed asked me to marry him, as we lay in the grass . . . Yes.*

Is this the way he used to kiss her?

I pull back. It is all my strength to sit up. A leaf is caught in my hair and it's crinkling against my ear. "Judas, I—"

"I'm sorry," he says, but I don't believe him. His eyes have taken on a sleepy delirious quality, and for all my guilt, it thrills me to think I am the cause.

"You shouldn't have done that," I say. "I don't belong to you. You don't belong to me."

He plucks the leaf from my hair. "We don't belong to anyone, you and I."

The insects are singing in the grass and in my blood. I want to tear away the ground around us like a drawing on a piece of paper. Then we can float away in the sky, leaving behind an empty space that bears our shape. I want to live forever in this little place we've created without rules or consequences. I want him to kiss me again.

But memories of the smoke at the harbor are pervading my senses, and back at the hotel a window has opened on its track, and someone is calling my name.

"Morgan?" In the distance, Celeste is leaning out the bedroom window. "Morgan? Are you out there?" She doesn't see me.

"I have to go," I say. My legs are numb, and I stumble. Judas rights me. "Thank you," I say.

He lets me go. I move for the hotel as fast as I'm able. I feel Judas watching me, and, standing behind him, the ghost of the girl he was meant to love.

Celeste is staring through the open window when I enter the bedroom.

"I'll miss the rain most of all," she says. "And the big creatures—elegors, giramos. I never saw a whale, though, or a mermaid. Fish with human hair. Imagine."

"Though, if it's on a fish, can it be called human?" I say.

"I've been wondering that, but I've never asked Nim. There are many things I haven't asked him."

"You'll be back," I say. "The reason I told you about the phosane was so that you could help us all get home."

"I wanted to talk to you about that." She turns away from the window. "When that jet leaves the ground, I don't know what's to become of me or any of us. But I want you to know that I'll keep my promise. I'll tell my father all you've done to help me, and he needn't know that Pen was the one to hurt Azure. I'm sure he wouldn't have told either, if he's still alive."

"You must be worried for him," I say.

"There's wind between his ears, my brother, but I am rather fond of him." She tries to smile. "Every generation, a prince is born. A prince who will grow to be the king, who will bear the burdens of a city and be the one to speak to the god in the sky, and to hear the god in the sky speak back." Despite her sorrow, there's a flicker of excitement in her eyes. "But that's wrong. This time, it's me. Even if I never wear a crown, and whether I stand in the sky or on the ground, I've always felt that, of my brother and me, I was meant to do something important."

She came here thinking she could unite two kingdoms, and she's leaving as a political tool. Her eyes are sad, but I can see her spirit shining ever through. She's going to give all she has, even if all she has are a few honest words.

"I'll be waiting for you," I say. "And when you come back, we'll ride the ferry and use beads and pearls to lure the mermaids up from the depths. After we've saved our world, of course."

"I'd like that," she says.

"And, Celeste, I have a favor, if I may be so bold."

Her eyes are misting and she dabs at the tears with her fingertips. "Of course."

"My father may still be alive. I don't know if he's your father's prisoner, or if he's in hiding, but if you could just— just tell him that I'm sorry I left him behind. Let him know I'll try to come back for him. I know it may not be in your power to set him free, but if you could tell him I wouldn't have left him behind if I'd known."

She sniffs. "I will. Morgan, I'm so sorry."

I put my arms around her, and she tenses, surprised, before she embraces me. "Look at me," she says miserably, "falling to pieces like this."

"Anyone else would have fallen to pieces long before this," I say. "I've lost my wits about a thousand times since we've touched the ground."

She draws back just enough to look at me. She shakes her head. "You could have been royalty," she says. "You have the steel of a king and the heart of a queen."

I crinkle my nose. She gives a feeble smile. "Really," she says. "I would know."

"Let's hope you're right, then," I say. "I've a feeling I'll need both of those things for what's to come."

"I'll take care of the sky, and you take care of the ground, then," Celeste says. "I'll look for your father, and I'll do my best to convince my father that there's an alliance to be made. But you have to look after Nim while I'm gone, and keep Pen from burning this place down."

I laugh. "I will do what I can," I say.

Celeste puts her forehead to mine. "We haven't seen the last of each other," she says. "You'll see. Something big is going to bring these worlds together."

Dinner is silent. Jack Piper doesn't join us; the door to his study has been closed since Celeste was taken away. I can't be certain that his absence is connected to hers; for as long as Riles's and Gertrude's seats at the table have been empty, he has looked upon his son and daughters with great difficulty. His children all bear a strong resemblance to one another, as though they can sit around the fireplace and exchange expressions the way they trade trinkets and cards. A brother's quirked brow, a sister's toothy grin. The youngest girls know this, and they also know that their resemblance to their dead brother and ailing sister cannot be helped; they duck their heads when their father passes through the room; they do not giggle or welcome him home or ask him their new questions about death. I suspect that this is the only way they know how to love him. With contrition and penitence.

Nim, however, is bolder. He will raise his eyes that have seen explosions, and cross arms that held his dying brother and were stained with his blood, and he will stare at his father as though to say that he can see through him. *This was your doing,* the eyes say. *And you can hide for only so long.*

"I'm not hungry," Annette says.

"It's hotcakes for dinner," Nimble says tiredly. "Your favorite."

"I'm not hungry, either," Marjorie says, following her sister's cue.

Nim rubs his eyebrows. "Okay," he says. "What would you like to do instead?"

"Ride an elegor," Annette says.

"It's dark now," Nimble says. "The elegors are sleeping, and the rentals are closed."

"I want to ride it to the hospital," she says. "I want to see Birdie."

"She's sleeping," Nimble says. "Remember? We talked about this."

"I think you're lying," Annette says, her voice rising. "I think she's dead and you don't want to tell me."

If I hadn't heard it myself, I wouldn't think a little girl in ringlets was capable of such a dark thought. But she is frustrated with Nimble, because he is the only one left to provide her with any answers, and she knows that the answers are incomplete. He and Birdie were a team, caring for the younger ones, shielding them from their world's horrors, making sure they were happy and healthy and dressed in time for breakfast. Birdie's presence was gentle and quiet, but her absence is violent. The pristine portrait the younger children knew has crumbled to dust, and now they see what was hiding behind it all along.

"That isn't true," Marjorie says. "She isn't dead. Right, Nim?"

"No," he says. "I've told you the truth. She's asleep. But it isn't a normal sleep where she'll wake up in the morning. She's having a very long dream."

Marjorie has started to cry. "I want to have a long dream, too," she says.

"No you don't," Annette says. "You won't wake up." She sweeps her arm across the table, knocking her plate to the ground. Nimble closes his eyes to the sound of it shattering. She runs off, and he doesn't try to stop her.

Marjorie whimpers. Her face is red. She throws her plate

on the ground, too, though it seems an act more of solidarity than of anger. Annette is younger, but she's the leader of their little duo. "I'm sorry," Marjorie says. "Nim, I'm sorry." She climbs onto his lap and worms her way into his arms.

His eyes are red and weary. "It's all right," he tells her. She's wrapped around him like a vise, and she's still clinging to him when he pushes himself from the table. "I think it's time for you and Annie to go to bed," he tells her. "And you'll have normal dreams, and things will look much better in the morning."

We all watch him carry her from the room. Judas looks at me, and my cheeks are burning. Whether it's guilt or desire, I can't be certain; I only know I want to be rid of it. I push myself away from the table, and I kneel down to pick up the shards.

"Don't," Basil says, kneeling beside me and taking my wrists. "You'll cut yourself."

"I'll get a dustpan," Alice says.

I stare at the porcelain on the floor. This is what it's all come to. Pieces. Even a child can see that.

21

That night, I'm kept awake by the ticking of the clock on the night table. It's the sound of time moving away from me, drifting up into the sky in ribbons of jet fumes. Celeste's bed is empty. Pen tosses and turns. Floorboards creak. The youngest Pipers have taken to wandering the house at night. I think they're afraid that they won't wake up from their dreams. They whisper and play with their toys by lantern light. Tin biplanes and helmets like the ones that fuel this war. The other morning I found Annette asleep in the claw-foot tub, hugging Birdie's kaleidoscope. She said she had spent the night hunting pirates. "More gold than you've ever seen in your life," she told me, "but the money's all bloody."

Everyone in the hotel has fallen into a kind of madness. There is nothing to do but wait and be restless. Wait for news of bombs or jets or alliances. Jack Piper, unwilling maestro of this wayward order, makes himself scarce. I've begun to dread any evidence of his presence; the rustle of papers behind a closed door, the clearing of a throat, or hard shoes against the floorboards. Something awful happens whenever he's around. Someone goes away or is dropped into a hole in the ground.

He has also taken away the transistor radio that the cooks kept in the kitchen. We aren't allowed to go far from the hotel. The ferry and elegor rentals have stopped. The city has finally gone to sleep, and we aren't made to know anything about what's happening, or what's going to happen.

The clock is always ticking, louder than ever.

Pen sits up with a gasp. "Morgan—" Still in her dream she reaches for me, but then she sees where she is and collapses back against the pillow.

"Bad dream?" I say.

"I heard a bomb falling," she says. "I didn't want you to get killed." She yawns. "I'm losing my mind. I still hear it."

I sit up. "I think I hear something, too," I say, but she has fallen back to sleep, if she was ever awake at all.

I go to the bedroom window, but there's nothing but a placid spring night. The sound is coming from the other side of the building.

Pen doesn't stir as I walk past her bed and turn the doorknob. She's able to recover more quickly from her nightmares about the harbor.

The sound is louder once I've descended the stairs. Nothing at all like the bombs at the harbor, but more of an engine's rumbling.

I step outside, crossing my arms against the chilly night

air, and I make it around the corner of the hotel just in time to see Nimble back his car into the fire altar. The tires dig into the earth and there's a grating sound as the back of the car is forced onto the stone platform.

Even from where I'm standing, I can smell the fuel, as though the car has been coated in it. Nimble climbs out of the driver's side, and a moment before he does it, I realize what's happening. He draws a match from the breast pocket of his pin-striped pajamas and strikes it, and in an instant the car is burning.

He stands as close as he dares, arms folded.

Head bowed, his lips move to form what can only be a prayer of offering.

"Oh, Nim," I whisper, even though I'm too far for him to hear me. He loved that car. This hotel is his floating city, his father his oppressive king. That car was his only freedom in this world.

I approach slowly, in the tracks the tires burnt into the grass. My eyes are watering from the stench of the rubber and the smoke.

When he's finished with his prayer, he turns toward me.

"When Birds and I were kids, we used to look up at the floating island and hold our breath when a big cloud passed under it," he says. "It was a game we had. She could always hold her breath for longer than I could. I feel like that's what she's doing now, holding her breath until a dark cloud has passed over us."

Something pops in the flames and I flinch, but he is as stoic as the altar under all that fire.

"Do you think what Pen said is true? About my prayers being able to reach my sister."

Thick black smoke disappears into the darkness of night, blotting out patches of stars. Somewhere up there, higher than his world and mine, is the place where all things go when they have stopped breathing. It is a place my brother visited, and perhaps Birdie has seen it too. Up where it's quiet and calm, and it takes something greater than voices to reach them.

"I do," I say.

It really was an exquisite machine. The metal glistens still.

The roof collapses in on itself, and the sound is absorbed by the roaring fire. It is violent and ugly and beautiful. Nothing at all like the wreckage at the harbor.

Nim's eyes are steely and filled anew with prayers. There is no choice for him but to believe. He has nothing left to give in offering.

A child's shriek awakens me in the morning.

Pen groans and pulls the blankets over her head as we hear what must be Annette and Marjorie running down the stairs.

"Your car!" Annette says. "Father is going to blow a gasket."

Nim shushes them, and the voices are too faint to hear after that.

"What about his car?" Pen asks.

"He set it on fire last night."

She pushes the blankets away from her face. "What?"

"On the fire altar, in offering so that Birdie would get better," I say. "He took your advice."

She stares at the ceiling, blinking. "Wow," she says. After a long moment she turns to face me. "I didn't think he would take what I said to heart like that."

"There are people who would give anything to have faith like yours," I say. "It's hard to come by."

"You're not going to get saccharine on me, are you?" She crinkles her nose. "Just because we've shared a few near-death experiences and personal tragedies."

I watch her sit on the edge of the bed and carefully undo her plaits. The curls fall perfectly into place. "I should probably get out of here early," she says. "The last thing I need is Jack Piper hearing I'm the reason his son set fire to his car. He'll probably set fire to me."

I sit up. "Go where?" I ask.

She shrugs out of her nightgown and studies the dresses in the closet before selecting one that's black with large polka dots. It's dreary on the hanger, but it becomes something elegant once Pen has wriggled into it. She looks so much more grown-up now that we've been here awhile, and I wonder if I do too.

"Pen? Where are you going?"

She looks over her shoulder at me. "Morgan, I adore you. Stop smothering me."

I cannot keep trying to follow her around this world, checking her breath for tonic, looking for her in alleyways. We aren't the children we were back home. I can't be her guardian, only her friend.

"Promise I won't find you floating facedown in any large bodies of water," I say.

She shoulders the window open. She means to avoid everyone with her exit, then. "If I were to do anything extremely foolish, you wouldn't find me at all."

And then she's gone.

I get dressed and tread carefully through the house. I don't know what sort of mood Jack Piper will be in once he's seen what happened to his son's car. He seems the sort of man to value possessions.

If fire altars were a part of Internment's culture, and if I'd owned something as extravagant as a car, I'd have done the same thing to save Lex when he needed it. And my parents would have joined in, because life is always worth more than things. Because their children were everything to them.

Fighting tears, I stand at the top of the staircase. I spent my life fascinated by the ground, but now that I'm here, I would give anything to undo what I've seen: a man who has five children and values none of them. Endless land destroyed by bombs.

I don't belong here, and this place has changed me, made me forget pieces of who I was before I left home.

That's why, rather than going downstairs toward the sound of breakfast chatter, I head for my brother's door.

"Alice?" he says as I turn the knob.

"It's me." He always used to know when it was me.

"Oh," he says. He's sitting on the floor by the bed,

tracing his fingers over the paper from his transcriber. "She's supposed to bring me breakfast."

"Why don't you come downstairs and get it yourself?" I ask. I try not to sound angry, but I hate when he carries on like an invalid.

"Because I want nothing to do with the Pipers," he says. "Sort of the way you want nothing to do with me."

"If you're going to feel sorry for yourself, I'm leaving," I say.

His dramatic huff is his apology. "Please, come in. Stay. Talk to me." His tone is caustic, but I believe he's being sincere, and I sit on the floor across from him.

"I'm running low on transcriber paper," he says, rustling the page in his hands.

"Is the story almost through?" I ask.

He smirks. "I don't think this one is meant to have an end," he says.

For a moment, it's as though we're in his office above my bedroom, and everything between us is as it was before.

His head is down. He says, "I hear the princess has gone back to Internment."

"Yes," I say.

He pauses. "Morgan, I need for you to understand why I didn't tell you about Dad."

"I hate to admit that I do understand," I say. "But that doesn't make it right. You wouldn't have left Alice behind, left me behind. Why Dad?"

"It was what he wanted," Lex says. "He didn't risk everything just to have his children die trying to rescue him."

I squeeze my eyes shut against the tears that come. I focus on my breathing so he won't know that I'm starting to cry. "Maybe that's what he wanted, but what I want is to find him," I say. "I don't know if I'll ever go home again, but if there's an opportunity, I'll take it."

He runs his fingers over the pages of his unfinished story. "Remember your promise to me, then. You said you'd always come back."

I pat his knee. "I remember."

Alice brings him a breakfast tray, and I leave to find Basil, who is surely wondering where I've been all morning.

We meet at the bottom of the stairs, and before he can say a word, I take his hands. "Let's go outside," I say. "I much like the smell of the air on days like this."

Contrary to the claustrophobic feeling this hotel has taken on, the spring air is sweet. Almost like home, but more fragrant.

We walk the perimeter of the hotel, and when we reach Nim's ruined car, Basil winces.

"An offering," I say. "For Birdie."

He stops walking, studying the charred remains. It looks like one of Pen's sketches if she were to use a crude piece of pen stone on a dirty piece of paper.

Basil's mouth twists like he's trying not to frown. "I really hope it works," he says. And because I've known him all my life, I know that he's staring at Nim's offering and he's thinking of his own family, up in the floating city that's a faded scar in this blue sky.

"There might still be a way for us to get back home,"

I say. "Celeste said she had a plan. Granted, her plans are always terrible, but it's all any of us have got right now."

"I'm not sure that would be for the best," he says.

"I'm still going to try," I say.

"I know you are." He starts walking, and I find myself sprinting to keep pace. "Morgan, I've had plenty of time to think down here. I've seen what Internment does to its people—how it nearly killed you—and I've seen what this world does."

"More of the same, isn't it?" I say.

"Yes," he says. "And even if a ladder were to appear one morning between this world and Internment, I would be at a loss for which world to choose."

"The climb would kill you first," I say, trying to make a joke. It makes me nervous to see this side of him. So serious. He's starting to get angry in a most uncharacteristic way.

"I don't know which world to choose," he repeats, "but I see no sense in trying to stop you from returning home if you can. I wouldn't be able to anyway. I was never able to tell you what to do." He slows his pace and glances at me. "Not that it's a bad thing. It's who you are. I very much like who you are."

"I like who you are, too," I say uncertainly. Where is he going with this?

He shields his eyes and looks skyward for a moment, and then back at me.

"Internment's rules never seemed to have suited you," he says. "And I've come to realize that it's unfair for me to hold you to our betrothal. I'm not going to invent any rules forcing you to love me if you don't."

I grab his arm to stop him from walking. He staggers and then faces me.

"It isn't that I don't love you," I say firmly. "Don't think that. That was never the truth. It's just that, all my life, I've watched Alice and Lex, and my parents, and even Pen and Thomas sometimes. And I've thought—what's wrong with me? Why aren't I brave enough to say 'I love you' when it's so easy for everyone around us?

"But I see now that we can't have what other people have. I don't want us to. I've grown up feeling my own way for you, and it's just something that's in me, and I've always known it, like the way I love a song I hear for the first time, even before I know all the words, the way I love my favorite color, and the way that the train would speed past my bedroom when it was very quiet and I'd feel it in my stomach rushing through me. I love you in a way that I've never felt needed to be said."

"You've just said it now," Basil says.

"I suppose I have." I look at my shoes and then at him. "So there it is."

He touches my cheek, and I lean against his palm. I feel the cool glass of his betrothal band against my warm skin.

I can't imagine marrying somebody else. Who else could know me the way that he does? There are infinite boys down here in this world, boys who aren't promised to anyone else. But none of them have grown up beside me. None of them know me the way that Basil and I know each other. Perhaps none of them are for me at all. Perhaps I'm meant to be alone.

"I suppose this isn't how you imagined it would be when I told you I love you for the first time," I say.

"I've never known what to expect with you," he says, and smirks. "So in a lot of ways, it's exactly what I imagined."

I think he's going to kiss me, but instead he moves his hand from my face.

"You can call what we have a betrothal, or not," Basil says. "But I'll still be here."

I let out a little laugh. "Yes, well, we're both stuck down here, aren't we? But the same goes for me. I'm still here when you need me." I do want that much. Need that much.

"And it suits me to keep my betrothal band," I say. "It doesn't have to mean what Internment's rules meant for it to mean, but that doesn't make it worthless. I just need—I need time."

"Time," Basil says, musing. He looks out to that vast expanse beyond the hotel. "This world goes on forever until it circles back to where we're standing; it should seem that time is infinite here, but I don't know that we'll have much of it. I don't know what's in store for us at all."

He looks back to me. "Just—whatever comes, promise you won't do anything to get yourself killed."

"Certainly going to try not to," I say.

I don't know what's to come, but I do know that he will give me all the time he has. He would give me until the end of the world if I'd take it. I want to give him something just as important in return. I want to bring him back to his family. I want him to be happy, whether or not it's with me.

We spend the rest of the afternoon at each other's side, admiring the strange bright flowers and trying to skip stones in the ocean and squinting to see our home up in the sky. But something has changed between us.

At dinner, Annette wears a collander as a helmet and pretends her utensils are controls in a jet. Her father isn't there to scold her. She likes to challenge this chaos that has ensued in her family, though it really seems to frighten her at the same time.

Pen doesn't return. Thomas has spent the day searching for her, walking to town and back. I know he blames me, though my guess as to her whereabouts is as good as his. My worry for her increases every time she runs off by herself; on Internment there were only so many places one could go, but here it would be so easy to get lost forever. I don't know how the people down here don't live their lives in fear of it.

After dinner I distract myself by reading the heavy black book on Pen's nightstand. I've landed on a story about the people of the ground naming their stars after their heroes. These are the same stars that shine over Internment, but with different stories behind them.

The love I have for my home hasn't diminished but has instead hidden itself in things like this story, to make me remember in a new and more painful way each time. Even the stars on the ground cannot comfort me.

I flip through the thin pages for a new story. A scrap of

paper flutters away, and when I catch it, there is another reminder of home in my fingers. It's a piece of request paper, its texture not like any of the paper I've seen on the ground. It is meant to be set on fire and to fly up into the sky, bearing the one thing we get to ask of the god in the sky each year. Pen must have been carrying hers when we fell from the sky.

I don't mean to read it. I mean to tuck it back into the page it was marking. But her drawing catches my eye, and my admiration turns fast to something that gives me chills.

Footsteps come to a stop in the doorway, and I look up.

Pen sees the paper in my hand, and all the light leaves her face. She looks from it to me.

"So there's to be no privacy in this world, then," she says.

"What is this?" I ask.

It isn't a traditionally written request, but Pen has never taken to paper in a traditional way. She has written the word "die" in delicate slantscript. And all around that she has drawn flames and bones and bottles. The bottles and the plumes of smoke all contain the same word in different sizes and shades of black: die, die, die. There is a tiny city in the background, and the buildings are all made of the same word: die, die, die.

"May I have that back, please?" She holds out her hand. A hand that has scaled trees with me, and crawled into the cavern with me, and handed me that first bottle of tonic meaning to help me cope with my worries. Her hand is small and pretty and soft, and I can't bear to give it such an ugly piece of paper.

When I do nothing, she stomps forward and reaches for it, but I back away. "Pen. Tell me who this is for."

I hold the page over my head to keep it away from her, but she's exactly my height and when I refuse to free the paper from my fist, she forces me to the ground. Her knees straddle my hips and the fall has knocked the air from my lungs, but something keeps me from unclenching my fingers even as she pries at them.

"Morgan!" Her voice is desperate. "You can't have this. I've given you sixteen years of secrets. This one belongs to me."

Instinct forces me to curl up my knees and kick at her until she's off me. I try to stand, but she digs her nails into my wrist. Her face is red and there is something in her eyes that makes her all at once a stranger.

"Let me go," I say.

"You can't have that," she cries.

"Tell me what it means."

I manage to yank my arm from her grasp, and the force of her release sends me backward into the night table, taking down the transistor radio. She comes at me again, but I'm able to get to my feet. There is a throbbing pain between my shoulder blades.

"Was it Thomas?" I say. "Has he hurt you?"

"Of course not."

"Someone did." I back against the door. "And we're not leaving this room until you've told me who."

She doesn't come after me. She sits down on the floor where I've left her, and her breaths come, shallow and hard. I think she may faint.

"Pen."

"I needn't answer," she says. She's looking at the ground, panting. She waves her arm at the paper. "You have it all right there, don't you? You're a clever enough girl."

I smooth the paper in my hand. The sweat from my palm has done little to smudge it—request paper is especially resilient. I let myself travel into Pen's brain, along the paths of lines she drew in secret. The flames and the bottles all point to the tiny city made of words. And now that I am really looking, I see that the city is familiar. It's a city within a city. The glasslands, of which Pen has a perfect view from her bedroom window.

I remember the coloring she did of the glasslands also, and the way she crumpled it up and stuffed it into the recycling tube.

She's staring at me when I take my eyes from the paper. She doesn't make a move for me.

"I have made only one request for as long as I can remember," she says. "And it has never been fulfilled."

She grimaces, recovers.

"My father brought me there, when I was little," she says. "He said I was a clever girl with a clever mind, and I should see how things go."

"You never told me he took you there." It's exactly the sort of thing she would have wanted to tell me; most of Internment will never get to see the inside of the glasslands.

I can't imagine why she would hate the glasslands so much. Why she would hate her father so much. She has never uttered an unkind word about him. Or any words at all, really.

"Oh, Morgan, don't be stupid." She staggers to her feet and rubs at her arm, which must have been hurt in our struggle. "A horrible thing happened that day. You wouldn't have understood. You were only a little girl."

Shame. That's the word that comes to me when I look at her. That's what's so strange about her face. She isn't angry or about to faint. She's ashamed.

"We were both little girls then," I say cautiously. "Anything you could have understood, I could have understood."

"But I didn't understand," she whispers.

My heart is in my throat. The thought I'm trying not to have cannot be right. I don't mean to say it aloud, to make it real, but it tumbles out. "Your father has been hurting you. And it started the day he took you to the glasslands."

She looks sharply at me. "You aren't in a position to talk about normal families yourself, though, are you?"

"I am waiting for you to tell me I'm wrong."

She stares at the paper in my hand, and I stare at it, too. It's a tiny world in which she has been trapped and from which I've been unable to save her.

Pen. What has he done to her? There are never any bruises. I grew up in the apartment just upstairs and never suspected a thing.

The knife under her pillow. The way she spurns Thomas's advances. All the expensive gifts from her father that she barely acknowledges. Drowning herself in tonic.

I feel sick. "Tell me what he did to you," I say, although it's a feeble request, and one she won't grant me. Whatever it was, her mother, drowned in her bottle, couldn't stop it. All Pen had to turn to was a piece of request paper.

"I never knew, Pen. You never seemed at all afraid of him."

"I was not afraid of him," she says. "I was afraid of being declared irrational. You'll understand I wasn't in a hurry to have my reputation discredited and be fitted with an anklet so that I could never leave home until I was old enough to be married off to Thomas."

She has pointed out one of our world's most dangerous flaws—how it treats those who argue or question or fight. Yet she would defend Internment until her death. She loves our city the way Alice loves the child she was forced to bleed away, and the way the prince would love the freedom to find his prince, and all the other things that label us as broken.

Her expression has gone sour as she looks at the paper. I have never seen such hatred in her eyes. "Keep that if it means so much to you, then," she says. "Perhaps it will be a cozy reminder of home."

She pushes me away from the door. I stagger.

"Pen, please," I say.

She leaves me there. The Pen I've known all my life has hurried from the room, descended the stairs, and slammed a door. A stranger is left staring back at me on the page.

22

The stars are the only things the sky cannot devour. I've seen the way that even my floating city can disappear into the murky whiteness of a cloudy day and be a hostage there all winter. I've seen birds fly up into the blue until there's nothing left of them. And now the sky has swallowed a jet that carries Internment's only princess, and with her all our chances of going home.

Yet the stars remain. I wonder if they are the true gods. Either way I don't ask anything of them. Pen has shown me that a lifetime of devotion does not mean a request will be acknowledged, much less answered. It wasn't a god's duty to protect her. I was the one who should have seen.

I try to imagine what terrible things she's endured, and she disappears into something less than dust in my imagination. I suppose that's what she'd want, to be burnt up like the request she never got to set on fire.

The door creaks open, letting in just a moment of light before it's closed again. Then my mattress moves with the weight of her climbing in behind me.

She wraps her arm around me and rests her forehead against the back of my neck.

Her skin is chilly from the night air. I don't know where she's been all evening. Perhaps something about her is supposed to have changed, but she seems the same to me.

"I'm quite fed up with words tonight," she says.

There are many things I would like to say to her, and so very many questions I'd like to ask, but I don't know which are the right ones, if any of them are. So if she would like silence, for tonight, I will give her that, because she has been my solace when I've needed it.

I move my fingers between hers, and she squeezes my hand.

All my unanswered questions are in the smoke and bottles she drew, begging to be burnt away.

23

I have envied my brother all my life.

As a child I followed him everywhere he'd let me, and I would hold his thick textbooks open in my lap in the evenings, quizzing him for his exams just so that he would speak to me in that distracted, madman's way of his. Even then, I felt that he had some sort of rare intelligence that could not be taught, and that if he had been any boy born of any other world, he would still have that same immovable wisdom.

After the edge wounded him, I wondered if that part of him was gone forever. His eyesight was gone, and his vivacity. I mourned him. But soon Alice brought him that transcriber, and he returned to his furious writing, and I realized that he hadn't changed. Only the view had changed. He had grown exhausted of our tiny world, had explored more than he cared to have seen, and now he was free to retreat into his mind with a luxury of abandon the rest of us would never have.

I have envied him this as well.

Morning light comes in through the window. A season called spring is in the process of thawing the frost from the grass and the bright weeds. This world takes weeks to awaken. Lex spent his life wanting to know what was beyond our world, and now that we're here, he has given up. He prefers fiction, lost as he is in his own mind. He has made peace with his darkness, because it isn't darkness. Not truly. It's only something the rest of us can't appreciate.

But for all my envy, I have overlooked something that he has tried over and over again to make me understand: Lex is Lex, and I am me. I may wonder at his curiosity, but I have a curiosity of my own. And I may try to understand his blindness, but I know that I wouldn't be at home there.

Despite its cruelty, I want to know life.

Lex has had his fill of society, and perhaps one day I can persuade him otherwise, but until then, I haven't had my fill of new things. I suspect I never will.

Pen has shown me this. Our world has hurt her, too, but still she visits new places and draws her maps so that they'll always be with her, inside her somehow.

I lie still so as not to wake her, until noises begin to fill the halls as the Piper children awaken. Annette no longer makes rounds knocking on the doors and calling, "Up and at 'em."

Someone slams the bathroom door, and Pen flinches as she wakes. Then, her mind not granting her so much as an instant of peace, she sighs. "Morning," she says, and pushes herself up.

"How do you feel?" I ask.

"You mentioned a church," she says. "It's got my curiosity, if you'd like to go."

"Would it be open now? After what happened at the harbor?"

"It's nowhere near the harbor," she says. "It's three blocks from the library. And, according to what I've read about them, churches seldom close. Times like these are just when people visit them the most."

"We could go," I say.

She grabs a dress from the closet and moves behind the changing screen. "I'm still cross with you," she says.

"I'm still not sorry," I say.

"Good, then. So long as we're clear."

"Should we invite the boys to come with us?" I ask as I slip into a dress. Back home, it was almost always a given that Basil and Thomas went along with us, and I'd like to cling to that familiar custom, but I'll understand if Pen doesn't want to be around Thomas, with last night's argument still lurking in her mind. He can tell when she's troubled, sometimes even when I can't.

But she says, "Sure. Yes. Though, try not to take it personally if Thomas gives you the cold shoulder. He's been moody lately."

Ever since she nearly drowned, she means. He was perfectly cordial to me most of the time back home, though Lex's jumping put a strain on things. That was the moment when he began to suspect that I was like my brother, that I would one day do something equally daring.

Pen stands with her back to me as she studies her reflection. She draws a deep breath, hesitates. I hope that she is going to say something about last night, or tell me to ask my questions and get it over with. But what she says is, "I saw you a few days ago. With Judas."

It feels suddenly hard to breathe.

"How long has that been going on?" she asks.

"It isn't," I say. "Nothing is going on. It just happened once."

She sits on her bed and looks at me. If this were something that had happened on Internment, perhaps there would be fear in her eyes. Perhaps she would tell me that a kiss with anyone other than Basil is dangerous. But we have spent so many days in this world without reason that she has become almost fearless. She leans back on her arms. "What was it like? Being wanted by one boy when you're promised to another?"

"What a word," I say. "'Wanted.'" But I realize that she's right—that something in his eyes when he looked at me, when he kissed me, even when he plucked the leaf from my hair, was wanting.

"Wrong," I blurt out, trying to rid my mind of the memory. "It felt wrong."

"Morgan," she sighs. "For the first time in your life, you do something dangerous and you regret it even before you've had a chance to enjoy it."

"There's nothing about it to enjoy," I say. "It happened, and if I could take it back, I would."

"You're lying," she says.

"Even if that were true, you're no better about telling lies," I say. "And it would break my heart if Basil did the same thing with another girl."

"Would it, now?" Pen says. I don't like this combative tone of hers.

"Don't," I say. "I'm going downstairs."

She follows me and says nothing, but all through breakfast I feel her smirk whenever Judas makes so much as a sound. She's wrong about him, though. There would be no future with him. Though, right now it's hard to imagine what any of our futures will be like.

After the breakfast dishes have been cleared and the Pipers have left the room, Pen says, "Morgan and I are going to visit the church, if you're interested in coming along."

She isn't looking at Thomas when she says it. She hasn't seemed able to meet his eyes all morning, so she doesn't see the concern on his face.

"Why now?" he asks.

"To admire the historic detailing, Thomas, I don't know. Because it's something to do."

"It seems dreary," he says. "Surely we can think of a more cheerful way to spend an afternoon."

"Cheerful?" Pen says. "The harbor is in ashes, and the only friend Morgan and I have managed to make in this world is dying. Internment is about to be destroyed, and you want cheerful?"

"Pen," I say. My tone is a warning. I don't want Annette or Marjorie to hear her say their sister is dying.

She looks at me with the same ferocity she showed before she lunged at me last night. "I'm going," she says. "You can come along or not."

She pushes her chair from the table and moves for the front door. I go after her, and just as she reaches for the handle, the door is pushed open.

Jack Piper stands at the threshold, as gray as storm clouds. Since the bombings at the harbor, he's become more ghost than human.

"The car will be coming around in ten minutes," he tells us. He only ever appears after he knows breakfast has been cleared, if he appears at all. He doesn't meet anyone's eyes.

"Who are you talking to?" Nim is standing in the doorway now, his sisters at his heels. They are forever following him these days, as though he will also be taken from them.

"I was speaking to our guests," he says. "The king is back and has requested the audience of five residents from Internment."

"Why five?" Annette asks. I suspect she has no interest but that she's grasping an opportunity to speak with her father for the first time in days.

"Because that was his request," he says. "I suspect a higher number would be overwhelming for what he intends. It's no matter which five. Decide among yourselves. Ten minutes." He's gone before the last sentence is even completed.

"I'm going," I say immediately.

"What?" Basil says. He lowers his voice and leans closer to me. "You can't—you don't know what he has planned.

It could be a public execution, for all any of us know."

"I did this," I say. "I'm to blame for telling about the glasslands, and Celeste being gone, and I'm sure that, whatever this is, I'm to blame for it, too. I'm going."

Basil opens his mouth to argue, but Judas says, "I'm in."

"And me," Pen says.

"And me," Basil says. He sees that it's useless to argue with me.

"I'm not letting you go," Thomas tells Pen. "Hasn't this madness gone on long enough?"

"It's just getting started," Nimble says. "Better hurry up and decide. You're down to seven minutes."

"I'll go," Amy says.

"Uh, no," Judas says.

"Why not?"

"I'll go," Thomas sighs. I wonder if he ever curses the decision makers for betrothing him to a girl like Pen, who is always and forever in motion when all he has ever wanted is for both of them to stand still.

By the time the king's driver has arrived, we're all assembled at the front door. Alice fusses with my collar.

"Don't tell Lex," I say. "There's no need to upset him, and I'll be back soon. I'll bet I'm gone an hour, tops."

Furious as I am with him, he is still my brother, and I still worry after him.

"You look so grown-up," Alice says. I think she'd like to say more, but her eyes are brimming and the driver has just honked the horn to summon us. I hug her before I run down the steps.

Nimble watches us from the doorway, and his pitying expression unnerves me. His sisters peek out from either side of him, wide-eyed and silent.

"What's with the dramatics?" Pen mutters. She straightens her skirt as the car begins to move. "We're not walking off to the edge of the ground."

It's the last thing any of us says for the rest of the drive.

I've been in this world for so long that I know its roads. I know, even before we arrive, that we're headed toward the city, and that if we drive far enough, we'll reach the harbor.

But as the city comes into view, it becomes clear that driving to the harbor would be an impossibility. The road ends where heaps of bricks and walls and splintered boards begin. And though there are few clouds today, the city air is murky and dark.

Basil draws a sharp breath, and I realize that I'm clinging to his forearm. He came straight to the hospital after the bombs hit, but he never saw what I saw. What killed Riles and left Birdie broken.

Pen stares out her window for a long moment, and then she sighs, looks at me. "Ready for whatever this is?"

"As I'll ever be," I say.

"Where were you when this happened?" Judas asks.

"I can't see it from here," I say. "Somewhere on the other side of whatever that building was."

"I think that was the brass club," Pen says.

"It can't be."

"It is," she says. "Look; I can see some of the lettering."

But I don't look. I can't stand the sight of this place anymore. I can feel Judas's eyes on me; since our kiss, he has been hovering just outside my airspace, driving my senses insane without uttering a word. I don't want his words. I want him to kiss me again, even here in this awful place, and I hate myself for that.

The door is opened for us, and we file out. There's a bitter smell in the air. Blood and skin and stone have been ground into nondescript piles of ash. I'm breathing in death and spirits.

The king's driver leads us down a pathway that has been carved from the rubble.

"Is anyone else hearing voices?" Pen asks.

I had thought the distant mumbling was my imagination or an apparition, but Thomas says, "I hear them, too."

"Is that—" Basil shields his eyes against a ray of sun that has found its way into this mess. "Is that a stage?"

My dread is mirrored on Pen's face when she looks at me. Her prediction has come true. Even before we make our way up the rickety steps to a makeshift stage assembled from fallen buildings, we know what this is.

I step over a trail of wires at the top of the stage. A crowd has assembled before us, and suddenly they are silent.

The king stands where the wires meet a sort of copper horn, much like the one he used to speak with King Furlow. One of his men steps forward to adjust the wires, and a horrible screeching comes from the horn before the king is able to speak.

"You've asked for hope," he tells the crowd. His

mechanical voice echoes. "And it stands before you now. Here is proof that there is a city atop the magical floating island."

He does not say the city's name, nor does he bother to introduce us. Instead he goes on about an alliance with the floating city's king—something the kingdom of Dastor can never provide its people. How very lucky they are to be a part of something so spectacular, he says. How lucky all of us are. This is, after all, the dawn of a new age: jets that can take us to new heights, and a tiny floating world offering to share its wonders. It will be something for the history books, he says.

There is no mention of the new stones in the cemetery. There is no mention, even, of King Erasmus. King Ingram manages to make it all sound so cheerful, as though there will be a staircase that spirals from the ground up into the clouds. But he can't promise a staircase. He can only present the lot of us as evidence. We have seen what this war is doing, he says, and we want to help. We want to bring it to an end.

The crowd is less than jubilant, grieving their own losses at the harbor, sleepless from their own recollections of bombs and the fear of more. But they believe what they've been told. Their desperation has made them soft, putty in his hands, just as he planned it. And we are his demonstration, also just as he planned. He never meant to kill us or to take a bomb to our magical little island; he intends to turn it into a novelty, like one of Birdie's snow globes. She keeps them on her window ledges in her bedroom so they'll catch the light. On Internment, I dreamed of the endless ground, while somewhere below my stratosphere she was collecting those tiny little worlds she could watch from all sides.

Pen takes hold of my hand. It isn't a show of weakness, but of defiance. If she's made to stand here and be a prop in a foreign king's speech, she's going to choose what's worth holding on to. Thomas takes her cue, and Basil, and even Judas, until we're all holding on to one another. We were brought here, the lot of us, at the same time and all for different reasons, but this world of spinning teacups and sinister kings will never take from us who we are and where we've come from. Even when we're frightened, even when we're angry with one another, on Internment people are loyal to our own kind. We are dangerous dreamers, and we are strong. The desperate crowd fades to darkness beneath us. I imagine that we could step through the wall of clouds that touches the horizon, and go home.

Morgan, Pen, and Basil have seen
corruption and tragedy in their worlds
above and below, but what will happen
when the two collide?

*Take a sneak peek at the epic conclusion
to the Internment Chronicles*

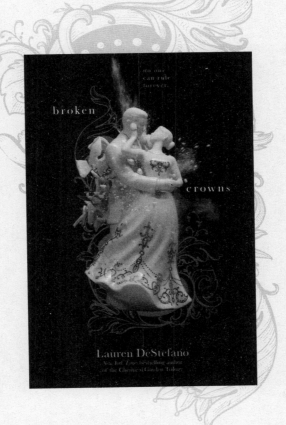

"The city is falling out of the sky," Professor Leander said. They were his last words. The medicine of the ground was not enough to cure an old man of the sun disease. He refused most of the efforts anyway. He told me that he'd already accomplished what no one else had been able to do. He'd gotten us to the ground. He was quite curious, he said, to know if his spirit would be taken to the tributary, or if he'd go to whatever afterlife the ground believed in, or if there was nothing at all.

Amy was with him when he died, and she called it a peaceful death. A fitting death.

Down a labyrinthine set of hallways in the same hospital, Gertrude Piper opened her eyes after a month of sleep. It was as though the two gods had made an even trade—the life of a man from the sky in exchange for the life of a girl on the ground.

Before that, we all thought that Birdie Piper would die. After I landed in Havalais at the dawn of winter, she was the most vibrant thing in her strange world. She offered her friendship to Pen and me without question; she snuck us through our bedroom window and showed us the wonders of Havalais. The mermaids in the sea. The glittering lights cast upon the water at night. The spinning metal rides in her family's amusement park.

And then the cold war between Havalais and its neighboring kingdom of Dastor advanced on us all at once, in the middle of the spring festival. I watched as an explosion swallowed Birdie. I saw her body, broken and bleeding and burnt, being kept alive by some coppery machine. Even worse than my brother had been when he'd come too close to the edge.

But nothing is certain, not even death when it's hovering over a girl. Not in my world, and not in this one. Birdie came back slowly. It took a month for her to open her eyes, and even longer for her to speak, serene in her delirium.

She told us about a spirit that would come into her room late at night to sing to her and to tend to the flowers on the table by the window.

When she had faded back to sleep, Nim slouched forward in his chair and rubbed his temples, anguished. "It wasn't a spirit," he told us. "Our mother's been here."

Mrs. Piper disappeared some years earlier to see the world. The same madness that brings so many to the edge of Internment haunts the people on the ground as well. One place is not ever enough for anyone, it seems.

It's August now, and Birdie no longer talks about her spirit. Instead she has returned to solid ground along with the rest of us. She asks her brother about the war. She wants to visit the grave of her other brother, Riles. She is getting well and she is ready to face the grimness that often comes with being awake. She doesn't wallow in her despair, and does not mind that her soft face has been forever scarred.

Pen is different. She doesn't seem ready to face anything these days. It has been months since King Ingram left for Internment, taking Princess Celeste with him, and in that time, Pen has been prone to more and more moments of distance. Jack Piper's guards surround the premises, and we are scarcely permitted to leave unescorted. Not until King Ingram returns with his instructions for us. But every week, Pen gives Nimble a new list of books she'd like from the library. Physics. Calculus. Philosophy. She is drowning in pages and pages of things she never shares with any of us. And that's when she isn't off someplace where none of us can find her, even within the confines.

The sun is starting to set, and after nearly an hour of searching, I find her at the amusement park. It would normally be thriving in August, the Pipers have told us, if not for the king's absence and the war. Now it's locked. But Pen and I sneak in sometimes.

"Pen?" I step onto one of the metal bars, preparing to climb over the locked fence.

She's standing high up on the platform with the telescopes that face Internment, and she turns to me.

"What are you doing?" I say.

She shrugs. She presses a piece of paper against the telescope and writes something down, then tucks the paper into her dress. "Nothing. Don't climb up. I was just leaving."

She descends the staircase, the steps reverberating under her stacked leather heels that make her taller than me. A girl our age would never be permitted to wear such things back home.

She comes to the fence and grips the bars and leans close, so that her forehead is almost touching mine.

"What are you doing all the way out here?" she says.

"Looking for you. You didn't come in for dinner."

"Who can eat?" she says, and hands me her shoes and hoists herself up over the fence. "The food in this place is nauseating. A different animal a night. I'd rather chew on grass." She lands on her feet with a thud, and goes about straightening her skirt. She takes the shoes but doesn't bother putting them back on.

I hate myself for trying to smell the tonic on her breath, but it must be done. She finds ways to steal gulps of it. We've fallen into an unspoken understanding that I will dispose of anything she tries to hide, and it will never be mentioned.

But if she's had anything to drink, I can't tell. Her eyes seem bright and alert when she looks at me. "Has Thomas been trying to find me?"

"Isn't he always?" I say.

She tugs my hand. "I don't want to go back inside just yet. Let's go to the water. Maybe there are mermaids."

Birdie told us that the mermaids never come close to the

shore. They prefer to stay where the water is deep, where they cannot easily be captured or get their hair ensnared on a fishing line. But I don't mind pretending we'll spot one. I try to keep pace with her as she runs.

With my other hand I hold my hat to my head. But eventually I let it go, and it escapes. When I'm with Pen, it seems I must always leave some small thing behind.

We are in a valley of green, with shy bright flowers poking their way through. In the wind I see dotted lines. I see red lines and blue lines. I see the maps that my best friend is always drawing as she moves, as she thinks.

"Maybe if we hold our arms out, the wind will carry us up," she says, and I think she believes it to be true.

Eventually we stop to catch our breaths somewhere along the ocean's shore. Pen rests her elbow on my shoulder and laughs at my wheezing. I have never been a match for her.

The wind is so loud that I can scarcely hear her laughter.

She drops onto the grass and pulls me down after her. Once I've caught my breath, she leans back on her elbows and looks at me. "What is it?" she says. "What's that worried look for?"

"I don't like all this wind," I say, over a roar of it. "It doesn't feel right." This time of year is so mellow on Internment. It is surely beautiful back home, the pathways all traced with bright flowers.

"A lot of the breeze comes from the sea," Pen says. "That's all."

"I know."

"Morgan, we aren't on Internment. Things are bound to be different. We've been here for months. We survived all that snow; this is just a little wind."

"I know." What I don't say is that I'm afraid she'll be swallowed whole by this whirling sky. This world already tried to kill her once, and Pen is fearless and foolish enough to let it try again.

A flock of birds flies high above us, in a uniform formation. Pen stretches her arms straight up over her head, her fingers arranged like a frame. I rest my head next to hers and try to see through that frame from her perspective.

After the birds have gone, she says, "Suppose Internment were to fall out of the sky."

"What?" I say.

"Suppose it couldn't stay afloat any longer and it came down all at once, hard and fast. I think it would coast at an angle, rather than straight down. I've been looking at the way the birds come down from the sky, and it's sort of a sixty degree angle most times."

"I don't give it any thought," I say.

She turns her head in the grass to look at me. "You've never thought about Internment falling from the sky before?"

"I have, I suppose." I stare up at the graying sky, where shades of pink and gold still cling to the sparse clouds. "But more as a nightmare, not something that will happen. I don't weigh the probability or try to picture what it would look like."

Pen stares up at the sky again.

"I think it would fall on King Ingram's castle," she says. "I think it would kill him and all his men. But the impact would destroy Internment, too. The foundations for all the buildings would shift. They'd likely collapse."

"Internment won't fall out of the sky," I say. I am gentle with her, but firm. I have heard Amy wonder about Internment coming down. I wondered myself, as a child. But Pen is different. She gets ideas like these in her head and they become real to her. She forgets what's in front of her and sees only what's in her mind, and just like that she's lost.

A mechanical growling from somewhere high above us disturbs the tranquil gray sky, and I flinch. Not even the largest beast on Internment could make a sound like that. The sound comes from the king's jet, descending from Internment for its monthly fuel delivery.

At the start of each month, the king's jet returns to Havalais to deliver more phosane that it has mined from Internment's soil. A refinery was built in Havalais to process that soil into fuel. In the mornings when I step outside, I can see the plumes of black smoke billowing out into the air, and sometimes I can smell it, too—like compost and metal.

But in six months, King Ingram has yet to return with his men, and after the delivery is made, the jet flies back to Internment for more. It's a wonder there is any city left up there at all.

The warring kingdom of Dastor has seen the jet's comings and goings. Nimble tells us that the war has moved to the home front. Boys even younger than he is are being recruited to fight. If Dastor means to have Internment and its fuel source, it will have to take ownership of Havalais itself.

"It won't happen," he's told us. "Havalais is bigger, more advanced."

I'm not so certain. I see nothing of the war from the confines of this sheltered world where Jack Piper raised his children, but sometimes when the air is still, I think I hear gunfire.

Pen puts her hand over mine, and I realize that I've been holding my breath. I know she's trying to keep me calm. She has heard me tossing and turning in my bed at night as I worry what news this king will bring when he returns from Internment. Only, I don't feel worry now. I don't feel anything, not even the dread that King Ingram usually ignites in me.

"We should go back and tell the others," I say.

Pen gnaws her lip, and even as she sits up, her face is still angled skyward. "It's probably just another delivery," she says, and she is likely right. Five times before this, the jet has returned, and five times we have all waited in silence for word of the king's arrival, and it never comes.

I pull Pen to her feet, and we make our way back to the hotel, both of us looking over our shoulders as the jet moves at an angle. Like a bird. Like a city falling from the sky.

Basil and Thomas arrive at the front steps moments before Pen and I do. Back on Internment, Pen's and my friendship was the only bond between them, but since coming here they've forged something like an independent friendship of their own, perhaps because if nothing else they have home in common.

They wouldn't have been able to go very far. Jack Piper has forbidden us to leave the grounds, for our own protection, all on the king's orders that we are to be kept away from anyone who may have sinister intentions for us now that it's revealed that we come from the magical floating island above this world. Though, the people of Havalais have more cause to distrust their king than to harm us.

Truth be told, I don't mind the restriction half the time. It makes me feel safe. Reminds me of the train tracks that surrounded me back home.

Other times, my wanderer's spirit comes out for a visit and I wonder at when this will all be over.

"We were walking back from the theme park when we saw the jet," Thomas says. "Did you see it?"

"Yes," I say.

Princess Celeste became a pawn when King Ingram needed access to Internment. King Furlow up in his sky has only two weaknesses, and those weaknesses are his children. He would allow King Ingram to have anything he asked for in exchange for Celeste's safe return.

I have worried for her in silence. Pen would be angry if I so much as brought her name up. But I do hope that she's well, and that her decision making abilities have improved.

Basil's standing close. His eyes are on me, and whether or not he knows it, he still sets my stomach fluttering.

Another gust of wind comes, and even the fearless Pen hugs her arms across her stomach and shivers.

Thomas frowns at her. "I've been looking all over for you."

"Not all over, clearly, or you'd have found me," she says.

He stands at a pace's distance from her, and I can see the worry in his eyes. I can see that he is trying to get a whiff of tonic on her breath. When he can't find one, he looks to me, and while Pen isn't watching I give a slight shake of my head. She's sober.

The jet has quit rumbling in the sky; presumably it has landed.

"Come on," I say to Pen, and hold the door open. "Let's see if we can find something in the kitchen you're willing to eat."

She follows me into the house, past the smallest Piper children, who are playing a war game in the living room. Annie is a soldier whose legs were blown off in an explosion, and Marjorie is a nurse applying a tourniquet. I have seen them play this game a dozen times, and it is anyone's guess whether Annie will survive her wounds. Last time, an explosion hit their pretend medical tent and all the nurses and soldiers were killed.

I hate this game, but I think it makes them feel closer to Riles.

Up at the top of the stairs, Amy watches them from between the bars of the railing, not quite ready for human interaction. She has been quiet since her grandfather's death, and she's added another cloth around her wrist beside the one meant to symbolize her sister.

"Let's say I lost my arm too," Annie says.

"Which one?" Marjorie asks.

"The left."

"Would you girls like to help me in the garden?" Alice calls down from the top of the stairs. She cannot bear this game of theirs.

Annie sits up from her deathbed on the hearth. "Why do you tend to the garden? We have a gardener."

"It just makes me happy, I suppose," Alice says. She reaches the bottom step and holds her hands out to them, and they forget their game and happily follow her outside.

In the kitchen, Pen and I sit at the small table reserved for the maids, and Pen bites into a raw carrot from the cold box.

"I wish you'd stop looking so worried," she says.

"I can't play it as cool as you, I suppose."

She stares at me for a long moment, and then she says, "You're not the only one who has nightmares about what's happening back home. Just because I don't talk about it doesn't mean I don't care."

"I know that you care. That's what's so frustrating," I say. "We've hardly spoken in months."

"What are you going on about 'we've hardly spoken'? We share a room. We speak every day. We're speaking right now."

"You know what I mean."

She takes another bite of the carrot, with a crunch I swear is meant to be pointed. "You'll forgive me if I don't entirely trust you with my secrets these days."

I know just what she means. It has been a source of

contention that's never fully gone away these past several months. She discovered that Internment's soil contains the very fuel source King Ingram wants for his kingdom, and she confided this secret to me. But after she nearly drowned, I told the princess everything, hoping an alliance could be forged between Internment and Havalais, giving us all a chance to return home.

Instead, King Ingram used the princess as a hostage and has been depleting Internment of its soil as he pleases.

I don't know the enormity of what's already happened and what's to come, but even so I wouldn't take back what I did. I'm still holding out hope that I'll be able to return Pen home to her family, to the city that she loves so much that she's been going to pieces without it.

So I say nothing, and Pen can see that she's wounded me. "Nim says Birdie has had her last surgery, and can come home soon," she says to change the subject. "She'll still be confined to her wheelchair, but I doubt that will last for long."

I push my chair away from the table. "I'm going to make some tea for Lex."

"Oh, Morgan, don't be cross. I didn't mean it. I'm just on edge because of that bloody jet."

"I know," I say softly.

I hope that this time the king has returned, and the princess as well, alive and safe. Whatever news they bring will surely be better than all this wondering and fear.

I don't know what sort of mood Lex will be in when I reach the top of the stairs, but he's been especially sour lately. He's running low on paper for his transcriber, and soon he will no longer be able to spend his days hiding in his fictional worlds.

I knock when I reach his door.

"Alice?" he says.

"No, it's me." Back home he always knew when I was the one approaching him, but something about this house and its noises disorients him. "I've brought some tea."

"Oh," he says, rather unenthusiastically. "Come in."

He's sitting in a wing chair near the open window, and the worry on his face mirrors my own from earlier. He doesn't care for the wind; perhaps it reminds him too much of the edge. "The weather down here takes some getting used to," I say. I press the teacup into his hand, not letting go until I'm sure he's got a grip on it.

"I have a bad feeling," he says.

"Me too."

I hesitate, standing before him, debating with myself whether to tell him what I saw in the sky.

But in the end I'm not given a choice. Even without his sight, Lex is clever at sensing when anything is wrong. "What is it, Little Sister? What's happened?"

I wring my skirt in my hands. "We saw the jet about an hour ago. Pen, Basil, Thomas, and I. We've been waiting for someone to come home and tell us what it means."

Lex is silent for a long moment. "I heard." He takes a sip of his tea and then with minimal fumbling he sets it on the window ledge. "So it begins," he says.

"There's no need to be so theatrical," I say. "It may be good news."

"A greedy king in a wasteland of wealth holds a princess hostage so that he may invade a tiny floating city, and you still think he may return with good news. My sister the optimist."

I am tired of being called an optimist as though it were a bad thing. Pen has used this word against me as well. "I'm merely trying not to panic, Lex." I hold myself back from saying anything too combative. I don't want to fight, and it has taken me so long to stop hating my brother for lying to me about our father being dead. I would like for us to be reasonable with each other.

"Where is Alice?" he asks. Maybe he wants to avoid an argument too.

"She's in the garden."

"And she knows about the jet?"

"I told her when we came back inside. We're all waiting now. Drink your tea, all right? Alice will be up to check on you in a bit."

As I cross the threshold, he says, "Morgan?"

I turn.

"Be careful."

"I'm only going downstairs."

"I never know what mad and wild adventures you'll get off to on a whim."